For Ross

Y040810

THIS CHANGES EVERYTHING

HELEN MCGINN

Boldwood

First published in Great Britain in 2021 by Boldwood Books Ltd.

Copyright © Helen McGinn, 2021

Cover Design: Alice Moore Design

Cover Photography: Shutterstock

A CIP catalogue record for this book is available from the British Library.

Paperback ISBN 978-1-80048-352-1

Large Print ISBN 978-1-80048-348-4

Hardback ISBN 978-1-80162-613-2

Ebook ISBN 978-1-80048-346-0

Kindle ISBN 978-1-80048-347-7

Audio CD ISBN 978-1-80048-353-8

MP3 CD ISBN 978-1-80048-350-7

Digital audio download ISBN 978-1-80048-345-3

Boldwood Books Ltd
23 Bowerdean Street
London SW6 3TN
www.boldwoodbooks.com

PART I

Annabel Armstrong had loved James for as long as she could remember. But on this particular morning she wanted to tip the contents of her half-full cereal bowl over his head. It wasn't that he was being deliberately unhelpful, but rather he was so busy rushing around the kitchen asking who'd moved his keys (answer: him) he didn't seem to notice Annie could really do with a hand. The boys had to be fed, teeth and hair needed brushing, and everyone needed to be in the car ready for the school run in the next twenty minutes. Meanwhile, chaos reigned. The noise – shouting from the boys, whining from the dogs, mewing from a hungry cat – was ridiculous. Annie contemplated sitting on the floor under the kitchen table, closing her eyes and covering her ears.

'Come on, Rufe, eat up!' she managed.

'I am! I can't eat any faster,' Rufus replied dramatically. He really was the slowest eater.

'I've finished all of mine,' said Ned, wiping the last of the cereal from his mouth across the sleeve of his newly washed school jumper.

Annie sighed, reaching for a cloth. 'Good boy, Ned. Now let's get going, otherwise we'll be late.'

'You never say good boy to me when I finish my breakfast!' protested Rufus.

'If you finished it, I would,' said Annie, immediately feeling mean.

'Thanks a lot.' He looked distinctly huffy.

'What's your plan today?' Annie called after James as he headed down the hall.

'Oh, you know, the usual,' he replied over his shoulder. 'Get in, be driven to distraction by people much younger than me. Try not to shout at people. Come home.' James was having a work mid-life crisis of sorts. Having spent twenty years working in advertising, changing company a few times as he worked his way up to a management position, he now seemed no longer to be doing the work he loved. As he saw it, he was a glorified babysitter for (just about) grown men and women who all appeared to be younger, hungrier and better equipped to get ahead than he was. Cue resentment, inevitably leading to a 'what's-it-all-for' phase. And now he'd started talking about retraining as a woodcutter, or something like that; Annie couldn't quite remember.

'Oh, come on, Jimmy, you love it when things are going well. Maybe this is just a, you know, down bit? Things will get better, they always do.'

'Annie, I love you for your optimism, I really do.' He came back to kiss Annie on the top of her head and shout goodbye to the boys.

''Bye, Dad!' they hollered before careering off into the garden.

The sun was out and it was already warm, despite the early hour. They were still just under half a term away from the summer holidays but there was already a holiday feel in the air. Annie watched them run, dogs in tow, into the garden before she turned to attack the kitchen table. The boys' cereal of choice had a habit of attaching itself to that table like barnacles. A blow-torch really would have been more appropriate than the damp cloth she held in her hand.

Her phone rang. It was her sister, Jess, the flashing screen announced.

'You OK?' Annie always started her phone calls with her sister with these words. Most of the time everything was, indeed, OK. But with Jess, calls often came with a generous dose of drama, sometimes with a side order of flakiness. Annie adored her only sister; eighteen months younger and a few years off forty.

'Oh God, Annie. You won't believe what I've done. Seriously, I have even surprised myself this time,' Jess sighed, and Annie could hear her dragging furiously on her e-cig.

Annie wedged the phone between her shoulder and ear, ditched the cloth and started to throw hastily made Marmite sandwiches into lunch boxes for the boys.

'Go on, I'm all ears.'

'Well, you know that small, bald, irritating little man in accounts?'

'Brian?' said Annie, fearing the worst. 'Oh God, Jess. Please don't say you...'

'No! Of course not,' said Jess. 'But he was buying endless shots last night and I seemed to be drinking most of them. And, er, things got a little out of hand and I ended up, you know... with Rob.'

Annie's shoulders tightened. Rob was drop-dead gorgeous. She didn't know that for a fact – she'd never met him – but according to Jess he was. He was also married. And as much as

Annie berated Jess for doing what she was doing, Jess insisted she was better off being with someone she didn't *have* to be with. Basically, it meant she didn't have to commit, which, Jess said, suited her perfectly. It was, Annie thought, a very sad situation for everyone concerned, most of all Rob's wife who, presumably, had no idea.

'Please don't expect me to say anything nice. You know how I feel about it.'

'I don't expect you to say anything nice – I know it's *not good* – but this time it was different.'

Annie's heart sank. This was the moment Jess was going to announce Rob was leaving his wife and they were going to be together officially. Annie waited for the crashing punch line to what was, so far, one of the worst jokes she'd ever heard from her sister. Jess always had someone in tow, usually impossibly good-looking, mostly a good deal younger. She was surrounded by them at work; her job meant spending long hours in the City, followed by many more hours drinking after work. Having started as an intern in a PR company, Jess now ran a successful business of her own. She worked ridiculous hours, was surgically attached to her phone, owned one of the most envied address books in the City and was both loved and ever so slightly feared by those who worked with her. No doubt about it, Jess was incredibly good at what she did.

But years of working in such a brutal environment had left Jess with skin so thick she couldn't remember the last time she'd cried in a movie. Actually, she couldn't remember the last time she'd even seen a movie. Unless you counted the soft porn film a lovely young man called Tom (was it Tom?) insisted they watch in a hotel room in-between meetings during a recent conference. But Jess knew that didn't really count.

Anyway, back to the punch line. Annie braced herself.

'I realised that Rob is, in fact, a bit of a dick.'

Annie did a silent air punch.

'Annie, are you there?' Jess was thrown by the silence.

'Yes, yes. I heard. God, I'm so relieved,' Annie said. 'I'm not saying you have to get married or anything, but getting involved with someone like that, who's capable of doing whatever it is you do behind his wife's back is just a complete waste of time. Not to mention potentially life-changing for all concerned when the truth comes out. Which it always does,' she added.

Jess took a deep breath, determined not to rise to her sister's predictably pious delivery. 'It's not always that simple, Annie. There's more to it, though I don't expect you to get it.' But however much Jess wished otherwise, she knew Annie was right. No matter how good Rob made Jess feel, he was cheating on his wife. This was her first affair with a married man and though she had thought she could do it, she had since realised she just wasn't able to live a lie.

It had been the sight of Rob in her flat just a few hours earlier, trying to put on his boxer shorts and tripping in the dark as he'd made his way to the bathroom to make a hushed phone call. At that moment, he had looked ridiculous rather than ravishing, as he'd done in the bar. The shots had become a distant memory, unlike the hangover she'd then nursed as a consequence.

'I'm just so glad you've seen him for the slimy grease ball he obviously is. You deserve so much better,' said Annie.

'Well, just don't go on about it. Let's just pretend it never happened. And don't, whatever you do, tell Mum.'

''Course not. Have you spoken to Mum?'

'Why, what's she done?' It was Jess's turn to sound weary.

'Nothing. She's fine, actually. But I know she'll ask me if I've spoken to you in that "she-never-rings-me" kind of way.'

'Tell her I'll be down in a few weekends' time. I'll book a table at The Fox. We'll go for lunch and have a proper catch-up.'

Annie knew there was only a very slim chance of this actually happening but the idea that it might cheered her immensely. Despite Jess's flakiness – and serious lack of moral compass at times – Annie loved her sister deeply. And she desperately missed Jess's company. Although separated by just a hundred miles of motorway, their worlds seemed so very far apart.

Annie hadn't always lived in the country. Once upon a time, she had lived and worked in London, racing to the Tube in trainers, ready to be at her desk by 9 a.m. despite often nursing a considerable hangover. Having taken a temping job covering for a sick friend at an art gallery, Annie had gone on to become the first port of call for all the artists the gallery represented, a role she loved. It might be a great British artist on the phone one minute, followed by a complete unknown who hadn't sold a painting for years the next. And Annie's skill – not that she'd realised it – was treating each artist exactly the same. From her quietly spoken, pinstripe-suited boss, who used to tell her jokes and deliver the punch line in Latin, to the extremely beautiful, willowy PA, Caro, with whom she'd shared an office, along with all the wonderful artists she'd dealt with daily, Annie had adored everyone and everything about working there.

Now she sighed, sweeping a look across her kitchen, which, she noted, was once again liberally decorated with small pieces of stray Lego. The white-painted walls looked two-tone, bearing the marks of sticky fingers and the odd felt-tip pen scrawl from about child's head height downwards. Plates, pots and pans balanced precariously by the sink, evidence of the seemingly endless meals Annie had to dole out every day to people both big and small. A basket of washing sat on a chair, the arms of crumpled shirts hanging out as if making a half-hearted attempt to escape from the mess.

Standing in the middle of the kitchen was a worn, zinc-topped oak table. It had been found years ago in an antique shop whilst Annie and James were on holiday in Cornwall, and Annie had insisted on tying it to the roof of the car to transport it back to their first flat in London, where it took up most of the main room. Securing it to the roof rack had severely tested her and James's knowledge of knots but here it stood, as it had done for the last six years since they'd left London for a small cottage in the country. Luckily, the kitchen was the biggest room in the house. To Annie, their table was a rock in a sea of washing, toys and noise. She picked at a piece of stuck-on cereal as she spoke. 'OK, I will. I'll ring you later in the week.'

'Sorry for being such a fucking nightmare.' Jess sounded genuinely contrite.

'Don't be silly. Big kiss.'

''Bye.'

Annie glanced at the clock on the oven. 'Come on, boys, we'll be late,' she shouted.

The boys ran in, mud on their knees and grass stains on their school jumpers. Deciding it was too late to do anything about that, she chucked the dirty plates in the sink, grabbed their lunch boxes and her bag and headed to the car. As the boys piled in, shouting and jostling for position, Annie remembered her phone, left on the side. 'Seatbelts, boys.' She ran back into the house to get it, finding it on the side, ringing. Her mother's name – Julia – flashed up on the screen.

'Sorry, Mum, it'll have to wait,' she muttered, stuffing the phone into her back pocket and running back to the car.

As she went through her usual mental checklist – boys, bags, coats, check, check, check – Annie set off on their school run.

'Haven't you got your Show and Tell this morning, Rufus?' she asked.

'Yep, and I'm going to talk about Colin,' he said, sounding confident. He held up a jam jar stuffed with leaves.

'OK, but make sure people don't frighten him,' she pleaded.

'Mum, snails don't get frightened!' Rufus said, laughing.

'How do you know? They might. Just make sure you bring him back safely and then we'll put him back with his friends under the flowerpots later.'

'Fine,' said Rufus, with a sigh.

'Are snails born with their shells?' asked Ned, and Annie realised she had absolutely no idea. Just as she was about to embark on a completely made-up answer, her phone pinged in her back pocket. She knew it would be a text from her mother. A missed phone call from Julia was always followed by a text. Too late to read it now; it would have to wait until after the school run.

As the sun shone and the boys continued to argue as usual, Annie reminded herself to catch Clare at the gates. They'd been friends since meeting at a pregnancy yoga class in a nearby village hall, both carrying second babies. Annie had fallen asleep during the deep breathing exercises. Clare had nudged her and she'd opened her eyes to find Clare's kind face informing her via stage whisper that the class had, in fact, finished. To this day, she was in Annie's phone under 'Yoga Clare', despite neither of them having been back to a single yoga class since. In the months that followed, Annie and Clare had bonded over a love of strong coffee and, in the later stages of pregnancy, a craving for pastries. In those tough early years, when Annie had found herself stuck at home with very small children, permanently tired and often incapable of finishing a sentence or cup of anything hot without needing to do something for someone small, Clare had been exactly the friend she needed. Funny, warm and definitely more relaxed about the whole parenting thing than Annie, Clare had been a proverbial breath of fresh air when the Armstrongs first left the city.

As she dropped the boys at the school gate, Annie scanned the playground for her friend's familiar figure, usually the only one dressed head to toe in faded black among an ocean of blue jeans and stripy tops. As the kids ran across the playground into school, she spotted her across the other side.

'Annie! Coffee!' yelled Clare.

'Yours or mine?'

'Yours,' Clare said, as she got closer. 'Mine looks like it's been burgled.'

'Done, see you in a mo.' Annie watched the back of the boys as they disappeared into class and, walking back to the car, remembered the message waiting for her. She took the phone out of her back pocket and waited for it to ping onto the screen.

DARLING I AM GOING AWAY FOR A FEW DAYS. WILL EXPLAIN.
CALL ME ASAP PLS. M XX

For reasons she'd never really understood, her mother always sent Annie text messages in capital letters. Either she'd never found how to take off the caps lock on the phone, or Julia just liked texting in capitals, but Annie always felt that her mother was shouting at her. Julia going away at short notice didn't worry Annie. She was always going away at short notice. Annie loved that her mother was an active, sociable woman in her seventies with a ton of friends and a seemingly endless number of lunches to attend. What did worry her, though, was that Julia felt it needed explaining. The 'WILL EXPLAIN' bit of the message was a concern. She dialled Julia's number and waited.

* * *

Half an hour later, Annie sat at her kitchen table, a mug of very strong coffee in her hand and the remaining crumbs of a couple of croissants on the plate between her and Clare.

'I mean, what the actual fuck is she thinking?' Annie shook her head slowly.

'I'm sure she knows what she's doing,' said Clare.

'Oh, come on, Clare, you know what she's like. She really doesn't! I mean, it's like she's decided this is what she's been waiting for. Prince Charming finally shows up, three marriages too late, and she goes running!' Annie had thought that nothing her mother could do would surprise her any more. Clearly, she'd underestimated her.

'So, what did she say, exactly?'

Annie sighed. Julia had answered Annie's call with her usual, cheery 'Hello, darling!' before saying 'Now', in a way that made Annie sense that what was coming next was going to be anything but run-of-the-mill.

'Essentially, Mum's just told me that she's planning to meet the man she says is her first love. She's not seen him for more than fifty years. *Fifty years!* And they're not meeting in any old place. Oh, no, they're meeting in Rome. Bloody Rome!' Annie lifted her eyes to find Clare with a huge smile on her face.

'But that's *so* romantic!' Clare sighed. 'I mean, she's a single woman, presumably he's a single man, what's so bad about that?'

'Because she's my mother, Clare. Things are never that straightforward. As you well know.' Annie raised her eyebrows at her friend.

When it came to surprises, Julia had form. Over the last few years, Annie and Clare had in turn each filled in the other on various chapters of their lives and the characters in them. One of Clare's favourites was Annie's description of her mother's romantic history to date, including the part where she married Husband Number Two, Simon, whilst on holiday in the West Indies. And according to Annie, Julia was slightly drunk on rum punch at the time and the taxi driver, a man called Winston, was the witness. On returning home, they announced the news to the assembled children on both sides: Annie and Jess, by now both teenagers, and their new twin stepbrothers. Jess had stormed off, Annie had burst into tears and the boys had simply asked if they could go and watch TV. Not a roaring success, really. Just like the marriage, which lasted less than three years. Then there was Husband Number Three, a kind man called Andrew. Ruddy-faced and permanently dressed in a holey green jumper and mustard-coloured cords, he hadn't lasted long either. Too boring, according to Julia. Annie had once asked why her mother hadn't realised that before marrying him but Julia's answer was typically brusque. 'Darling, he was a fantastic Bridge partner. I just shouldn't have married him.' And that was that.

There was, of course, another husband. Number One was Annie and Jess's father. His name was David and Annie had just turned eight when he left. Jess was six. Annie didn't remember it as a particularly traumatic event in her life. There were no arguments. She didn't remember either parent staging a dramatic exit. Rather, she mostly remembered them being what she assumed was a normal, happy family. Until one day, he just wasn't there any more. Over the years that followed, as she'd grown up and come to understand what her parents were like as people, the idea that they had been together long enough to have two children amazed her. They were so incredibly different. As much as her father was calm and straightforward, her mother was flamboyant and unpredictable. Their wedding photo, one of Annie's favourite pictures, showed Julia standing in a very short miniskirt, David in a sober suit, proud-looking parents on either side. Both bride and groom wore shy smiles. They'd met in a pub in London, when the town was in full sixties swing. Julia worked behind the bar; David was there by mistake.

When Annie thought about her parents as a couple, she didn't really have many memories to go on. Even when she really concentrated, she couldn't picture her parents together, other than in that one wedding photo.

Anyway, now there was another man in the picture, according to Julia.

'Apparently, he's called Patrick. They met as teenagers and Mum says he was her first love,' said Annie.

'So, why Rome?' asked Clare.

'God, I don't know. I didn't ask. What I don't understand is why he's got in touch now, after so many years. And why Mum thinks it's such a good idea to go. I mean, she's got no idea what he's like now, where he's been all this time. Who knows what he's after?' cried Annie.

'But that's the thing. She obviously does know what he's like, if they were in love once,' said Clare, encouragingly.

'It's just so... so...' Annie's voice trailed off.

'Julia!' replied Clare. 'It is just so Julia.' Annie had to smile at that. Her friend was spot on. 'So, how did he get in touch?'

'He wrote a letter.'

'Oh, that's too gorgeous!' Clare clasped her hands together in delight.

'Yes, maybe, but it creeps me out that he knew where to find her. I mean, he might be stalking her.'

'Hardly. You don't stalk someone by asking them to meet you in Rome. How did he know where to find her?'

'God knows. I didn't think to ask her that either. I'm still getting over the fact that she's going to meet him.'

'Oh, come on. Try not to worry; she's a grown woman. She'll be fine. And she'll have a wonderful time. I mean, it's Rome...' said Clare.

'I know, I know. But to be honest, I'm just not sure I can face meeting Husband Number Four.' Annie picked at the last of the crumbs on the plate and drained her mug of coffee. 'Talking of which, it's our wedding anniversary tomorrow. Ten years!'

'Oh, wow!' Claire cried. 'That's a big deal. Are you going to do something to celebrate?'

'Not sure. James usually plans something. Not that he's mentioned it yet.' Annie smiled.

Clare hoped he hadn't forgotten, not least for his sake. Given that Annie had seemingly already decided that another stepfather was on the horizon, Clare thought she might just need something to take her mind off that.

2

'Are you going to ask me or not?' were the words Annie had said after kissing James for the first time, standing outside the local village hall after a friend's birthday party. They were both seventeen. Annie remembered him wearing an old oversized long coat, the underlying mustiness disguised with a generous dash of Dunhill aftershave. Annie was in her brown suede jacket, bought in a second-hand shop in Kensington Market. With the faint sound of Bryan Adams singing about everything he did in the background, James and Annie found themselves outside together, talking as they shared a turquoise cocktail cigarette stolen from Julia's stash in a drawer in the kitchen dresser. The smoke curled slowly in the cold autumnal air and the two teenagers talked about life as they knew it. About James taking his driving test, which he planned to do as soon as possible. Of course, this wasn't the only reason that Annie had liked him but, looking back, she had to admit it was a contributing factor. Having been friends through school for years, a run of teenage parties had thrown them together more than usual. Both made braver through warm beer, this time they had ended up in the car park in a slightly awkward teenage embrace. Annie was thrilled. And, prompted by Annie, James had asked her out. Not that they went anywhere in particular in those days – the odd trip to the cinema, the occasional walk with the family dog in order to talk without parents around. And smoke more (stolen) cigarettes, obviously.

Annie's university years took her to Scotland to study Art History. James, on the other hand, couldn't wait to get on with it (his words) and soon got a job with a small advertising firm in London. Despite the distance between them, the relationship worked. There were a few tricky patches but ultimately, they were mad about each other. Whenever they could afford it, they'd meet up and spend hours in a tiny restaurant in James's neighbourhood in north London, making a bottle of wine last for as long as possible so they could stay and talk without having to go back to the flat. Not that the flat was that bad; rather James's flatmate, Stig, an old university friend of his brother, loved to do yoga at night. Naked. James and Annie would put off returning to the flat until they were sure Stig had finished his sun salutations and downward dogs.

By the time Annie moved to London three years later, she knew that she, too, wanted to share a flat with some friends. So it was that she lived with two university friends, Bee and Louise, in a dingy place near Vauxhall, where cups fell off the shelves every time a train went past. There was always a bottle of sparkling wine in the fridge, thanks to Bee's job with a city catering company. Louise was studying medicine and knew exactly what to do to shift a hangover. They worked hard during the week, partied on Saturdays and slept on Sundays. It worked perfectly.

By the time they reached their late twenties, Annie and James had been together for over ten years. So when he proposed, no one was surprised. Apart from Annie, that is: it was almost as if she wasn't expecting it.

'But how could you not know he was going to ask you?' cried Bee, as they sat on the sofa of their flat just a few days after the proposal.

'I don't know. I know it sounds weird, but I just didn't want to assume it would happen. I mean, I knew. I *knew* it was going to be him. But I couldn't be sure he knew that too.' This was Annie's best explanation.

'But can you really marry someone if they're the only person you've ever been with? And that includes sex, by the way,' said Louise, in her usual no-nonsense, medical manner.

'Well, I'd always thought that if we met someone else along the way *before* we were married, that would be the test. But the thing is, the idea of being with anyone but him makes me feel a bit sick. I've loved him since I was seventeen. Being apart from him all that time, surrounded by lots of other people, made me love him more. Does that make any sense?' Annie looked at her friends for some kind of understanding.

'Darling, I think it's the most gorgeous thing,' said Bee, with tears in her eyes.

'Personally, I think you're both mad. It's not normal. But you're so happy. Cheers to that,' concluded Louise, topping up her pint glass with more free Moët.

The wedding was a spit-and-sawdust affair, much to Annie's in-laws' disapproval. Their budget was spent mostly on lots of booze and a really good band. The marquee (more a big tent) was borrowed from the village cricket club and decorated with branches pinched from the nearby woods. Old jam jars were crammed with meadow flowers. It was June, but it poured with rain. The photographer got lost, so most of the photographic evidence from the day was thanks to Stig, a keen amateur photographer. He'd been close enough to capture the bride and groom as they left the church, both with enormous grins on their faces and an undeniable light in their eyes.

This particular picture was now framed, just one among a sea of faces crammed onto the biggest wall in the house, at the far end of the kitchen. The wall had started with just a few photos in odd frames when Annie and James first moved into the cottage, but over the years the collection had grown. There were plenty of dodgy haircuts and questionable outfits on display during Annie and James's late teenage years. There were shots of Annie or James, rarely both of them (this was pre-selfie days), in various locations from Venice to Vietnam, all holidays before the children were born. After children appeared, the backdrops behind them were noticeably less exotic. But the grown-up faces in the photographs were just as happy, if a little more tired.

And for Annie, it was the tiredness that tested their relationship the most. Nothing had prepared them for the sheer exhaustion of having small children. From the day they brought their first-born back to their minute, hastily bought one-bedroom flat, life had not been the same.

'Where shall I put it?' asked James, motioning to the car seat. It was as if a new but unexpected piece of furniture had been given to them, and they didn't know where it should go.

'Him, you mean. Not "it".' Annie eased herself into the only armchair in the room. 'Leave him in there for now, so we can look at him.' They both stared in wonder and slight shock at the tiny creature in front of them, fast asleep in the seat. The baby's hat had slipped over one eye; his fingers curled into tight little balls.

'Hello, Rufus,' James whispered.

'Hi, Rufus,' said Annie, barely audible. She felt her heart

would burst with love. She was elated and terrified all at the same time.

Those early days with just the three of them, in that flat, went by in a haze of broken nights along with the smell of those hideous little plastic nappy bags. Annie spent hours sitting on various sofas in friends' flats and houses across town over the next few months as they drank endless cups of lukewarm tea. Swapping birth stories, Annie realised hers was mercifully straightforward – the epidural was so effective, she was able to read an old copy of *Hello!* magazine that James had found in the waiting room – in fact, she sometimes felt obliged to make it sound a little more dramatic than it really was. The nearest they'd got to a moment of drama was when James had sprayed deodorant in Annie's face instead of water, having got the cans in the hospital bag mixed up. But then the drugs had kicked in and the baby appeared before Annie had even got to the cookery pages.

By the time Rufus started walking and talking, the decision to move to a bigger place had been made. Except that finding somewhere even remotely in their price bracket in the area was impossible. When another mother at Rufus's nursery suggested Annie change religion to get Rufus into a good school – bearing in mind he was still in nappies at the time – she knew it was time to move. Not just down the road, but really move. Out of the city to the countryside.

Annie really hadn't grown up thinking she would end up living in the same village as her parents. In fact, she'd spent most of her teenage years thinking how unbelievably boring it was. But when her mother turned up on the doorstep for a last-minute visit ('I might be in the area, darling'), she brought with her a copy of her local paper. And Annie spotted a cottage just outside the village where Julia lived, available for rent. It was utterly beautiful, with a small garden and a duck pond on the village green nearby. Suddenly, the idea didn't seem so bad after all. It wasn't as if Annie was going to have her mother there all the time; Julia was far too busy. But she would be nearby, and that felt right. Putting the idea to James had been planned with precision. Beef stew, mashed potato and lots of red wine first, propose move to the country second. It meant an hour's daily commute for James to work, who was by now in the office of a much bigger firm of advertisers, but it also meant more space than they could ever have dreamed of. That and the promise of the odd free night's babysitting from Julia swung it. James agreed it was time to make the move.

Pulling the van up outside Wisteria Cottage just before Rufus's second birthday on a warm day in July was marred by just one thing. The week before, as Annie and James sat in the waiting room of the London hospital waiting for their scan appointment, she'd known something was wrong. What had started as a dull ache in her stomach the night before was now so painful it scared her. Running to the loo in the hospital just before her scan, Annie saw the flash of red in the water and, feeling like her skin was actually crawling, called out quietly for her husband. What followed was a blur of voices and pain as Annie had a miscarriage right there in the hospital on the day of her twelve-week scan. Waking up after the D&C operation (had two letters ever sounded so cruel?), she looked out of the hospital window at a cloudless blue sky. She'd felt hollow. Depleted. James was at her side. He was pale, his eyes red-rimmed. She squeezed his hand, and he squeezed hers right back.

A year and a half later, Ned was born. Not quite the stress-free delivery enjoyed with Rufus. Instead Ned made an early appearance, two months before his due date, thanks to preeclampsia. Annie spent weeks in hospital, both before and after the birth, most of the time by Ned's bedside, once he'd arrived. Eventually they brought him home at a healthy weight. As he grew older, he grew fast. To everyone else, Ned was bulletproof. But for Annie, the memory of watching his frail little body attached to wires and monitors, with the incessant beep-beep-beep and steady flashing lights was never far away. The sounds of those machines should have reassured her, given that they signalled everything was as it should be, but instead they had made her feel sick. Still, with two healthy boys, Annie knew she had much to be grateful for. And she really was.

* * *

Just as soon as she'd finished folding at least the top layer of the basket of washing on the table, Annie planned to head to the shed at the bottom of the garden to do some work. The shed was stuffed with old bits of furniture, pots of paint and dustsheets, and had a strong smell of white spirit. As much as she wished she could earn a living as a painter, it turned out that sanding down old bits of furniture and painting them was more lucrative in the short term. In the corner of the shed stood an easel and a blank canvas, which she hoped one day she might find the time to paint for pleasure. But in the meantime, she had a set of bedside tables rescued from the tip on the go, which would be perfectly sellable once she'd given them a makeover.

As she fished around the basket trying to find the partner to the sock she had in her hand, her phone rang. It was Jess.

'You will not believe what Julia's doing now. I mean, for fuck's sake, seriously, she's...'

'I know,' said Annie, calmly.

'Oh my God, has she told you?'

'Yes, I got a text from her this morning. In capitals, obviously.'

'Same! Did you tell her she's completely mad?' cried Jess.

'Not exactly, no. I don't think that would have stopped her. She's very bright and breezy about the whole thing, like it's the most normal thing in the world to go all the way to Rome to meet someone she hasn't seen for over fifty years. It's weird, but it was like she was telling me she's going to the shop down the road to pick up the paper and a pint of milk, only she'll be gone for a bit longer.'

'Did you ask her *why* she was going?'

'Yes, but she just said it was something she had to do. And that if we were in her position, we'd do the same.'

'What position does she mean? I just don't get it. I mean, do you think she's being blackmailed to go? He might be a lunatic! He might cut her up into pieces and put her in the boot of a car, for all we know!'

'Jess, I think that's definitely the worst-case scenario,' Annie laughed.

'Well, you read these stories and God only knows what might happen... What if he really is a lunatic? Or even a conman? Seriously, Annie, please can you talk some sense into her?'

'I don't think it'll do any good, honestly. Sounds like it's all organised. She's going next week.'

'Next week? In that case,' said Jess, inserting a dramatic pause, 'I'm going to follow her out there.'

'You're what? Why? What about work?'

'Well, actually, I was planning on taking some time off anyway. I need to—' another pause '—get away for a few days. From the office, I mean.'

'Why? Jess, what's happened?' Annie frowned.

'Nothing dramatic, I just need to... I think it's a good idea if I... I'll tell you when I see you. It's complicated but, really, nothing bad. It's just... I could do with a change of scene. Stalking Julia in Rome will be a fantastic distraction, if nothing else.'

'What are you going to do? Hide behind statues? How will you find them? You don't even know where they'll be!' cried Annie.

'Oh my God, why don't you come, too? We could go together! It'll be amazing! Come on, Annie. We never get to do things like this. Just for a couple of nights. I'll pay.' Annie started to protest but Jess went on. 'Seriously, please let me. I don't have any time to spend my money, let alone anyone to spend it on.'

Annie laughed, put Jess on speakerphone and continued to search the washing basket for the missing sock. 'It's a lovely idea, Jess, but I can't. Who'll look after the boys?'

'Can't James help?'

'He's at work. No can do. And anyway, I've got a fancy dress costume to make before next Monday. For Roman Day, ironically.'

'Buy one on Amazon, for God's sake. Life's too short to not do stuff like this, Annie!' Jess was not going to let it drop.

'Well, I guess that's exactly what Julia's thinking.'

Jess sighed. 'Well, if you change your mind... I'm going to look into flights. Can you find out when she's going and where she's staying?'

'I'll do my best, but you know how vague she can be.'

'Really? I hadn't noticed.'

* * *

Jess hadn't ever meant to get involved with a married man. But too many failed relationships had left her feeling that she just wasn't right for marriage. She was too selfish, a fact that she was entirely comfortable with. There had been one, years before, that everyone, including Jess, thought would be *The One*. His name was Ben and he proposed to Jess on her thirtieth birthday. So it came as a surprise to her as much as anyone when she turned him down, instead taking a job in New York for the next three years. Over time, Annie had learned not to ask why, when it had all seemed so perfect. Julia had never asked in the first place, of course, regarding it as a decision Jess would explain as and when she ever needed to. All Jess would ever say about it was that it didn't feel right. She loved Ben, but she didn't want to marry him. To her, it was as simple as that.

Since then, Jess was rarely single but as far as Annie could tell, never really *with* anyone either. At least, not long enough for Annie to meet them properly; to know what they were like. And when Rob had come along, Annie found it difficult to hold her tongue. It was just not like Jess to do anything that might hurt somebody other than herself. They both tried to avoid it but whenever the subject of Jess's relationship came up, the conversation rarely ended well. Eventually, it became an off-limits topic, which Annie hated because she wanted Jess to be happy. And she wasn't sure her sister was as happy as she should be, indeed could be if she was with the right person. Specifically, someone that wasn't married to someone else.

* * *

Jess stood up from her desk, slipped her feet back into her black high heels and smoothed down her knee-length black skirt. With it, she wore a simple silk shirt and subtle but achingly expensive jewellery. Her long, caramel-coloured hair was swept up loosely. She was tall and whippet-thin, like her father. Glancing at her watch, Jess realised that she had to be across town in half an hour for lunch with one of her favourite clients and was running late. She popped her head out of her office and asked her PA to get a cab ready to meet her at the door in two minutes. The green juice hadn't helped the hangover. Nor had the coffee or the handful of painkillers. Hopefully, a plate of shepherd's pie in one of her favourite restaurants would sort her out. Grabbing her coat and bag, Jess checked her phone – one missed call from Rob – and headed for the lift.

As the taxi weaved its way through the streets of Soho, Jess was oblivious to the gorgeous early summer day outside. The sun shone, coats had been shed by both tourists and workers alike. With her eyes glued to the screen of her phone, she scrolled mindlessly, scanning the first lines of emails to make sure there wasn't anything that couldn't wait until after lunch.

'Here you go, love.' The cabbie's voice was her cue to shove her phone in her bag and make for the door. Tapping her card, she thanked him and hopped out onto the pavement. The sight of the enormous revolving door to the restaurant was a welcome one. Jess knew she was minutes away from the comfort of a corner booth and, quite possibly, a cold glass of champagne. She waited for the door to turn, seeing someone coming out as she did. The glass was thick, the wood dark, brass gleaming. In that moment, as she stepped inside, she caught sight of the person going out. It was a split-second look, but enough to make her catch her breath. Tall, dark but definitely not a stranger – it was Ben. As the door delivered her into the foyer of the restaurant, she turned to look back. The door continued to turn slowly, but there was no sign of him. She went to go back out, but stopped. Could it have been him? She ran through the probabilities: on a trip back to London from wherever he was living now (some-where in Asia, she had thought). Presumably a work trip, given that he was on his own.

They'd not spoken for years. Jess knew she'd broken his heart. But she also felt, back then, that he deserved someone better, someone who *really* wanted to marry him. Basically, someone not as selfish as she was. They'd kept in contact briefly after Jess left for New York but after a short while, the emails stopped. She filed what she'd done away mentally under Major Fuck Ups and tried not to revisit it too often. But seeing him in the flesh put it right back on top of the pile.

Gathering herself, she tried to think about the lunch she had ahead. She checked her watch – the client would be at the table – and headed to the cloakroom. Passing the bar, she caught sight of a youngish man sitting alone with what looked like a Martini in front of him. He smiled and winked. Jess was completely thrown. Did he know her? He must be looking at someone behind her, she thought. But, dear God, no, she realised he was now walking towards her. His face was so familiar but out of context, she struggled to place him. With a few steps between them, Jess suddenly remembered.

'Hi, Jess. Long time no see.'

'Hello, Tom.' Was it Tom? Too late now, she thought.

'I've been hoping to see you again but I didn't have your number. You left so quickly.' Yes, it was Tom, from the confer-ence. Right at that moment, Jess wanted to be anywhere but standing there. In fact, she wanted to run. First Ben, then Tom. It was like some kind of hideous nightmare, featuring the men most likely to make her feel like a failure. But her client was waiting and when it came to her work, she was nothing if not professional.

'Good, thanks, Tom. Yes, I did but you know how it is. I'm

really sorry but I'm running late, so do excuse me. Lovely to see you, though.'

'Oh, of course. Don't let me keep you.' Jess ignored the edge to his voice. 'Take care.'

'I will, thanks. And you.' With that, Jess slipped through the tables towards the cloakroom and was gone.

Standing at the basin a few moments later, Jess looked at her reflection in the mirror. She peered at the slight dark circles under her eyes. She thought about Ben, how seeing him for just that moment had made her feel so... what was it? It had made her feel sad. Sad at the thought of what might have been, sad at making him feel so wretched. Sad at the idea that she could simply put it to one side and get on with life. Sad that, in the end, Jess didn't seem to need anyone at all.

* * *

Annie cleared the last of the plates from the table and sat down for a moment, determined to take a sip of tea whilst it was still hot. The boys had taken themselves off into the garden. Despite the mess, the house was peaceful enough. She reached across the table for the pile of papers, on top of which sat a rather hideous anniversary card, picked up in the village shop. It was the best of a bad bunch, covered with pink hearts and 'You & Me' written in embossed, curly gold letters. Still, it's what's on the inside that counts, she reassured herself as she searched, fruitlessly, for a pen that actually worked. On the way home from school, she'd stopped by the local farm shop and picked up two lamb chops and some cheese. Annie was looking forward to the prospect of a simple supper, together with a more-decent-than-usual bottle of red wine and a chance to catch up properly over dinner.

With the card written and the tea drunk, she wandered into the garden to pick some fresh sweet peas for the table. She could hear the boys playing in the tree house that James had built for them soon after they'd moved into the cottage. The sun was still high in the sky and the breeze was warm. Perhaps they might even get to have a glass of wine outside before dinner if James got home early enough. She called for the boys, bracing herself for the bath/bed hour-long marathon that lay ahead.

'Rufus! Ned! Time to come in!' Predictably, her order was met with a barrage of protestations.

'But, *Mum*! We haven't finished our game!' cried Ned.

'Please can we just finish this one? We've only just started,' pleaded Rufus.

'Ten more minutes, then bath – deal?'

'Deal,' they both replied before turning and racing to reach the football first.

Annie went inside to go and run their bath, stopping on her way through the kitchen to put the flowers in an empty jam jar. Once she'd hidden the pile of papers in a drawer, scrubbed the spaghetti off and put a few tea lights on it, she knew her beloved table would look perfect.

* * *

It was after 9 p.m. when she got the text.

Got stuck with clients, I'll be late. Am so sorry. Don't wait up x

Tears pricked Annie's eyes. She felt her cheeks flush with colour as she tossed her phone across to the empty end of the sofa. She'd gone from pottering in the kitchen, enjoying the peace and quiet of the house post-boys'-bedtime to feeling angry, upset and disappointed in a moment. It was clear to Annie their wedding anniversary wasn't even on James's radar. Too tied up with his work, specifically his mid-life work crisis, to remember, she thought crossly. She poured herself another half-glass of red, put the lamb chops back in the fridge and grabbed her laptop. She knew exactly what she had to do. She typed 'cheap flights to Rome' into the search bar, retrieved her phone and replied to his text.

I won't. Happy Anniversary x

Hours later and both in bed, the silence lay heavy over James and Annie like an unwanted blanket. James had returned full of apologies, of course. Annie knew he was genuinely mortified. Still, forgetting a landmark wedding anniversary was going to take more effort on his part to make things right. His words were met with a frosty 'It's fine' before Annie turned on her side and closed her eyes.

Tomorrow morning, she'd tell him she was off to Italy with Jess for a few days and that his mother was moving in for the duration to help him look after the children.

3

One of Julia's greatest joys was walking round her garden, in her dressing gown, before anyone else was up. She loved watching the birds, stopping to inspect or deadhead a flower, depending on the season, waiting for the rest of the world to wake up. Her cottage overlooked the village green, with a walled garden at the back. For a modest-sized cottage garden it was crammed with plants. Roses, camellia, verbena and hellebores all fought for space in the borders, with fruit trees standing solidly at the back. Julia was a natural gardener, and over the years she'd created a beautiful space. Just outside the conservatory doors at the back of the house stood a wooden table and four chairs, covered in striped cushions she'd picked up years ago from a market whilst on holiday in Provence. Now faded and well worn, they provided comfort for a steady stream of visitors to the house. It was only at this early hour that Julia could be sure of having the garden and table to herself, along with a pot of hot coffee. Having lived here for years she was surrounded by old friends, although numbers were falling due to natural wastage, as she liked to put it. And whether it was coffee or, later, wine being poured, Julia was happy to sit and listen or talk to whoever dropped in on their way past.

It was Saturday morning and a little quieter than usual. Empty cup in hand, Julia wandered back into the kitchen to tackle the pile of washing-up in the sink. Last night's impromptu drinks with her divine old neighbours, Pam and Dicky, had ended with her digging out a fish pie from the freezer, followed by a game of cards and plenty of cut-price Chablis. As she collected the empty glasses from the kitchen table, the phone rang.

'Hi, Mum, it's me.'

'You're ringing early, darling.' It was just past eight o'clock.

'I know, sorry. But I knew you'd be up. Are you in this morning? Thought I might drop by on my way back from taking the boys to football practice.'

Annie clearly had a plan. Julia smiled to herself. 'Yes, of course. I'm not going anywhere until lunchtime.'

'Lovely. I want to know all about your trip to Rome.'

'Are you checking up on me?' Julia couldn't help herself.

'Not at all... I just thought it would be nice to hear about where you're going, what you'll be doing, who you're meeting. So, yes, I suppose I am checking up on you. But only because I'm interested... I'll be round in a bit.'

* * *

Annie had woken up that morning to the sight of a cup of tea in her favourite blue striped mug and a few hastily picked cornflowers from the garden in a glass. There was no sign of James but the bed was still warm. She could hear voices from the kitchen along with the clattering of bowls and spoons. James had clearly picked up the breakfast mantle and Annie decided she would definitely leave him to run with it. She pulled the duvet around her and reached across to turn the radio on. Her head ached slightly, thanks to the more-than-usual amount of red wine she'd had last night. No doubt about it, she thought, motherhood made hangovers a whole lot worse. Three glasses used to be a warm-up; now it counted as a fairly heavy night. And then she remembered: Rome. She'd booked a flight to Rome. Then there was Patty, James's mother. Annie had asked her mother-in-law if she could come and stay for a few days the following week. Of course, Patty had been delighted, only too happy to move in and have her much-adored grandsons to herself for a few days. Not to mention time with her only son. And so it was decided, she would come on Monday evening. Annie's flight was early on Tuesday morning and she'd be back on Thursday evening. Annie remembered feeling pleased with getting everything organised so quickly. But now, as she lay in bed with the quietly spoken headlines from the radio washing over her, she couldn't ignore the fact that she'd never done anything so impulsive in her life. And she didn't even know exactly when Julia was going to Rome, or for how long.

So it was that just over an hour later Annie sat on one of the faded cushions in a chair in Julia's garden, with a strong cup of coffee in her hand. She looked around her at the garden, so full of the promise of summer. On the table sat a small wooden trug of weeds, the result of Julia's early morning turn around the borders.

'Are you all right, darling? You look tired.' Julia always started with a summary of appearance.

'I am, actually. James didn't get back until late. I was already in bed.' Annie took a small sip of her coffee. 'Mum, he forgot our anniversary.'

'Oh, but you're both so busy! You with the boys and your

work, him with his job... It's no wonder sometimes things get forgotten.' Julia was clearly taking James's side. Annie smarted.

'Mum, it was our ten-year anniversary. Ten years! I mean, I'm not saying I was expecting a firework display and a unicorn but I was expecting *something*. Ten years is a bit of a milestone, isn't it?'

'Yes, I suppose it is different from any old year but I am sure he was mortified when he remembered, wasn't he?'

'He really was, actually. Got tea in bed this morning, and he did the boys' breakfast. And folded a pile of washing.' Annie smiled. 'I'm sure I'll get over it, but last night I just felt so angry. I mean, I know we're busy, I know we're tired, but still, that's no excuse to forget about the person you're in this together with, is it?'

Julia let out a small sigh. 'No, you're right to feel cross about it. But, darling, don't drag it out. It's such a waste of time and effort on both your parts.'

This was the side of Julia that Annie had never quite understood. Somehow, Julia was able to put any feelings she didn't like to one side and move on. She supposed this was down to having one husband leave her and two who she had left. Julia simply seemed to pack up her feelings about a particular situation and get on with whatever came next. Annie found it incomprehensible.

'Anyway, I don't want to talk about it. Tell me about Rome. I mean, come on, Mum. Why Rome?'

'Why not?' Julia smiled.

'Why not? Oh my God, Mum. For a start, you have no idea who you're meeting. I mean I know you know this Patrick but you haven't seen him for fifty years! He might be a complete nightmare, and you'll be trapped with him, in a foreign city, miles from home, with no easy escape.'

'Goodness, Annie, you sound almost as bad as your sister. Look, I wouldn't go if I didn't think it was safe to. I don't expect you to understand, but Patrick is one of the few people on earth I would do this with.'

Annie sighed. 'What I don't get is why you'd go and do something like this with a man we've never even heard you talk about.'

'I did have a life before your father, you know. It's just not something you tend to talk about once you're married. Especially not with your daughters.'

'I understand that part. It's just that this man appears out of the blue, says, "Come to Rome," and you say, "OK then. I will."'

'I know. Lovely, isn't it?' Julia picked up her cup, hiding the smile that played on her lips.

'Mum! Seriously! Aren't you at all concerned it's a bit, you know, weird? That he might be weird? I mean, do you know what he's been up to for all those years in between?'

'Darling, I don't expect you to understand. But, honestly, I knew him very well indeed. We were together for a while. I was young, but I loved him. He was wonderful.' Julia gazed across the lawn, eyes settling on the bird feeder. 'Ooh, look. A chaffinch.'

Annie ignored her mother's attempt to change the subject. 'So why didn't you stay together?'

'Circumstances. It just wasn't meant to be.' Julia took another quick sip from her coffee cup. 'Top up?' She offered Annie the pot across the table.

'No, thanks. I'll be on the ceiling if I have any more. Point is, Jess and I are just a bit worried – understandably, I think – that you were going off to meet a complete stranger. Or worse, that you'll come back married. Again.'

'Annie! What do you take me for? Of course I'm not going to

come back married. It really is just meeting an old friend and he happens to think that a few days in Rome is more exciting than a garden centre in Guildford. Anyway, I don't need to marry again.'

'That qualifies for understatement of the year. Sorry, couldn't resist.' Annie slipped in the apology before her mother could protest. 'Anyway, you can't get married again without our written consent, remember?' Annie gestured inside with a nod of her head.

'Oh, you're not still going on about that, are you? I can over-turn that anytime I like,' Julia laughed.

After Andrew had left, taking his holey green jumper and cords with him, Annie and Jess has made Julia sign a piece of paper. In fact, it was the back of a cigarette packet; Julia was never far from a Silk Cut and an ashtray in those days. And written on the paper, the following:

I, Julia Shield, hereby promise not to marry again without both my daughters' written consent.

The paper was signed, dated and crumpled, the result of a few glasses of wine, much laughter and Julia's attempt to then dispose of the contract in the bin. Jess had immediately fished it out, laminated it with sticky tape and stuck it to the front of the fridge, where it had stayed ever since. 'Three's enough,' Jess would say, jabbing a finger at the front of the fridge on her rare visits.

'Where are you staying?' Annie desperately tried to sound casual.

'It's called the Locarna, I think. Not sure exactly where it is but it sounds perfect.'

'What about him?'

'He's staying there too, I think.'

'What? You're staying in the same place? Mum!'

'Annie, I'm old enough to decide whether to stay in the same hotel as a man if I so choose.'

'In the same room?' Annie was now wide-eyed.

'No, not in the same room! Give me some credit.'

'Oh, OK. For a minute I thought you were, you know. Oh, I don't know. Awkward.' Annie drained the last of her coffee. 'Will you let me know when you get there so I know you're safe?'

'Yes, of course I will. I'll book a taxi to the airport. I'm flying out on Monday afternoon.'

'What time?'

'About two o'clock, I think. From Heathrow.'

'And you're back on Thursday?'

'Yes, quite late. Sandra's coming in to feed the cat and water the plants whilst I'm gone.' Sandra was Julia's neighbour on the other side.

'And what will you do when you're there?' Annie was aware she was starting to sound a little too interested.

'Oh, I don't know. Walk around, take in the sights, eat and drink too much, I should think. I'll show you a picture.' Julia got up slowly and moved towards the house. Annie watched her mother go through the conservatory to the sitting room. Every surface was covered in trinkets, vases, candles or photo frames with faces – some old, some young, but always happy. Books filled the shelves from floor to ceiling, mostly biographies, Julia's favourite genre. Well-thumbed novels fought for a spot on the lower shelves as she couldn't ever bear to part with a book once read. The walls were barely visible as paintings and framed pictures and photographs jostled for position, telling Julia's life story, albeit not in chronological order. After a few minutes, Julia returned with a photo in her hand. It was an old black-and-white picture showing a young man with windswept hair and smiling eyes. Annie guessed he would have been in his late teens. He was grinning broadly at whoever had taken the photo – must have been Julia, thought Annie – and behind him was a beach. With the white horses in the background frozen in time, the man wore a large fisherman's jumper and striped scarf around his neck.

'That was taken in Cornwall, in the summer of 1961. I was nearly seventeen. He was nineteen. Our families both holidayed in the same small village on the south coast, not far from the top of the river. We'd known each other since we were about ten. That summer, he and I went back to stay there and on that particular day, a beautiful sunny one as I remember, we'd walked from the village all the way along the river path and over the headland to a cove round the corner. There was no one there but us. Patrick had borrowed a friend's camera so that we could take some pictures. That was my first attempt.'

'Why didn't you stay together?' Annie had tears in her eyes. One look at the picture and she knew, simply from the way he was looking at her taking the picture, that he'd really loved her mother.

'Well, it just wasn't meant to be. We were too young, really. He was away at university in one city and I went to work in another. That's it.' Julia shrugged her shoulders, her eyes not leaving the photograph.

'So what made him get back in touch?'

'A funeral, actually.'

'Whose?'

'The friend who lent us the camera that took that photo. Richard, his name was. Apparently, it made Patrick think of me and he wanted to, you know, get in touch before it was too late.'

'How did he find you?'

'There's this thing called the Internet...'

'Ha, ha, very funny. So, he stalked you online?'

'Yes, I suppose he did.'

'Bit creepy, don't you think?'

'Well, only if you then don't get in contact. He was trying to find me so that we could meet, catch up, talk about old times, find out what happened to our lives... I don't know. I've not spoken to him. This has all been done by letter.'

'So, he finds you on the Internet but doesn't think to contact you by email?'

'No, I just got a letter from him telling me about Richard's death and saying that he'd love to see me to catch up. Like old friends, I guess.'

'Except you're not. You said he was your first love.'

'He was. But we've obviously gone on to live our lives, and been very happy, so I like the idea of, you know, coming full circle.'

'As long as you don't get married, Mum.'

'Stop it, of course I won't. Actually, I'm rather looking forward to seeing Rome. I've always wanted to go. Just never got there.' Julia looked far away for a moment, before collecting herself, smoothing down her dressing gown and reaching for the empty coffee cups.

* * *

Dear Julia,

My sincere apologies if this comes a bit out of the blue but as you may have heard, Richard Fern died recently. He was diagnosed with cancer about a year ago and his health deteriorated very quickly in the last few months. I lived not too far from him so managed to visit every couple of weeks for a catch-up over a pint (if he could, depending on treatment). Anyway, we talked about old times at length, our old friends especially. Your name came up often; Richard adored you, as I'm sure you'll remember! It's the only reason he lent us that blessed camera of his when we were in Cornwall. But thank goodness he did, because the photographs I have of our time together there are so very important to me. They remind me of one of the happiest times of my life.

Before he died, Richard told me that I should get in touch with you. Sadly, the fact that life is short had been brought a little too much into focus for him. But I haven't been able to stop thinking about it, about you, and would love to see you again.

I feel I should tell you my story, briefly. A few years after we last saw each other, I met and married a wonderful lady called Kathy. We met when I was briefly back from Paris, where I was working as a photographer; she went on to be a lecturer, and mother to our two children, Oliver and Emma. We were married for more than forty years. Kathy died just over five years ago. That too was cancer, which I suppose is why I resolved to try to help Richard through his illness.

I've had a very happy life and really, don't have any reason to feel hard done by. But the one thing I've always wished turned out differently is what happened to us. I realise it is too late to change anything but in the time that we have left (sorry if that sounds a bit maudlin, I don't mean it to), I'd love to hear what's happened in your life.

So, I have a proposal. Do you remember how we always talked about going to Rome? You were passionate about your history of art; I wanted to go and see the architecture of the place. And, of course, we never got there. I realise this might *come across as the ramblings of an old, slightly mad man but the thing is, Richard asked me to make sure his ashes were scattered somewhere more exotic than Gerrards Cross, where he lived. And his favourite city in the world was Rome. I can think of nothing I would love to do more than meet you there, and we can scatter Richard together. Or, if that's rather grim, I'll scatter him first.*

If you are still reading, I'm a) thrilled, b) slightly surprised and c) hoping you might say yes. Let me know when you've had time to think about it.

With fondest love,

Patrick

Julia held the letter in her hand. She hadn't shown this to Annie, knowing it would have meant yet more questions. But when Annie had gone, Julia had read it once more. What surprised her was how normal it felt to be holding something written by Patrick. His writing was just as she'd remembered. Maybe she'd always expected he would be in touch again at some point. She couldn't be sure. But what Julia did know was that she very much wanted to meet Patrick in Rome. Which is why she'd replied, yesterday, to the email address written on the letter, the day after receiving it. They'd agreed to share the cost (he'd offered, Julia had said she'd pay her own way), staying at a hotel he'd suggested and made plans to meet at four o'clock in the afternoon, to the right of the front of the Pantheon as you look at it, on the following Wednesday from the date on the letter – and Julia had said she'd wear a purple scarf so that Patrick could spot her in the crowd.

He'd explained everything perfectly in the emails that followed so making the arrangements was done without fuss. Julia was excited at the prospect of discovering a new city; one she'd always longed to visit. And she loved travelling alone: no one to insist on arriving at the check-in gate first (Husband No. 2, Simon, had always done that); no one jabbering away for the entire flight (Husband No. 3, Andrew, was a terribly nervous flyer, never stopped talking); Julia was looking forward to going away; she was ready for an adventure, even if it was only for a few days.

Julia put the letter back in its envelope, sat down at the computer on the table in her conservatory and typed 'Rome weather' into the search bar. If she was going to travel light, she needed to make sure she packed the right clothes.

* * *

Annie's phone vibrated in her pocket as she stood on the sidelines, watching the boys finish their game of football. It'll be Jess wanting an update, she thought. But it was James.

'Hi.'

'Annie, I'm so sorry. Again.'

'I know you are.'

'But I have to ask, did I miss the part about my mother coming to stay?'

Annie laughed. 'Shit! Has she been on the phone already? Oh God, I'm sorry. I was going to tell you when I got back this morning.'

'Tell me what? Are you leaving?' James sounded truly panicked.

'No! Of course not. Don't be so ridiculous. But it's a bit of a weird one, I must admit.'

'Just tell me!'

'OK, well. Mum has been asked to go to Rome with her first boyfriend. Patrick is his name. He's written to her out of the blue and asked if she'd like to go. And of course it's a *crazy* idea but Mum being Mum has said how lovely and she can think of nothing more exciting than an unexpected trip to Rome for a few days. Except Jess thinks he might be a complete weirdo, or worse, she'll come back married. Again.'

James was laughing now.

'I'm being serious! You know what she's like. Anyway, Jess has decided to go too, not that Mum knows, and begged me to go with her. Follow Mum out there just to keep an eye on her. And she offered to pay for the tickets on the grounds that she's, well, loaded. I think she's actually excusing herself from a slightly awkward work situation so is desperate to get away for a few days. You know, with that idiot Rob. I told you about it. Anyway, that's not the point. So I know it's mad and I should have talked to you about it first but I was so pissed off with you last night that I drunk-booked a flight and then called your mother and asked her to come and stay. Not actually drunk, but too many glasses of red wine. So, you know, bit reckless. But technically it's partly your fault. I'll fly on Tuesday, back on Thursday. I'll get everything ready for Patty so the boys are sorted...'

'Annie, it's fine. But just so I get this right, you and Jess aren't planning to tell Julia you're following her out there?'

'No, of course not. She'd have a fit.'

'Well, she'd have a point.'

'We're just going to keep an eye on her, that's all. Make sure she doesn't end up being abandoned in Rome. I mean this Patrick might not even show up! What then?' Annie sounded genuinely worried.

'Look, I think you and Jess will have a brilliant time and you should go regardless of Julia being there. And I'm not saying that just because I forgot our ten-year anniversary.'

'Although there is that...'

'I know, I know. Don't milk it. Anyway, fill me in when you get back. I'll see you in a bit.'

'See you in a bit.' All things considered, that could have been worse, she thought. Now all she had to do was make enough Bolognese sauce to feed the boys for a few days. That and rustle up a Roman costume before Monday morning.

4

Jess stood in front of a make-up counter mirror under the harsh light of the Duty Free area, hair tied back, peering at her reflection. 'God, my Botox bruises are bad.'

'I don't know how you can do that to yourself,' said Annie. 'I mean, what if your entire face collapses when you're older?'

'Don't be so ridiculous!' Jess pulled at the skin on either side of her cheeks.

'I'm serious! Surely injecting poison into it is going to have consequences somewhere down the line?'

'Maybe, but I'd rather have smooth features for now. Anyway, it's only the tiniest bit around the mouth to get rid of the smoker's lines.'

'Even worse!' Annie laughed. 'And anyway, you're gorgeous without it. You really don't need to do anything. Me, on the other hand...' Annie grabbed her tummy.

'Oh, now you're being ridiculous. You've had two babies, for God's sake!' cried Jess.

'Maybe so, but still...' She wobbled it for effect.

'Come on,' laughed Jess, 'we've got time for a glass of champagne if we're quick.'

'But the flight's boarding in a minute.'

'Annie, we've got plenty of time. Just a splash in the lounge before we go to the gate. It's on the way.' Jess had insisted on upgrading Annie's ticket to business at the check-in desk, which of course she'd been able to do with one flash of her gold flying card.

Once seated with a glass of free cold champagne in front of each of them, Annie decided it was a good moment to broach the subject of Rob, to get it out of the way. Keep it brief, she thought. And besides, they were in a public place so it couldn't end in an argument.

'So, why the sudden exit stage left?'

Jess took a small sip, swallowing quickly. 'What do you mean?'

'Come on, Jess. You know what I mean.'

'Well, to be honest, I'd just had enough.'

'Of Rob?' Annie couldn't keep the hope from her voice.

'God, no. Not him. That's not even, you know, a thing. It was stupid. I was stupid. I know you don't approve and, honestly, I'm not very proud of myself *at all*.' Jess took another sip, longer this time. A pause, then: 'I ran into Ben.'

'When?' Annie's eyes widened. She put down her glass.

'Last week. We didn't speak.'

'Why ever not?'

'He didn't see me. Well, I don't think he did, anyway. I was on my way in; he was on his way out. Revolving door.'

'Didn't you call out to him? I mean, if he'd known you were there...'

'What, Annie? What do you think he would have said? What would I have said?' Jess took a large slug of champagne.

'Well, "hello" would have been a good place to start.'

'It's not that simple, Annie. You know that.'

'But how will you ever know if you don't see him?'

'I know, but I was the one who ended it. It's not my place to start it again. He's got a whole life that doesn't involve me now and it's definitely not for me to fuck it up. Again.' Jess drained her glass. 'Come on, let's go. Last call.'

'Shit!' Annie scooped up her bag and followed her sister towards the door, grabbing a last handful of free cashew nuts as she went.

Once on the plane, Annie couldn't help but run through the list of things in her head one more time. Food? All done. A few hours of batch cooking Bolognese sauce and banana cake on Sunday morning had made her feel better about being away for a few days but, as it turned out, Patty had turned up with enough chicken casserole, lasagne and apple crumble to feed them all for weeks, let alone three days. There were clean school uniforms in the boys' wardrobe and food for packed lunches in the larder. Clare was on standby to have the boys after school on one of the days if Patty fancied a break and James promised he would be home in time to say goodnight to them.

'Please stop worrying. We'll be fine,' James had said, as they'd travelled up early on the train together that morning.

'I know you will but it just feels so weird, going off.'

'Don't complain, make the most of it.'

'You're right, I will. Thank you.'

Sitting on the plane with her sister beside her, in the front row of all places, Annie's thoughts turned to Rome and of what lay ahead in the next few days. 'Do you know,' she turned to Jess, speaking in an almost whisper, 'I've been so preoccupied about the logistics of getting here, I've not even thought about what we're going to do once we get to Rome. I mean, where do we even start?'

'Good question. I was thinking a stroll down the Via Condotti followed by a glass of something cold and sparkling, looking out over the city from the hotel near the top of the Spanish Steps.'

'Jess, I mean Mum. How do we go about finding her?'

'I think we'll leave that until tomorrow. First, we need to enjoy a drink and watch the world go by.'

'When in Rome...' Annie couldn't help herself.

'Exactly that,' smiled Jess. 'Now if you'll excuse me, the diazepam is kicking in. I might just shut my eyes for a bit.'

'When did you pop those?' Annie looked aghast.

Jess laughed. 'Same time you were pinching the free cashew nuts. Washed them down with champagne. Just to take the edge off. Lovely.' With that, Jess lowered her sunglasses and tipped her head back.

Annie sighed, picking up the glossy magazine lying in Jess's lap. A whole two and a half hours lay ahead and the only question she might be asked is what she'd like to drink. The flight alone was practically a mini break.

As they stepped out of the airport, the wall of warm air hit them with force. The sight that greeted them was one of complete chaos. There were banks of white taxis but none seemed to be moving. Drivers on pavements talked fast and furiously, gesticulating wildly at the gathering crowds around them.

'Oh God, what's happening?' cried Annie.

'*Sciopero*. Shit.' Jess reached for her phone. 'There must be a strike on, probably the buses or the trains. The roads will be completely blocked with cars. Looks like we're stuck, at least for a bit.'

On the plane, Annie had been planning an afternoon taking

in the sights of the Colosseum, the Pantheon, the Trevi Fountain and the Spanish Steps with the odd glass of Prosecco thrown in for good measure. Clearly that wasn't going to happen.

'What shall we do? I mean, could we call the hotel, see what they say? Or maybe go and get a coffee or something and come back in a bit?'

'No, we're just going to have to sharpen our elbows and get to the front as quickly as we can. Follow me.' Jess grabbed Annie by the arm and together they made their way into the throng.

* * *

Julia sat at a table in the shade outside a small bar with a condensation-on-glass of chilled white wine in front of her – and Patrick opposite her. The intense heat of the day had started to ease a little but the sun still blazed, the sky was azure blue, and Julia was very happy indeed. She had arrived the evening before, taking the train from the airport into Roma Termini, the central station. From there, she'd taken a taxi to the hotel – the taxi driver, Stefano, had told her she was lucky to arrive when she did because the following day the train drivers were due to call a one-day strike – and she had enjoyed her first full day in Rome immensely.

On landing, she'd received instructions from Patrick via text to go to a different hotel than originally planned, a small guest-house tucked on the side of a cobbled piazza in Trastevere, on the other side of the Tiber away from the crowds. Run by a heavenly husband and wife, Antonio and Isabella, the house was stuffed with art and antiques. Barely a patch of paint could be seen for the picture frames of all sizes hanging on the walls. Her room looked out over a piazza and on the roof was a small terrace with a handful of tables and white canvas umbrellas. On checking in,

Antonio had handed Julia a note. It was from Patrick, saying that, if she wasn't too tired, he would meet her for a drink on the terrace at 8 p.m. Or if she wasn't keen to meet tonight, maybe they could bring forward their original plan and meet the following afternoon by the Pantheon. Julia didn't see the point in wasting time. She had days ahead of her to explore the city.

Julia had had time to hang her handful of clothes in the large wooden wardrobe before taking a bath and changing into fresh clothes. To her surprise, as she headed to the terrace, she didn't feel the slightest bit nervous. Rather, she couldn't wait to see Patrick, to hear how he'd been and what he'd been doing all these years.

As she made her way up to the roof in the old lift, she checked her lipstick in the mirror and took a deep breath. The lift door opened and there, sitting at one of the tables, his head in a book, was Patrick. His frame slowly unfolded as he stood to greet her. He was tall, despite the slight stoop that age had put upon him, and his hair was thick and grey. His blue eyes matched the faded colour of his gently crumpled blue linen shirt. Still kind eyes, just as they always had been, thought Julia.

'I'm so pleased you came,' Patrick said, taking one of Julia's hands and holding it in both of his.

'So am I, Patrick.' Julia looked at him. Tears sat just behind her eyes but they didn't fall. She opened her arms and they stood for a while, lost in a warm embrace.

Two hours later than they'd hoped, Annie and Jess pulled up in a taxi outside their hotel, just a few streets to the west of the Piazza del Popolo, at the northern end of the Centro Storico.

The building was tall and narrow, with an air of faded glamour. Outside, rows of bicycles and *motorini* sat on the edge of the cobbled street looking like a suddenly abandoned cycle hire shop. Small orange trees sat in huge stone pots on either side of the heavy black double doors of the hotel. As hassled and hot as she was, the scent of orange was not lost on Annie as she passed them and climbed the steps into the hotel.

But the sight that greeted them was not quite what they had expected: a crowd of bewildered tourists all asking questions in different languages. The two women sitting behind the desk were apologising profusely.

'*Scusi*, please can you tell me what's going on?' Jess had her best smile on.

The older of the two women cupped her hand to her ear.

'We have a reservation. Is everything OK?'

'Unfortunately, the hotel is closed. We have a crack in the wall. The city authority tell us we have to close immediately. I am sorry, there is nothing we can do. We must find you somewhere else to stay.'

'Seriously? Just like that you're closing?' Jess's raised voice brought the room to silence.

Annie stood at the back of the room, mindlessly looking at the rack of free postcards on the wall. Not exactly what I had in mind for our Roman holiday, she thought. Still, at least she was here and not, for once, picking fish fingers, toys or wet towels up off the floor, which is what she'd normally be doing at this time of day at home.

'I am sorry, madam, but as I already said, there is nothing we can do. We have to close. We find you another hotel as soon as we can.'

'Where? Near to here?'

'Please. Give us some minutes and I can organise it for you. How many rooms did you have booked?'

'Two. I'm here with my sister. And we think my mother is staying here too.'

'You *think* she's staying here?'

'Yes, long story. Can you tell me where she's moved to?'

'What's her name?'

'Shield. Julia Shield.'

The woman pulled down her glasses from her head and slowly ran her finger down the list of names in front of her. 'There is no one of that name on the list. When did she arrive?'

'Yesterday, I think. With a man called Patrick... Patrick... Annie!'

Annie turned.

'What's Patrick's surname?'

'I've absolutely no idea.' Annie shrugged.

Jess turned back to the woman, who now had her glasses firmly back on her head. The younger woman was also now interested, along with the German couple to Jess's right. 'We don't know. But there must be a booking for Julia Shield.'

'I'm sorry, but there's nothing under that name. I find you another hotel now.'

'OK, thanks.' Jess sighed. 'Annie, I'm going outside for a mo. Hang on here until we know where we're going.' Clutching her e-cigarette, Jess pulled down her sunglasses and headed for the door, completely unaware of the stunned gazes that followed her.

Moments later, Annie was called to the desk by the younger woman. She spoke softly. 'So, I have a room for you in a hotel not far from here, it's called the Mellini. There is a taxi outside that will take you. It's just a few minutes but you have your bags so it's easier to go in the car. The room rate is the same as here so you just pay them and we'll refund your deposit. We are sorry about this.' The woman smiled apologetically.

'It's fine, really. It's not your fault, just one of those things. Thank you.' Annie scooped up her bag, grabbed Jess's suitcase and made her way outside. 'That's our car,' she said, nodding to the taxi as she passed Jess on the steps. 'Come on, hop in. We're off.'

Soon they were speeding through narrow cobbled streets before crossing a bridge, the murky yellow-green water of the Tiber snaking steadily below them. Turning left onto a wide street, they pulled up outside an enormous, anonymous-looking building. Only when the taxi driver opened the door did Annie see the name Mellini across the plate-glass door. Realising this was, in fact, their hotel, she couldn't help but feel a little disappointed. The Locarna had looked every inch the hotel of her dreams and now they were staying in what looked like a government building.

'Brilliant!' Jess looked up.

'Really? Don't you think it's a little drab?' Annie was surprised by her sister's calm acceptance of it all.

'The wifi will be good, as will the constant supply of hot water. Unlike the Locarna, no doubt. And we're closer to one of the best coffee places in Rome here; it's just across the next bridge down. Anyway, we're not going to be here much. We've got shopping to do.' Jess grinned at her sister.

'And finding our mother, Jess. Don't forget about finding our mother. At least we had some hope of doing so if we'd been in the same place.'

'Oh, yes. Of course. That, too. Now, shall we throw our bags in the room and go and get a drink somewhere?'

* * *

Given the stressful journey they'd had to get there, the functional nature of the Mellini did indeed turn out to be a blessing in disguise. After the chaos of the previous three hours, Jess and Annie were checked in within minutes. With their bags hastily dumped on enormous beds, they headed out into the city, ready to fill their senses and stomachs with whatever Rome had in store for them. As they crossed the bridge, heading back towards the heart of the city, the heat of the day now seemed to lie in the cobbles below their feet. The air was still warm, the sky pale blue with a whisper of pink creeping in from the edges.

Jess grabbed Annie's hand as they raced across a busy street, narrowly avoiding being mown down by a couple on a Vespa. They seemed to be travelling against the tide as workers passed them, walking back to their homes with soft leather briefcases in hand.

'Where are we heading?' Annie could sense Jess was on a mission.

'About halfway up this next street,' Jess replied. They came to a small door. 'Ah-ha, just as I thought. Negroni?'

'It looks like a bank, Jess.'

'Look up.'

Annie raised her eyes, spotting corners of beautiful thick canopy umbrellas above. The gentle hum of the crowd reached them in the street below. 'Definitely time for a Negroni,' she said, following her sister through the door.

* * *

The waiter placed the glasses on the table, each small tumbler filled with drink the colour of blood oranges, along with a bowl of indecently green olives and a small plate of bruschetta topped with basil.

'*Grazie.*' They reached for their glasses.

'*Prego.*' The waiter smiled at them both, before snaking off between tables. Annie took a small sip and felt the bitterness of the drink take hold of her taste buds immediately.

'Oh my God, that's good.' Jess shivered in her seat.

'Like a short, sharp slap across the tongue.' Annie was more used to the gentle lemony notes of a nice-enough Pinot Grigio on hers but right here, right now, this little *aperitivo* was perfect.

'So, how are the boys?' Jess loved them madly and they, in turn, adored their favourite aunt.

'Oh, all good. Rufus is doing really well at school. Ned is yet to realise that there is no coming-back-to-life potion. I have tried to explain that if he runs into the road or climbs a really big tree, and something goes wrong, then that's it, game over. But he doesn't get it.'

'Well of course he doesn't! He's five!'

'Six, actually.'

'Near enough... Shit, did I miss a birthday?'

'No, not unless the remote-controlled car that got delivered that day wasn't from you. I mean, honestly, Jess. That must have cost a fortune.'

'Oh, thank God for that. For a minute I thought I'd forgotten.'

'You never forget, Jess. It's just a shame that you're not often there. They love you so much.'

'I know, I know. But work, it's insane at the moment. Actually, it's like that all the time. Which is why I'm looking for someone to help me.'

'Jess, that's great! You are the world's worst delegator and you can't expect to keep working at the pace that you do and not keel over with the stress of it all at some point.'

'I know, but it's so hard even imagining handing someone my

baby. But if I'm going to keep the business going, I've got to find someone who can work with me and then, one day, take over.'

'Look, I can't pretend to know what it's like. I paint furniture for a living...'

'And you're raising two kids! Come on, Annie, what you do is amazing...' Jess downed the other half of her drink and signalled with a dazzling smile to the waiter for two more.

'I'm not belittling what I do. It's bloody hard work. But it's also really, really boring sometimes. I mean, at least I get time to myself now they're both at school and that's very different from being at home with two small kids all day. But still, I can't help but think what might have been if I hadn't jumped off the career ladder.'

'You can always get back on it, though.' Jess realised she was on shaky ground.

'It's tough, Jess. The cost of childcare is eye-watering and the jobs that fit round school hours are hardly abundant. I do everything I can with the furniture but, to be honest, it's a slog. I'm just so tired. All the bloody time. Apart from now, with this in my hand I feel I could take on the world and win.' Annie drained her glass and noticed the Negroni doing its work.

'Well, the grass is definitely not greener from where I'm standing. Honestly, I hate to think I'm defined by my job but that's how it feels sometimes. As if not being married or having children by now means that I had no option but to throw myself into work. Which really isn't the case. I do it because I love it. Anyway, considering you were going to marry what's-his-name, the lead singer from that boy band you didn't do so badly.'

'I was not!' Annie look genuinely horrified. 'It was the other one, who was, by the way, the best dancer, if you must know. And I know we would have been very happy together.'

'Enough about what might have been. What we really need to talk about is what we fancy doing tomorrow.'

'You mean finding Mum? We haven't much to go on...'

'No, not that, we'll work that out tomorrow. For now, I can't think beyond a plate of antipasti. Let's walk up to the Spanish Steps after this one and find somewhere to eat. It's gorgeous at this time, now it's not so hot.'

The bar was busy, humming with the sound of Romans decompressing after a day spent in sweltering offices. Together, they soaked up their surroundings, enjoying the noise of people talking in Italian, fast and with feeling. The men were mostly without ties; the women immaculately dressed with expensive-looking sunglasses either covering their eyes or placed on their heads, keeping back their manes of luxuriously shiny hair. Annie couldn't quite put her finger on it but everyone looked both seemingly desired and desirable. Maybe that was just the Negronis.

'Come on then, I'll get the bill.' Jess looked round to catch the waiter's eye. 'Oh, just look at that sky!' Behind her the sky was pink as the sun prepared to take its leave for the day.

Annie sighed. 'It really is beautiful here. And after those drinks, I'm starving.'

The waiter placed a dish on the table with the bill, along with a card and a scribbled number under the name Mauro.

'Oh my God, I think he's given you his number. I mean, how? You've been here for less than half an hour and didn't even speak to him?' Annie looked at Jess, wide-eyed.

'Maybe he's just being friendly?' Jess placed a note on the dish and slipped the card into her bag. She smiled at Annie, grabbed her sister by the hand and together they headed further into the heart of the city.

5

Julia awoke to the sound of church bells and the low morning hum of human life on the street below. Wheels on cobbles, cheery greetings and teasing exchanges between locals; words she didn't fully understand but got the gist of. She reached for her water, suddenly regretting last night's final grappa – on the house, obviously – but as the previous day pieced together like a simple jigsaw in Julia's mind, she couldn't help but smile.

It had started with cappuccino on the guesthouse terrace, surrounded by pink-tiled rooftops and glimpses of freshly washed sheets billowing gently on washing lines strung between windows like spaghetti. She'd met Patrick in front of the fountain in the piazza below and together they'd set off towards the Aventine Hill. According to Antonio, this was the place to go for the best views across the city. The idea was to find the perfect spot to scatter their friend's ashes but they'd decided, over dinner the night before, that a recce was in order to give them a chance to find the right place and return there when it was less crowded.

Their first evening together after all those years had been all about filling in the gaps, talking about their lives, marriages – Julia's three had taken less time to explain than Patrick's one – and their children. But the following morning was spent very much in the present. As they headed away from Trastevere, crossing the Tiber by the Ponte Palatino, the noise of the busy city enveloped them. Then, as the hill approached, the traffic fell quiet and the crowds on the pavements thinned out. Up ahead stood a large church with enormous Y-shaped stone pine trees lined up on either side.

'That's it; that's where we're heading.' Patrick gestured up ahead. He took hold of the camera around his neck, a Leica. Years of working as a war photographer had left him completely incapable of going anywhere without a camera. He quickly lifted it and pointed it in the direction of the church.

They left the main road and the tourists on Segways and walked through a huge green door in the wall, stepping into the most beautiful garden full of orange trees. They passed a stone bath filled with fountain water trickling in from a comical carved face in the wall. The heat from the sun was warm but not yet hot enough to make them sticky, the sky clear blue and the scent of citrus hung heavy in the air.

'It feels like we've got Rome to ourselves for a moment.' Julia looked around at the high walls of the church beyond, the wistful stone figures that stood gazing not at her, but towards the sky.

'It really does. But not for long. I think we might find a crowd around the next corner but hopefully we're here early enough for it not to be too busy. I think you are going to like this view.' Patrick led the way, Julia following close behind as they crossed the garden and turned the corner. There, before them, lay the city. From here, Julia could see across the Tiber all the way to the unmistakable dome of St Peter's Basilica. The hum of the city lay far below; the only sounds to contend with, the backdrop of gentle conversations between other tourists as they too took in the view. Or rather, tried to. Julia didn't quite know where to start: the domes that dotted the line between city and sky; the imposing hills that lay behind and the beautiful combination of sun-washed oranges, off-whites, yellows and pinks of the buildings below. It looked so peaceful. Yet she'd been walking among the life that buzzed on the roads and pavements below only moments before. It didn't seem possible from here.

'What do you think? Worth the wait?' Patrick looked at Julia.

Julia sighed. 'Definitely worth the wait; I just can't believe it took me so long to come to Rome.' She stood, still as one of the nearby statues, drinking in the view, committing it to memory.

'Come on, let's take a look inside the Basilica before we go and find something to eat.'

Their walk back into the city took them down towards the vast open space of the Circus Maximus, where the path was dry and dusty underfoot. On they went through the paths of the Roman Forum, marvelling at the ruins that lay before them; so ancient yet so solid. They passed around the Colosseum, deciding to admire the imposing, sun-drenched arches from the outside rather than join the snaking queue of people waiting to catch a glimpse of the ruins inside. Turning north, they were relieved to find shade in the small, cobbled streets ahead where the hum of traffic fell quiet.

Spotting a small *taverna*, they settled at a table covered with a simple white cloth and a single set of cutlery at each place.

'*Buon giorno!*' A short, bald man with steel-framed glasses and smiling eyes greeted them. 'Please, I'll get you a menu. But first, wine. I bring you a glass of something to refresh you both.'

'Thank you, and some water too, please.' Julia hung her scarf on the back of the chair.

Patrick stretched out his long legs to one side of the table and picked up the menu. A young waitress – the owner's daughter, Julia thought, glancing at her features – put a small basket of herb-flecked bread on the table. The smell of fresh rosemary and sage filled the air. The man reappeared with a small silver tray and two glasses of orange-coloured sparkling wine, so bright they looked as if they had fairy lights in the ice cubes.

'Thank you! They look beautiful!' cried Julia.

'*Prego.* Now, today's specials, I must tell you. We have *tonnarelli cacio e pepe*, is like thin spaghetti with green olive oil, black pepper and pecorino. And before that, if you want, we have some fresh burrata with tomatoes.'

'Well, I don't know about you but that sounds completely perfect.'

'Absolutely.' Julia smiled at him. 'Thank you, signore.'

'Is a pleasure. Now, I leave to enjoy.'

'Cheers, Patrick.' Julia raised her glass.

'To you.' For a moment, he looked serious. 'Thank you for coming. I can't tell you how happy I am that you did.'

'So am I, Patrick. So am I.'

* * *

Walking off lunch, gelato in hand, they stopped to look in the windows of tiny shops filled with curiosities, beautifully crafted jewellery and towering piles of second-hand books. Now well into the afternoon, the heat was starting to ease but the light was still dazzling. As they rounded a corner, the magnificent dome of the Pantheon came into view, making everything around it look like small toy buildings.

'We're a day early. We'd said tomorrow. To meet here, I

mean.' Patrick picked up his camera and pointed it seemingly carelessly towards the centrepiece in front of them.

'Well, there's no point in wasting time at our age, is there?' Julia grinned and headed towards the huge doors, draping her purple scarf around her shoulders as she went.

Once inside, they stood side by side, looking around them, above them, in easy companionable silence. Sunlight streamed through the oculus above, throwing a perfect, giant golden ball of light against the wall inside. The air was cool and calm; the atmosphere matched it.

'Someone once told me that when the rain pours through there,' Julia motioned to the hole in the roof above them, 'it comes down and scatters raindrops across the floor like a million marbles.'

Patrick looked at her. 'That was me. Back when we talked about coming to Rome.' They spoke in soft whispers as people wandered around them, eyes drawn to the roof above.

Julia smiled. 'I know you did. I just wanted to see if you'd remember, too.'

'How could I not?' Patrick smiled and Julia took in the already familiar lines around his eyes.

'Patrick, I think I'd like to talk about that now.'

'Are you sure? I mean, I want to, too. But I'm just as happy leaving it where it is, if you'd prefer.'

'Yes, I'm absolutely sure. Also, coffee.' Julia took Patrick's hand in hers and together they walked out into the sunshine and back into the narrow streets.

* * *

The smell of roasting coffee hit them before they'd even stepped through the door. A long, dark wooden bar ran the length of the small room and a partition hid the waiters from view as they worked the gleaming silver coffee machines along the back wall. They appeared from one end, one after the other, with trays and saucers held high. Patrick ordered two *grandi caffè* and they waited in a small booth at one end, perched on burgundy velvet-covered banquette seats. No sooner had they settled in, than the coffee was on the table. Each one came with a small exquisitely wrapped sweet in gold tissue paper, tied with a thin ribbon on the side of the saucer.

'Even these are beautifully done. I mean, they could just come wrapped in clear plastic but really, for them it's as much about how it looks as how it tastes,' mused Julia.

'Exactly. Form and function.' Patrick placed his sweet on Julia's saucer.

'Patrick, I know we've talked about our families, filled in the gaps.' Julia took a breath, met his gaze. 'I feel like we both had the lives we were meant to have, given that we couldn't have one together.'

'I know. Your daughters sound like wonderful people. You seem as happy and strong as you ever were.' Patrick raised his cup; put it back down. 'But if there is one regret I've had in life, it's not doing everything I could to make it possible for us to have stayed together. To have challenged those who said we couldn't.'

'Me, too.' Julia twisted the ends of the sweet in her hands, admiring the way the paper glinted in the late afternoon sun. 'But regrets at our time of life are a waste of time. And energy. I'm so grateful for all that I have. And the fact that you've come back into my life now seems like it was always going to happen, even if I never dared imagine it would.'

Both were silent for a moment. The sound of empty cups hitting saucers on the bar as busy Romans drained their cups, shouting their greetings and goodbyes was all they could hear.

Patrick spoke softly. 'We were so young. But we were so sure. I hate that it ended like it did. Forced apart. Forced to do something we didn't want to do.'

'I know, but how could it have been any other way? We had nothing – and nowhere – to go to. We would have been helpless.'

'It still makes me angry thinking about it now.' Patrick drained his cup, adding his own sound of cup on saucer to the chorus.

'Patrick, honestly, we have to let that go. We have to remember what we had, when it was good. Not be cross for the things that were beyond our control. Doing that is the only way to live the rest of our lives and enjoy it, as we deserve to. You can't change the past.'

'When did you get so wise?' Patrick's blue eyes fell on her, a gentle smile on his lips.

'I surprise myself sometimes.' Julia laughed, raising her coffee to her mouth, letting the bittersweet aroma fill her nose before she sipped. 'Look, all I know is that I spent years wondering "what if" before realising that the more I did that, the less I could fully enjoy the life that I had. My girls, my husbands – even the bad ones had their good points. Anyway, feeling angry is exhausting. So I decided to let it go. I think you should, too.'

'But what if...'

'Don't. Just don't think about it. That belongs in the past. We have our lives now and I for one am determined to make the most of it. So, how about we go and find the hidden Caravaggio tomorrow?' Julia popped a chocolate-covered coffee bean into her mouth.

'You don't forget a thing, do you?' Patrick laughed.

'I think you'll find, if you remember correctly, that it was me that told you about that.'

'So you did.'

* * *

Jess had woken early to the sound of church bells, thankfully muffled by the functional double-glazed windows of the Mellini. The Negronis and cherry-scented red wine that followed had left her helpless in the face of tiramisu, which they feasted on after plates of *coscio di agnello* in a busy, bustling restaurant tucked away behind the Spanish Steps. She glanced at the hotel clock radio on the table beside the bed. The angry red numbers stared back at her: 05:03. Why could she *never* sleep in properly? She lifted the mascara-streaked pillow up and over her head, rolling onto her other side, cocooning herself in the thick duvet as she did. Finding the coolness she craved, she sighed and tried to find sleep again, at least for a few moments.

Down the hall Annie lay in bed, eye mask in place, snoring lightly. A few hours later than Jess, she woke to the sound of her mobile phone telling her there was a message. It was from James. She lifted the eye mask and squinted at the phone. The room was dark; the blackout blinds doing their job admirably against the breaking day.

Hope having a lovely time. All good here boys fed and dressed. Mum doing school run. I miss you.

Annie took the eye mask off with one hand and put the phone down, propping herself up on the pillows before texting back.

All good, Rome amazing! Dinner delicious, Jess on great form. Miss you all so much too. No sign of Mum. Give boys a big kiss from me xx

Next, she texted Jess.

Oi! Are you awake?

Yes, have been for bloody hours.

Breakfast in half an hour?

Roman breakfast for me.

What's that? Sounds delicious.

Coffee and a cigarette. Well, an e-cigarette.

Oh. I want coffee and pastries.

Let's skip the buffet here. Meet you in the lobby in half an hour.

Fab, see you in a bit.

Annie threw on the thick white towelling robe and headed for the storm shower. The Mellini, she thought, had its upsides. Half an hour later, she walked into the lobby dressed in her usual get-up – jeans, slightly shoddy white T-shirt, scruffy trainers. Jess swept in a few moments behind, similarly dressed but one look and Annie knew that everything Jess wore cost at least a few hundred pounds more than hers. The trainers were box-fresh designer ones compared with Annie's beaten-up versions. The crisp white T-shirt hung loosely, as only an expensive cotton-linen mix can, and a black blazer sat across Jess's angular shoulders. The sunglasses were enormous, adding a glamorous edge. Annie made a mental note to invest in bigger sunglasses next time she was replacing hers.

'Right, shall we go and find proper caffeine?' Jess led the way towards the hotel door.

'Good plan.' Annie followed.

They headed out along the anonymous, wide street and turned the corner back towards the Tiber, taking the bridge across as they'd done the night before. But instead of walking on towards the bar they headed south through narrow streets, now filled with carts of vegetables, fruit and flowers making their way, like the sisters, towards the Campo de' Fiori.

'You promised me a Roman breakfast.' Annie struggled to keep up with her sister, who was by now striding ahead, sunglasses firmly fixed on her face.

'It's just up here, I promise.' Jess had read about a little coffee place on the corner of a street leading to the square named after the hat makers who used to have workshops here. 'There, Via dei Cappellari.' They walked along the cobbled street, buildings on either side the colour of marzipan. Bars covered the big windows and peeling paint, and plaster added an air of faded glamour to the enormous doorways. *Motorini* lined the street on one side and, this hour being too early for most tourists, Jess and Annie felt let in on the city's secrets. A woman in an apron made pasta in an open doorway, the light catching the flour and the spray of olive oil in the air as she tossed it up and then down onto a cold, flat surface. As they drew nearer to the square, the noise of people and movement grew louder. They dashed into a café on the corner and made their way through the small crowd towards the counter.

'*Due caffè, per favore,*' called Jess, across the bar to the old man sitting behind an enormous gleaming silver cash register. She handed the money over. He took it, unsmiling and gestured for her to move down the bar.

'What about food? I'm starving!' cried Annie.

'Have this coffee and then we'll find something to eat. Promise.'

The coffees came, steaming hot and ever so slightly sweetened, in tiny cups on saucers. They both jostled for some elbow room at the bar, locals either side of them. Annie looked around, enjoying the noise, the smell of the place. Jess's glasses remained firmly in place.

'Those Negronis were quite strong last night.' Jess took a sip of her coffee. 'God, that's better. Right, food.'

Annie took a long sniff of her coffee. 'Got a text from James this morning: all good. So strange to think that life goes on when you're not there.'

'It'll do them no harm to manage without you for once. Enjoy it!'

'Don't you worry, I plan to.' And with that, Annie drained her coffee cup in one go.

Leaving money tucked under the saucer, they left the café and crossed the square, passing stalls heaving with wooden crates filled with sun-ripened courgettes and salad leaves, ripe purple artichokes and dark, wrinkled cavolo nero. Rows of flowers, boxes of tomatoes and piles of melons fought for space, just as the cries of the sellers behind them fought for air time.

Just then, Annie caught a whiff of freshly baked bread hanging in the air. The scent took her to the door of a small bakery at the side of the square. A queue of locals outside was enough to make her join it, seeing that what this place sold was worth queuing for. Before long she had, in a small brown paper bag, a couple of cream-filled *cornetti,* little Italian pastries. Once back out in the square, Annie perched on a stone step and, taking her *cornetto* from the bag, took a good look before biting into it, crumbs falling onto her lap.

Jess sat beside her and took the bag, helping herself to the other one. 'I wonder what this guy Bruno did.'

'Who the hell is Bruno?' Annie still had a mouthful. 'Hang on, before you bite into yours, I need to take a picture. It's not every day I get to Instagram my breakfast from Rome.' She held the remaining half of her *cornetto* in her mouth and reached for her phone from her back pocket.

'The guy behind you, eyeing up your breakfast.'

Annie turned and looked to see a formidable bronze figure on top of the stone plinth. 'He looks lost in thought.'

'He looks hungry to me. I don't know how you have time for that stuff.' Jess gestured towards Annie's phone.

'Try being stuck at home with two boys. Then you'd understand.'

The sisters soaked up the scene before them as they demolished their pastries, listening to the cheerful shouts and calls of the locals, feasting their eyes on the rich colours of produce and flowers. 'It's like watching the most brilliant play,' Annie mused.

'Last time I went to the theatre, I fell asleep. This is much better.'

'So, what's the plan? I mean we've lost our only lead now that we've all moved hotel.'

'Well, let's just see how it goes. We might not even find her. Fun, isn't it?' Jess grinned at her sister. 'Come on, where do you fancy going? Let's do some cultural stuff before the shops open.'

'Can't believe you're even thinking about clothes shopping when we're surrounded by some of the greatest art in the world! Seriously, I think we should head for the Forum, then to the Colosseum, then up to the Villa Borghese via the Trevi Fountain. I have a whole route mapped, here on my phone.' Annie stood up, brushed the crumbs from her clothes and hitched her bag onto her shoulder. 'Come on, time to go.'

'Yes, miss.' Jess grabbed Annie's proffered hand and glanced up at Bruno before turning and heading back across the square, her arm looped gently through her sister's as they headed back into the maze of the *Centro Storico*.

* * *

'What an extraordinary creation.' Julia stood in front of a statue in a museum in the grounds of the Villa Borghese that same morning. They'd made their way here to escape from the heat of the late morning sun. It showed the figure of a young man and woman in a seemingly tragic not-quite embrace.

'It's Apollo and Daphne. He loved her but she was destined to return to the earth at his touch. Well, turn into a laurel tree, at least.' Patrick looked up at Daphne's face.

'It looks like they're actually moving,' Julia whispered as she moved around the statue, taking in its detailed form. 'Look, her skin is turning to bark. Her feet are growing roots! Poor thing, she looks terrified.'

'Well, you would be, wouldn't you? Apollo is after you and you're repulsed, thanks to Eros playing dirty tricks. Daphne's father intervened and turned her into a tree. Not the happiest story.' Patrick spoke gently, his eyes now fixed on Apollo's outstretched hand.

'But to get such movement from stone... I mean, look at their faces. So sad... and those laurel leaves. To do that with a chunk of marble is just...' Julia shook her head gently as she, too, gazed at Daphne.

They continued wandering the rooms of the museum,

feasting their eyes on the rich colours and forms of paintings of Titian, Rubens and Raphael, which hung on marble walls at every turn. They stopped to admire Bernini's *David*, showing him poised to fire his slingshot at Goliath, his face epitomising intent.

'I feel like I don't even want to stand in front of this one. I mean, that rock looks like it's actually going to ping out and hit me any second.' Julia moved to the side of *David*, pulling her scarf around her shoulders as she did. The stone-cooled temperature inside the museum was in stark contrast to the skin-prickling heat outside.

Patrick reached for his Leica, taking a quick snap of *David* and Julia as she passed. The sound of the click pleased him, even after all these years. 'How about we go and find something to eat? All that walking's made me hungry.'

'I can't quite believe I'm saying this but I'm actually hungry again, too.'

'There's a great little place just round the corner from here. We should be early enough to get a good table outside, in the shade.'

'Perfect.' Julia took one last look at *David* from the side, his body twisted so that it seemed to fill the grey-flecked white marble stone with energy, before turning and heading for the door, Patrick a step behind.

* * *

'Not going to Instagram this one?' Jess elbowed her sister gently in the ribs.

They were perched side by side on a white stone ledge, while water frothed from the mouths of carved galloping horses behind them, tumbling with a thunderous roar into the pool below. They'd left the cool of the narrow side streets, turning a corner to find the Trevi Fountain nestling in a small square. Groups of tourists came and went in quick succession, standing momentarily before taking selfies, most of them adding peace signs and pouts as they pointed their iPhones.

'No, of course not! This is something you've just got to look at. Enjoy it. And try to commit it to memory. Not that I can remember what I came into the room for half the time nowadays.' Annie gazed at the gleaming white stone stallions. The soft salmon-coloured walls of the surrounding buildings stood in stark contrast to the white stone palazzo, a suitably dramatic backdrop to the fountain.

'Where does all this water come from?' Jess trailed her fingers in the pleasingly cold, pale blue water of the fountain.

'Aqueducts. The city is built on them. There's a whole network of them running underneath.'

'How do you know this stuff?'

'I'd love to say it's my old art history coming back to me but actually I saw it in a documentary ages ago. There are sinkholes everywhere, too.'

'That explains the Locarna hotel, maybe.'

'Exactly! That's what I thought. Not that it seemed like the best time to bring it up.'

'So where to next? And can we stop for a drink?' Jess took a surreptitious drag on her e-cig, the thick vapour hanging in the air with no wind to shift it. Annie clocked a group of tourists with selfie sticks drift away. Jess was oblivious.

'Not before we've thrown a coin in the fountain. And made a wish. I know what I'm going to wish for.' Annie rummaged in her bag, hoping to find some small change among the detritus that sat in the bottom. 'Obviously I can't tell you otherwise it won't come true.' The look on her face told Jess she was being absolutely serious.

'I love that you actually believe that.'

Annie tossed a coin over her shoulder, into the fountain, wishing for her sister's happiness as she did so.

They wandered north along small streets, grateful for the shade of the buildings. Even the narrowest street was lined either side with mopeds, small cars and tiny vans squeezed in wherever space allowed. They crossed the Via Condotti, lined with its boutiques, designer names above the doors glinting gold in the sun, glimpsing the Spanish Steps set back at one end as they did. The sight of the crowds spurred them back into the narrow streets and as they turned a corner, Jess walked slap-bang into the back of a tall man with a mop of dark hair.

'*Scusi!*' He turned quickly, reaching out to steady her with – she couldn't help but notice – a rather beautifully tanned forearm.

'Oh God, sorry! I wasn't looking where I was... oh God!' Jess's breath caught in her throat. 'You look... like someone I know. Used to know,' Jess corrected herself quickly.

'What's with the queue?' Annie gestured to the snake of people standing in front of him.

The stranger smiled. 'Ah, this is for the best takeaway in Rome. But it's a secret! The best pasta you will have from a plastic bowl,' he smiled and tapped his nose, 'so don't tell anyone I've told you about it.'

'Secret's safe with us.' Jess winked.

'So what do you recommend?' Annie was trying her best to peer ahead to see what people had in their bowls.

'Well, that's easy. There are only two dishes to choose from. But we won't know until we're at the counter.' He whispered, so as to not blow their cover in the queue.

Annie could hear the conversations among the young *Romani* in front of them, animated with words tumbling out over each other. The dress code was clearly smart-casual with the men in white linen shirts casually rolled up to the elbow. The women looked effortlessly stylish, like something out of one of the catalogues that landed on her doorstep from time to time, where everything looked relaxed but clearly well-cut.

'So, are you here on holiday?' The stranger fixed Jess with his dark brown eyes.

'Yes, we are. Well, we're looking for our mother. Actually, only sort of looking for her. She's here with a friend.' Jess lifted her sunglasses and perched them on her head, sweeping back her caramel hair as she did so.

'She lives here?'

'No, she's on holiday, too.'

'But you didn't come together?' The stranger was understandably confused.

'No, she came with a friend. And we just wanted to check she's OK. But we haven't found her yet.'

'I'm not surprised! There are three million people living here!' His eyes sparkled with amusement.

'I know it sounds ridiculous but, to be honest, I fancied a break and... oh, sorry, this is my sister, Annie...'

'Hi.' Annie raised her hand in greeting before craning her neck to peer into the next passing bowl.

'*Ciao, Annie.*' He returned the gesture. 'So, how are you going to find her?'

'Well, there are only so many places a tourist goes when they're here for a few days. Hopefully our paths will cross at some point,' said Jess, vaguely.

'Why don't you just call her?'

'We don't want to spook her. Just be here in case, you know, she needs us.' As she said it, Jess realised quite how ridiculous the whole thing sounded.

'The thing is, our mother gets married quite a lot – three times and counting – and, well, it's getting a bit tiring. That's why we're here. Because if she calls us to say she's getting married again, at least this time we might be here to witness it.' Not once did Annie take her gaze from the front of the queue whilst delivering her explanation.

'Well, yes, I guess that covers it.' Jess shrugged her shoulders at the now laughing stranger.

'*Ha perfettamente senso!* Seriously, it's not too crazy. Not in this city, anyway. And it means you get to eat lunch from here, something you won't ever forget.'

'Exactly! I'm actually going to pass out, the smell is so good,' Annie said.

Soon they were at the front of the queue, inside the small shop front where a family – they had to be family, thought Annie, with their matching features among five faces of different ages – moved around behind a glass-fronted counter at great speed, somehow managing to avoid crashing into each other in such a tiny space. Behind the counter sat two enormous silver trays filled with pasta.

Annie squinted at the menu, chalked up on a blackboard behind the whirling men. 'What do you recommend?'

'So, you have either gnocchi with tomato and sausage sauce or fettucine with *funghi porcini*. Mushrooms.'

'Fettucine for me, definitely.' Annie inhaled deeply, savouring the smells and sounds of the shop.

'Gnocchi for me.' Jess reached for her bag.

'No, let me get these for you, please.'

'You can't do that! We don't know you!' protested Jess.

'No, no, honestly, that's very kind but we really can...' added

Annie.

'Look, it's four euros a bowl. I'd like to. Then I am part of your Roman holiday, whatever happens with your mother!'

'Well, that's really kind of you. Completely unnecessary but really kind, thank you.' Jess moved to one side to let another customer out and seconds later had a bowl of warm pasta in her hands, along with a napkin and a fork.

As they left the shop, the sisters once again thanked their new friend as he took off back round the corner, waving and wishing them luck as he went.

'How do you do that, Jess?' Annie mused as they watched him go.

'Do what?' Jess replied, with a shrug of her shoulders. They headed to find somewhere to eat, the small tables outside the shop already taken.

'Get men to buy you lunch after a sentence.' The pungent, earthy smell of mushrooms seeped from the sides of the sealed bowl in Annie's hand.

'I didn't! I think it was you telling him what we're doing here that did it. Whatever, I can't wait to eat this, it looks absolutely amazing.'

As they walked past the Spanish Steps, teeming with tourists climbing up and down the giant staircase, Annie turned to her sister. 'I know who he reminded you of. I think you still love him, to be honest.'

'I do not!' Jess protested a little too vigorously. 'Seriously, I don't.'

'Whatever.' They passed the little restaurant from the night before, the only clue to its whereabouts a small menu behind glass on the wall beside the enormous – now closed – dark green wooden doors. 'Let's head to the gardens and find a spot in the shade to devour this.'

6

Filled with mozzarella and rich tomato sauce-topped pizzas and a couple of tumblers of Rosso Piceno, Julia and Patrick made their way from the tucked-away *osteria*, back through the labyrinth of narrow streets towards Piazza del Popolo.

Over lunch, they'd made plans to take Richard's ashes back to the spot on the Aventine Hill early the following morning, ahead of the crowds. The view was, they'd agreed, perfect; the city of Rome blanketed the ancient hills below them.

For now, though, they strolled comfortably arm in arm towards the huge oblong-shaped piazza. In the middle stood a gigantic Roman obelisk. Churches sat around the edges, and on one side an enormous white stone monument was decorated with statues and busts, which gave Patrick and Julia haughty looks as they passed.

'So where is the Caravaggio?' Patrick looked around, his eyes stopping at the smartest church at the end of Via del Corso.

'It's in the one behind you, actually.'

'That one? But that's so *ordinary*.'

'I know. That's the beauty of it. And there's more than one by him. And statues by Bernini, too. And another beautiful painting by a little guy, but I can't remember his name.'

'How do you know he was little?'

'Because his name means "little painter"... oh, what is it? It'll come to me in a minute...'

They entered the church through an enormous door at the top of a flight of wide stone steps. The cool of the air wrapped around them the second they stepped inside. Julia pulled her scarf across her shoulders and Patrick removed his beaten-up Panama hat from his head. They stood for a moment, taking in the impressive sight. White marble pillars and arches rose above simple wooden pews, an altar lying at the far end. Light came through small windows along the top, throwing sunbeams across the floor.

'This way. Follow me,' whispered Julia. She took a turn to the left, behind the wooden pews and along past the chapels lining the wall. Then, at the front of the church and to the left of the altar she stopped and stood at the entrance to a small chapel. Following her gaze, Patrick took in the riot of colour in front of them. Three enormous paintings dominated the walls. In the middle, the image showed the Virgin Mary, draped in a red dress, being held aloft – rather awkwardly, Patrick felt – by cherubs.

But Julia had her eyes fixed on the painting on the left-hand side. 'That's by Carracci, the guy who painted the ceilings of the Farnese Palace. All rather over the top, if you ask me. But these...' she looked from the left to the painting on the opposite wall, '... are by Caravaggio.'

Patrick looked up, taking in the dark and light of the painting, showing a man, upside down, on a cross.

'That's *The Crucifixion of St Peter*. He wanted to be placed upside down so as not to look like he was trying to be Jesus. Just look at the men trying to carry him. He obviously weighed a ton.'

'And what's this one?' Patrick gestured to the painting opposite, showing a man on the ground, his horse being held by another man.

'That's *The Conversion on the Way to Damascus*, St Paul's road to Damascus moment. He was so stunned he fell off his horse. Isn't the light in these paintings incredible? It's as if they're lit from behind.'

'My goodness, they really are.' Patrick was mesmerised. 'I mean, to have such pain on one side, and such pleasure on the other.'

'I'm not sure it's pleasure. He's just fallen off his horse.'

'You know what I mean.' Patrick nudged Julia, making her smile.

Julia grabbed Patrick's arm. 'Let's go and have a look at the little painter's efforts.'

* * *

The sisters sat on a bench in the park, in the shade of a towering umbrella pine, enjoying the relative peace and quiet of the surrounding gardens. It seemed a world away from the constant noise and movement of Rome's streets. In front of them was a lake, dotted with couples in rowing boats attempting, badly, to reach an islet on one side where a small temple stood. Beside it, an ancient oak tree towered above.

'What secrets that tree must have.' Annie took a swig of her water and glanced at her phone.

'Any news from home?'

'Long update from Patty via text: the boys are fine. Not missing me at all, it seems.'

'Well, that's good, isn't it? Better that they're having a ball than in bits because you're not there for five minutes.'

'I suppose. Oh, and another apology from James for forgetting our anniversary. That makes four so far. I think I'll have to tell him to stop now.'

'Nah, let him sweat for a bit more. At least it won't happen again.'

'True. Now, what do you fancy doing? I feel like I'm forcing you to look at paintings when I think you'd rather be doing something else.'

'No, I love it. Empties the head. I mean it empties it of stuff that's usually in it. I'm enjoying filling it with other things.'

'Well, there is one particular painting I would love to see, given that we're not far from the church it's in. It's a Nativity scene by Pinturicchio, really beautiful.'

'Promise me after that we can go and find a Bellini?' Jess placed her hands together in mock prayer.

'Yes, of course we can! Just a few more paintings and I'll be happy.'

They turned and headed through citrus-scented, statue-laden gardens towards the edge of the park, down a flight of wide stone steps into the piazza.

'This,' said Annie, angling her phone and pointing towards the obelisk in the middle, 'used to be in the Circus Maximus. God knows how they got it here.'

'You're talking about a city that built the Colosseum. I'm pretty sure moving *that* wasn't a problem.' Jess took in the wide oval space in front of her, the gate to her right, twin churches to her left. 'Where now?'

'Over there.'

'What, that?' Jess looked towards a rather plain-looking building standing quietly in the corner.

'Yep. That's the one.'

They climbed the steps into the church, the simplicity of the white stone pillars and wooden pews seemingly a foil to the colour and creativity housed in the chapels along each side.

'Now, I think it's this way.' Annie led the way, Jess following behind as she shoved her sunglasses onto her head. They turned right and headed towards the first chapel at the back. There, in the middle of the wall, was a Nativity scene, just as Annie had said.

Annie stood motionless in front of the painting. Her eyes moved from the scene – a baby, an adoring mother – to the surrounding arch covered in carvings of plants and flowers.

'I like the colour of the roof.' Jess motioned to the deep blue on the vaulted roof, painted with tiny golden stars. A voice from behind, so familiar and yet totally out of place, made them turn to one another, eyes wide.

'Now *this* is the one I was thinking of. Still can't remember his...'

'Mum!' Jess and Annie chorused, spinning round at exactly the same time. Both stood, gawping at their mother.

'Girls! What on earth are you doing here?' Julia's face was a picture.

'Oh, Mum, I'm so pleased to see you!' Annie threw her arms around her mother.

'Hi, I'm Jess.' Extending a hand to the obviously bemused man standing to the side of Julia, Jess flashed a smile at her mother.

'Er, hi! I'm Patrick.' He smiled back, putting out his hand to Jess, then Annie.

'Hello, Patrick.' Annie tried not to stare. He looked so like the photo her mother had shown her except for the hair, now grey rather than dark.

'Hello, darling.' Julia hugged Jess before standing back to look at them both. 'This is extraordinary! What are you doing here? Did you come to keep an eye on me?' She laughed, fixing them with a look: *I know you did.*

They spoke at once.

'No!' Annie replied, nervously.

'Yes, actually. We did.' Jess looked at Annie. 'Shit, we should have rehearsed that bit.'

'Yes, you should have done!' Julia turned to Patrick beside her. 'Patrick, meet my girls. How extraordinary!'

'It really is lovely to meet you. I've heard lots about you. Your mother is clearly very proud of you both.'

'How funny. Because we don't know anything...'

'Well, we hadn't planned to bump into you exactly.' Annie spoke over her sister. 'It was just that when you said you were coming to Rome, I realised that I *desperately* wanted to see the city, too. I've never been. And Jess had a few days off work...' Annie looked at her sister, hoping for backup.

'Yes, exactly.' Jess nodded. 'And we never get time away alone so we thought, well... let's just go! We didn't think we'd see you. Honestly.' Jess could feel the red rising in her cheeks as she spoke.

'Well, now we're all here, we should meet up for dinner tonight. That is, if you haven't got plans already?' Patrick looked from one sister to the other, then to Julia.

'Well, we... um...' said Annie, slowly.

'No, we haven't.' Jess sounded firm.

'Great. We were going to eat somewhere near our guest-house tonight, down in Trastevere.'

'We're staying at this end of town, just over the river. Could we go somewhere in the middle?' There was an edge to Jess's voice.

'Yes, of course. Do you know anywhere?' If Patrick thought Jess was being a little frosty he was too polite to let it show.

'Yes, I do, actually. A fish restaurant.' Jess racked her brain for the name of the place her PA had mentioned. 'It's called something like...'

'La Rosetta, I know it. We'll book a table for nine o'clock tonight on our way back this afternoon,' said Patrick.

'That's the one.' Jess forced a small smile.

'Great, see you there. Look forward to catching up, Mum.' Annie kissed Julia on the cheek.

'Me, too, darling.' Julia laughed, delighted at the kismet of it all. She hugged Jess. 'It'll be so nice to hear all your news. It's been an age since we've caught up properly. Make sure you see the Caravaggio paintings before you go,' she added as she headed towards the door.

'We will!' Annie called after her, only to be met with a glare from a fellow tourist, clearly trying to have a moment of quiet contemplation in one of the pews at the back of the church. 'Sorry,' she stage-whispered. '*Scusi.*'

Jess watched as her mother and the man they knew little about stepped out from the church and into the just visible bright light of the afternoon. Patrick placed a hand in the small of Julia's back as they disappeared from view. 'Oh my God. Sorry if that's inappropriate but...'

'I know. I wasn't expecting that. And Mum, acting like it's the most normal thing in the world!'

Jess dragged her eyes away from the door and back to Annie. 'Well, she looks like she's having a wonderful time. He doesn't look like a serial killer. He could still be a conman, though. I think they're more difficult to spot.'

Annie laughed, once again disturbing the tourist, still in not-so-quiet contemplation. 'She looked fine. And no engagement ring, at least as far as I could see,' she whispered, winking at her sister.

'Thank God. Right, can we please go and find a Bellini now. I've done the painting bit.' Jess started towards the door.

'Yes, just as soon as we've seen the Caravaggio paintings in the other chapel over there. C'mon, we'll be really quick.'

'OK. But after that, no more paintings until we've had a drink.'

'Deal,' said Annie, pulling a reluctant Jess by the arm to the front of the church.

* * *

'So, you really had no idea they were here?' Patrick couldn't help but show the amusement in his eyes.

'Honestly, I didn't. I mean, I know the girls worry about me from time to time, but that's because I'm getting old. And I think they worry about me being on my own. But to follow me out to Rome...'

'Well, they knew you were coming out to meet me. And they wanted to make sure you were OK, at least be on hand if you suddenly needed them.'

'I think you're being too generous, Patrick. They were definitely spying. To see who I was with, to make sure I didn't come back married, I should think.'

'Why, have you done that before?' He placed his camera on the table.

'Well, yes, I have, to be fair. I left that one out when filling you in the other night. It is the one I'd rather forget, to be honest.' Julia felt embarrassed, a feeling she wasn't used to.

'What happened?' Patrick handed Julia a small, chilled flute of sparkling wine. By now back in Trastevere, they sat alone on the rooftop terrace of their guesthouse, the dipping sun casting long shadows across the piazza. The tourists below walked slowly, the heat of the day and the miles covered having taken their toll on their now-tired limbs. The *Romani*, on the other hand, walked with a light spring in their step, having escaped their offices for the day.

Julia took a sip of her drink, the cool, frothy liquid spreading across her mouth. She swallowed, savouring the flavours. 'Goodness, that's gorgeous. Tastes of pears. Absolutely delicious.'

'It's from Cartizze, the best area for Prosecco. It's not easy to find at home; the Italians drink most of it.' Patrick raised his glass to Julia across the table.

'Cheers. I'm not surprised.' Julia took another sip and put her glass back on the table. 'So, the one I didn't tell you about was Simon. Bit of a monster, as it turned out.'

'What happened?' Patrick picked up his glass.

'Well, at first it was lovely. He was lovely. After David and I had separated, I was honestly quite happy to be on my own. I had the girls, of course, so I wasn't *really* on my own. But I was fine with my own company most of the time. And I certainly didn't think I'd marry again so soon. But then, we went on holiday and, well, I just got carried away. You know, with the thrill of it all. And I came back married. The girls were furious.'

'How long were you married for?' Patrick tried not to sound as surprised as he was.

'Not quite three years. Quite long enough, though. He was a drinker. And not a happy drunk.' Julia looked down at the table. She picked up her sunglasses and put them on, the orange light reflecting back at Patrick from her lenses. 'How long have you had that camera?'

Patrick accepted the deliberate change in conversation

without question. 'That one's almost thirty years old. I got it just before the Berlin Wall came down.'

'Were you there when it did?'

'No, I wasn't. I was in Afghanistan, covering the Civil War. I was there on and off for a couple of years.' Patrick took an olive from the bowl on the table, offering them to Julia as he did. She shook her head.

'When did you decide you wanted to be a war photographer?'

'Not long after you... we parted. I'm afraid I dropped out of university. My heart just wasn't in it. I went back home and started doing jobs for the local paper as a photographer. No formal training, of course, but somehow I managed to persuade the chap in charge I could do it. At first it was covering weddings, openings, that sort of thing. But then I got sent to the local court house one day to get a picture of a man accused of something or other, can't remember what exactly. And getting the picture was... well, it wasn't just about being in the right place at the right time. It was about capturing the moment, despite what was going on around me. That's when I knew I wanted to do more. The power of a great photograph, you know?' Patrick popped the olive in his mouth.

'How did Kathy feel about you doing that for a living? Being a war photographer.' Julia draped her scarf loosely around her shoulders.

'Well, obviously she didn't like it much. But she knew when she met me that that was what I wanted to do. In fact, by the time we met I was working as a photographer for one of the big agencies. I was away quite a lot from the beginning. And I was young then, I took risks. So I got good pictures. And good pictures meant more work. Vicious circle, quite literally. But I knew I didn't want to end my career wearing my boots, as it were. I knew that at some point, my luck would run out. The trick is getting out before it does.'

'So when did you? Get out, I mean.'

'The children were still relatively young. Coming back to "normal" life was hard. I loved the job. But I loved my family more. So I came back after about ten years and joined Kathy at the university as a researcher. But after a few years I knew I had to go back. My pictures made a difference. And as awful as it might be, wherever I was I had the option to leave.'

'You went back?' Julia was aghast.

'Yes, I did. And, well, that's when I got shot. Only in the leg, but enough to give me the wake-up call I needed. After that, I never went to the front line again.' Patrick finished his glass.

'I'm not surprised! I think you were one of the lucky ones.'

'We're all the lucky ones. Not living in a war-torn country, I mean.' He smiled across the table. 'I was a terrible dinner guest for years.'

'I can imagine.' Julia returned the smile. 'But for what it's worth, you're a wonderful one now.'

'Why, thank you.' He laughed gently.

'Now, I know I sound old but I'd quite like a quick nap and a long bath before we head out to meet Jess and Annie later. Would you mind?'

'Not at all. I might head out for a short walk. This light is going to be too good to miss.' Patrick glanced up at the sky, a pink glow now starting to creep across the blue.

'Of course. Wonderful idea. So, meet you downstairs in a couple of hours?'

'Perfect.'

* * *

Across the river, Jess and Annie sat at a table each with a small Bellini in front of them.

'Tosca threw herself from those walls. To her death.' Annie gestured to the giant round building standing guard on the bank of the Tiber behind them.

'How gruesome.' Jess reached for her glass and took a sip of her drink. 'God, at last. I've been looking forward to that for hours.'

'She was tricked into killing herself because she thought the man she loved didn't love her any more. But actually, he did. And he had all along. She just didn't know it,' Annie picked up her glass, 'until it was too late.'

'What are you getting at, Annie?'

Jess knew exactly what her sister was getting at. But however much Annie was dying to press her, Jess knew that she wouldn't go any further. The only person to really push Jess on her love life was Julia – and the last time she'd broached the subject it had ended in six weeks of angry silence. Annie had eventually brokered the peace deal. Again.

'Nothing! Really, I'm just pointing out that the ending of one of the most tragic operas ever written took place behind your right shoulder. That's all.' Annie took a gulp from her glass, looking up at the statue that topped the building, like a stone cherry on top of an enormous cake.

'That doesn't really narrow it down. They're all pretty tragic, as far as I can tell. Look at poor Carmen! And Mimi dies of TB. Give me a good ballet any day.'

'They're not much better. The Swan Princess and the Prince throw themselves into the lake! It's all too tragic. I can't think of one with a happy ending.'

'I guess it's easier to move an audience with a tale of tragedy than one of plain happiness. People love a drama.'

'I'm too tired for drama...'

'How long have we got until we meet Mum and Patrick?'

Annie glanced at her watch. 'A couple of hours. Shall we go back to the hotel for a bit? Quick shower and change... Oh my word, look at that...' Annie was looking beyond Jess towards the sky. Behind her sister, an enormous cloud of birds moved as one across the dusky backdrop.

Jess turned to watch the show. 'Starlings. Looks like some sort of weird organism, doesn't it?'

They watched for a moment, captivated by the constantly changing form and direction.

'Hypnotic, isn't it?'

Jess drained her glass. 'Come on, let's go.'

7

Patrick stood by the small fountain in the piazza across from their guesthouse, watching a series of small plays unfold. There was the husband and wife laying tables outside the front of their small *trattoria*. Although both looked to be in their seventies, they moved quickly, carrying trays loaded with glasses and crockery, stopping to place carafes of water on tables as they passed. The scent of bread wafted across the square; a few tables already occupied by hungry tourists.

Two young boys raced around the square, the older of the two holding a giant plastic wand that left a stream of enormous bubbles, each one floating gently out of reach, much to the younger boy's annoyance.

Looking up towards the tops of the buildings surrounding the piazza, Patrick saw an elderly woman take her washing off the line whilst her husband watered geraniums in pots placed around the edge of the terrace overlooking the piazza.

The sun was yet to set, the dark blue sky mostly clear bar a few streaks of cloud tinged with pink light. Patrick had just had time to change his shirt and throw water on his face. All that walking had left him hungry and thirsty. He checked his watch – a few minutes after eight – and looked across to the door of the guesthouse just as Julia stepped out.

Dressed in a pale green linen shirt, long white trousers and with her silver hair drawn back loosely off her face, she looked, Patrick thought, just as she had when they first met. Not exactly, obviously, but she had that same look; one that expected only good things to happen. He loved that about her. She smiled and waved at Patrick across the square.

Maybe he had seen too much, become too worn over the years. But being with Julia made him dare to look forward to what lay ahead for the first time in years. After Kathy died he'd gone through the motions; saw friends, tried to keep busy. He didn't want his children to worry about him, to be a burden in any way. But his life felt rather like a faded photograph, the colour drained.

Being here, filling his senses with different sights, smells and sounds was making him feel properly alive – something he hadn't felt for a long time. He wanted to engage with life again.

Earlier, on his walk back, he'd taken pictures of doorways, of rows of *motorini* lined up against the walls of endless narrow, cobbled streets and of people sitting on chairs at the bottom of stone stairways. Sometimes they were talking, others were simply watching. Around every corner was a new frame, seemingly waiting for Patrick to capture it. Life was everywhere; interesting, with form and energy. Watching Julia come out of that doorway, smiling and waving, was the most perfect shot of the day.

'You look wonderful.' He offered her his arm.

'Well, thank you, you don't look so bad yourself.' Julia laughed, putting her arm through his. 'Right, where are we off to?'

'It's about a fifteen-minute walk, back up near the Pantheon.'

'I think I can cope. Got my sensible shoes on.' She smiled and motioned to her silver trainers.

'So you have, very sensible. Right, this way. Watch out for the bubbles.' The two boys scampered past, the younger one shouting after the other, trailing them as he went.

The colours of the buildings around them looked different in this light, muted but still magical.

'I feel like I'm in a film. This looks like a set.'

'Thank goodness, then, the fountain's only small. Otherwise I think you might be in there.' Patrick motioned to the water.

'Have my Anita Ekberg moment? Wrong fountain...'

They crossed the Tiber on the Ponte Garibaldi and walked along the still busy streets. People took theirs seats at tables outside restaurants. Young *Romani* scooted past, sounding their horns as they weaved through pedestrians. As Patrick and Julia passed through a small park, they saw older Roman couples sitting on benches watching as dogs played on the small patch of grass in the middle.

'What did your children make of you coming here?' Julia thought of her daughters, their faces a picture when they met in the church.

Patrick laughed. 'I didn't tell them. I knew they'd be anxious. Ridiculous, I know. You'd have thought that doing what I did for years would reassure them, that I'm perfectly capable of looking after myself.'

'It's funny, isn't it? How we spend all those years worrying about our children. Then before you know it, it's the other way round. My daughters sometimes seem to forget I did manage to bring them up. I've been there, done that. Got the lines to prove it.' She touched a hand to her forehead, feeling the soft skin under her fingertips.

'But I guess they're just concerned about us getting old. Thing is, right this minute I don't feel old at all.'

'I think Richard would be very happy about that.' Julia put a hand to Patrick's face.

'God, Richard! Poor thing's been left on the shelf, quite literally, in the hotel since we've been here. But yes, I think he would too. Now, just up here on the right is the most wonderful sight. Shall we take a quick detour?'

Turning right, Patrick headed down a narrow, cobbled street and ushered Julia on ahead. There, round the corner, was a square stone basin with four marble shells and four young figures carved in bronze, each holding a turtle above its head.

'Oh, I've never seen this!' Julia walked slowly around the fountain. 'It's so pretty.'

'Isn't it? There's a love story that goes with it. Apparently a duke had it built overnight to impress a potential father-in-law who lived here in the palazzo, to win the hand of his daughter. Sadly the timings don't quite add up for it to be true – there was no palazzo then – but I love the idea of it.'

'But isn't that the thing about great love stories? It's all a matter of timing. And sometimes the timings just don't work.'

'Sometimes, sadly, they don't.' They held each other's gaze for a brief moment before Patrick placed his arms gently on hers. 'Right, come on. I'm hungry now. And your daughters will be waiting...'

The entrance to the Pantheon still boasted an impressive audience of tourists and the piazza buzzed with activity. Musicians played, children ran through the moving crowds fuelled by late ice creams, and groups of gazing tourists stood listening to tour guides, their faces turned to the building's façade.

They moved carefully through the crowds. 'It's just up here.'

Patrick gestured ahead. Turning down another side street off the piazza, they came to the restaurant. 'After you.'

Walking in, Julia noted the stark wooden tables, each set with a single white rose in a small vase. They were quickly shown to their table in the far right-hand corner. The waiter, smart in a white jacket and black bow tie, placed water down, followed by menus and a wine list.

'Should have known. Jess is always late.' Julia picked up the list.

'Well, we're not in any hurry. Let's get something to drink. What do you fancy?'

'I think a glass of their house white will do perfectly well. Oh, look, oysters!' A waiter passed carrying an enormous plate of shimmering oysters on a bed of crushed ice. 'My favourite.'

Patrick pulled a face.

'Are you not a fan?' Julia looked disappointed.

'Had a bad oyster once. Never again.'

She couldn't help but laugh. 'So you've survived some of the most dangerous places on earth but an oyster can floor you?'

'I know. I'm a wimp when it comes to oysters.'

'Then why on earth did you suggest this place?'

'I didn't want to offend Jess. And she seemed keen to try it. I didn't want to be rude. Anyway, there are plenty of other things on the menu. It's not all seafood.'

Julia squinted at the menu. 'It sort of is. And it does all look rather... goodness...' Julia noted the prices on the right-hand side of the menu. 'It's not cheap, either. Oh, Patrick, I am sorry. Not that you're paying obviously but—'

'Honestly, I'm very happy. Just don't take offence if I pass on the oysters.'

* * *

Annie checked the time on her phone again. She'd been waiting in the foyer of the hotel for Jess for over fifteen minutes. Since they'd returned, Annie had had time to have a shower and read some of her book before falling into a blissful sleep. The sound of her phone ringing had woken her up.

It was Patty, who reassured her that everything was under control. The boys, she said, were in high spirits. (Annie knew this was Patty's way of letting her know they were being a handful.) But James was due home soon and they were all looking forward to seeing Annie the following day. She, in turn, had been thrilled to hear their voices.

Then Annie had pulled on her jeans, a long-sleeved black sparkly top, put on some make-up – a slick of red lipstick and some black eyeliner and mascara – and pulled her hair out of its ponytail. She grabbed her khaki jacket, thinking it suddenly looked a little more worn that she'd remembered. Looking at her reflection in the mirror, she'd seen it wasn't quite the transformation she'd been hoping for but it would have to do.

Now, looking up from her phone, she watched Jess enter the foyer. She wore a long sleeveless orange silk dress, her hair was pulled back from her face in a ponytail, and there was just a faint touch of colour on her cheeks and lips. A long scarf the colour of clotted cream hung over her arm and her hand clutched a small black bag, the gold letters signalling its expense.

Annie suddenly hated everything she was wearing, from the too sparkly top to the scruffy trainers on her feet.

'Annie, you look gorgeous! Sorry, have you been waiting long?'

'Oh, I do not. I look like I'm trying too hard.' Annie tugged at the sparkly top.

'You really don't. Strong look.' Jess smiled reassuringly. 'Come on, they'll think we've chickened out.'

Annie feigned a laugh, but really all she wanted to do was go back upstairs, take off the top and make-up and throw on a T-shirt. But it was too late, and before she knew it Jess was pushing her through the revolving door and out onto the still warm street.

'So, what do you think he'll be like?' Jess was leading the way, across the river and back towards the *Centro Storico*.

'Well, I thought he seemed lovely. Polite, nice smile, clean clothes...'

'That's all very well but I still don't get why now, why here. I mean, if he managed all this time without Mum, why wait until you're going to bloody Rome to meet up?'

'You know why. It's their friend, whatshisname...'

'Richard.'

'Exactly, Richard. Mum said they were all friends when they were younger.'

'Yes, but I've never heard her mention him, or Patrick, for that matter.' Jess's clipped tone had returned.

'But you don't think about your parents before you were born, really. You know, who they were, who their friends were, unless they were in your life, too? It's like their lives started when yours did. Or is that just me?'

'I just hope she isn't doing an Exotic Marigold on us.'

'Jess! What do you mean? She's allowed a life. Just because she's in her seventies... I think we need to give her the benefit of the doubt.'

'Annie, she's been given that a few times since Dad. I'm not sure I can face another wedding.'

'Not your favourite thing, are they?'

'Uncalled for.' Jess shot Annie a look.

'Sorry, I didn't mean...'

'Ignore me. Let's go and see what he has to say for himself.'

'God, he sounds like a man condemned before we've even started.' Annie laughed. 'Be nice, Jess.'

'Of course I'll be nice! Honestly, I'm not that bad.'

'I know, just don't frighten him off. Not yet, anyway.'

They headed south along a long, cobbled street before crossing a small square and going down another narrow passage. The tables outside the restaurant, squashed up against the wall on one side, were all taken.

'No sign of them yet. Time for a quick drink over there before we go in?' Jess motioned towards a small bar on the other side of the road, clearly popular with the younger crowd, given the number of beautiful *Romani* standing outside, bottles of beer or glasses of wine in hand.

'No, we're late already. They must be inside. Thank goodness, it might be a little cooler in there.' The air was warm and heavy. Annie headed for the door.

'Coming. Just having one last go on this.' Jess grabbed her e-cigarette from her bag and held it up. 'Be right behind you.'

* * *

'What took you so long?' Julia stood to greet Annie. 'Where's Jess?'

'Sorry, Mum, it took a bit longer than we thought. Hello again, Patrick.' Annie smiled warmly before kissing her mother on the cheek and taking the seat next to her.

'Sorry, sorry, my fault...' Jess swept up to the table in a cloud of hastily applied scent, a habit she'd developed back when she was on real cigarettes. 'Hello, Patrick, I'm sorry to keep you waiting. Hi, Mum.' Jess blew a kiss across the table to her mother and swept into the seat next to Patrick, now half-standing, half-sitting as he greeted them both.

'Hello, darling, fashionably late as ever.' Julia blew a kiss across the table to her younger daughter.

'I try.' Jess shot back her response.

'Whereabouts are you staying?' Patrick took his seat again.

'Just across the river. It's called the Mellini.' Jess's seat scraped noisily across the floor as she moved it away from Patrick. She wasn't quite ready to be in such close proximity.

'It's just what we needed. Close to the centre and, to be honest, all we could get at such short notice.' Annie sounded a little too breezy. She was a hopeless liar.

'It's funny, we were meant to be staying in the most beautiful art deco hotel up at the other end of town, near where we met earlier. But a huge crack had appeared in the wall at the top of the building and ran all the way down to the bottom, apparently. And they were having to shut the whole hotel. Patrick, do you want to fill the girls' glasses up?'

Patrick reached for the carafe of white on the table but before he could get to it a waiter appeared and filled the glasses with a flourish.

'My goodness! What are the chances of that happening?' Jess caught her sister's eye. 'Probably a sinkhole.'

'That's what Patrick thought, too. Luckily he knew about a small guesthouse over in the... what's it called, Patrick?'

'Just by the Piazza di Santa Maria, in Trastevere. I used to stay there from time to time. Luckily, they remembered me and squeezed us in at the last minute.'

Oh my God, they're sharing a room, thought Annie.

'Oh, Annie, take that look off your face. We're not sharing a room, for heaven's sake.' Julia grinned and took a sip of her wine.

'I didn't say you were!' Annie raised her eyebrows in indignation.

'You didn't have to, darling.' Julia winked at her.

'So, Patrick, tell us about the ashes. I mean, can you just take them on a plane?' Jess reached for her glass of wine.

'Well, turns out you can do just that. As long as whatever you carry them in can be inspected easily, I guess they want to be able to make sure it really is a pile of ash and not a stash of anything else.'

'How funny, I just assumed it would be more difficult to take, you know, a dead person on a plane.'

'Jess, darling, do you have to be quite so... blunt?'

'Mum, I'm just saying. I'm surprised it's so easy.'

'Well, you need a death certificate, or at least a copy of one. But apart from that, it was fairly straightforward. They didn't even check the urn.' Patrick passed a couple of menus to Jess and Annie.

'It wasn't even an urn really. They're in a flask,' said Julia. She wasn't sure she'd be able to look at a Thermos flask in quite the same way again.

'Was your friend... forgive me, I've forgotten his name...' Annie looked apologetically at Patrick.

'Richard,' said Patrick.

'Yes, Richard... was he fond of Rome?'

'It was his favourite city in the world. So when I asked him if there was anything I could do to help, you know, at the end, he said yes, there was actually. His wife had died years ago, no children. He really was on his own. And so he asked me to take him to Rome one last time. Or rather, his ashes. And he adored your mother. In fact, it was Richard who suggested I get back in touch with her.' Patrick looked across at Julia.

The sisters glanced at each other briefly.

Jess turned back to Patrick. 'And what are you going to do with the ashes?'

'Well,' Julia removed an olive stone from her mouth, 'we thought somewhere with a view over the city might be best so we're going to head up the Aventine Hill early tomorrow morning. Before the crowds get there. We went yesterday – so beautiful. Girls, you really should try and see it before you go. When are you here until?'

'Trying to get rid of us?' Jess teased her mother.

'Don't worry, Mum. We're off tomorrow afternoon; it's a late afternoon flight. I think James might leave me if I stay any longer.'

'Oh, Annie, of course he wouldn't.' Julia turned to Patrick. 'You'd love Annie's husband, James. He's a wonderful man. Annie's very lucky.'

Annie bristled at being told she was lucky. It wasn't the first time, by any means. She swallowed her words and instead took a large gulp of wine, the coolness flooding her mouth. 'God, that's delicious. What is it?'

'House white. I think it said it was from Sicily.' Patrick turned the menu over, looking for the wine list.

'Tastes like peaches,' said Jess before taking another sip.

'Right, what are we eating?' Julia passed a menu to Patrick.

'Good, I'm starving. Lunch seems like a lifetime ago. How about we share the *gran misto di antipasti* – it's got a bit of everything. Tuna carpaccio...' said Jess, turning the menu over.

'Let's get that and a plate of oysters, then.' Annie looked up to catch the eye of one of the waiters whizzing past the table.

'Lovely. As long as I can have a plate of lobster spaghetti afterwards, I'm happy.'

'You can, Jess, as long as you don't mind paying a small fortune for it.' Her mother still hadn't got over the prices.

'No, I don't, as it happens. In fact, this is on me.'

'Don't be silly, darling.' Julia put a hand on Jess's arm.

'I'm not being silly, Mum. I want to. I suggested this place. So I'll pick up the bill.' Jess sounded firm. Julia telling her what she should and shouldn't spend her money on really annoyed her.

'So, um, Mum, Patrick, tell us a bit more about how you two met. Oh, hang on, there's the waiter. Let's order.' With food – and more wine – on the way, Annie prompted Patrick once more. 'So, go on. Where were you?'

'Well, we met on holiday in Cornwall – both our parents used to take us there on holiday as children – and we must have been about, what, ten?' Patrick looked at Julia.

She nodded. 'Yes, about that. It was a small village and all the kids used to meet at the bridge when the tide was high, to go crabbing. We met up every summer after that, until I was sixteen.'

'What happened after that?' Annie thought of the photograph, remembering the look in her mother's eyes.

'Oh, well, you know. We were young. Patrick was at university, then got a job. It was miles away from where I was going to be...' Julia tailed off.

'But I always thought of your mother, wondered how she was.' Patrick picked at a piece of bread. 'How... um, well, it's just so good to be here with her and to meet you both, of course.' He looked first at Annie, then Jess.

Nothing was ever that simple, thought Annie. Their connection was clearly so strong, even after all these years.

'Patrick was such a big part of my life, even if I was young and it was so long ago. People who are important to you, and you to them, remain so no matter where you end up or who you end up with.' Julia squeezed Patrick's hand.

'So are you going to get married again?' The words were out of Jess's mouth before she could stop them.

'Jess!' Annie stared at her sister across the table, open-mouthed.

'Not that I know of.' Patrick laughed awkwardly.

Julia glared at her daughter. 'Jess, there was no need for that.'

'Well, I'd just quite like to know this time. You know, rather than find out after the fact. I mean, at least with us here you've got a couple of bridesmaids to hand if you need them. Won't have to ask the taxi driver this time.'

'That's enough, Jess.' Julia's voice was hard now.

'Jess, stop it,' Annie pleaded with her sister. She could see this was not going to end well.

'Oh, come on Annie. It's not just me that's fed up with Mum doing exactly as she wants.'

'Jess, I said that's enough. I'm sorry, Patrick.' Julia glared at Jess.

'I'll just...' Patrick went to stand up.

'No, please don't move. You need to hear this.' Jess topped up her glass. 'Clearly I disappoint her. I'm always late. I spend too much money. And the thing that really annoys her, being the serial marrying kind, is that I didn't marry the one she wanted me to marry.'

'Oh God.' Annie dropped her head into her hands.

'It's all right for you, Annie. You've got James.'

Annie looked up sharply. 'Do *not* say I am lucky.'

'Well, you are! James, the boys, house in the country...'

'That is not luck, Jess!' Annie turned to her mother. 'You say the same. You're always telling me I'm lucky. Well, you know what? Sometimes you make your own luck. I loved my job. I loved my life before children. And I've worked hard to make our lives work for us now. I wouldn't change a thing but just know that it's not all down to bloody luck, OK?' Annie looked at the table, all eyes on her. The noise of other tables babbled on, oblivious to what was happening at theirs. She wasn't done.

'And you know what, Jess, you put Mum on the spot just then but what about you? When are you going to admit that you're still in love with Ben?'

'I am not!'

'Oh, for goodness' sake, of course you are. You saw him in London and now you can't stop looking for him. And the reason you think you're seeing him is because you want it to be him. Thing is, you're so bloody stubborn, you can't admit it. Even to yourself. You shut yourself off with work, so much so there's no room for anything else. And that includes being honest about how you feel.' Annie paused for breath, then let out a long sigh.

'Your *gran misto di antipasti...*' The waiter stood smiling, holding a huge plate of glistening seafood. Another stood behind with a plate of oysters. Julia started nervously moving glasses and cutlery.

'Actually, I'm not hungry.' Jess stood up. The waiters backed off. 'You carry on. I think I'm going to head back.'

'Oh, darling, please don't. Come on, we're all here now. Let's make the most of it. Annie, say sorry.' Julia looked at Annie.

'No, you go ahead. Sorry, Patrick. Not what you were expecting, I'm sure.' Jess grabbed her scarf from the back of the chair, scooped up her bag and headed for the door. They sat in silence as the waiters placed the seafood-laden platters on the table between them.

'Annie, I'm surprised at you. I've never heard you speak to your sister, or me for that matter, like that. What's got into you?'

'I'm sorry, Mum, but it had to be said. No one's pointing out the obvious to her. She relies on me not doing that, in fact. And I understand that, but honestly, she's in a mess at home. The only reason we came here, really, is because she was desperate to get away from London for a bit. You being here was just a good excuse. And I happened to be a bit pissed off – OK, a lot pissed off – with James so I didn't need much encouragement.'

'Why didn't you tell me?'

'Because I thought she was OK. And I thought it wasn't my place. Now I feel bad. I'll go after her.'

'Perhaps I should go?' Julia went to stand up.

'No, Mum. Let me. I'm sorry, Patrick. Clearly Rome hasn't brought out the best in us.'

'Please don't apologise. Anyway, we've got plenty of seafood to keep us going.'

Annie managed a small laugh. 'Thank you. Sorry, Mum, I'll text you later to let you know we're OK.'

'Thank you, darling.' She hoped the tears threatening to fall would stay in place, at least until Annie left.

Julia and Patrick watched her go.

'Just don't expect me to help you with those oysters.' It was all Patrick could think to say.

Julia sighed. 'Patrick, I think I need to tell them about what happened. It's time to tell them about our son.'

8

1961

'Come on, keep up!' Julia called behind as she half-ran down the steep path. The August sun was strong, throwing its light onto the sea, making it look like a million shiny milk bottle tops.

Patrick followed behind her, carrying a hamper in one hand, an armful of towels in the other and with a camera hung around his neck. 'Go ahead,' he shouted. 'I'll meet you at the rock. Hurry, before someone else nabs it.'

Julia headed down the stone steps towards the beach, her legs bare and brown. The waves rolled in to the bay, throwing stones onto stones as it did so. It was a sound she would come to long for.

By the time Patrick reached their rock, hidden just round the corner at one end of the bay, Julia had stripped down to her swimming costume.

'Last one in makes the fire!' she shouted, heading towards the water.

'Unfair advantage!' Patrick watched her run towards the waves, fearless as ever. He dumped the hamper and towels at the foot of the rock and followed her, pulling his shirt over his head as he ran towards the sea. By the time he got to the water's edge, Julia was already in up to her waist, rising and falling with the waves.

'It's bloody freezing!' he called, but she took no notice. Her arms were up above her head and with one swift movement she was gone, coming up a few seconds later further out than before.

'It's glorious! Honestly, as soon as you're in, you warm up!' Julia dived again, reappearing closer to Patrick, by now up to his chest in water. She swam towards him, hooked her arms around his neck and kissed him full on the mouth. He took her face in his hands, looking into her enormous green eyes, taking in the handful of freckles on her nose. To him, they looked as though they'd been hand painted.

'I love you, Julia.'

'I love you, too.' She grinned, wrapping her legs around him. 'I'm also absolutely ravenous. What's in the hamper?'

'Some mackerel – caught them this morning – and a few tomatoes and half a bottle of cider.'

'Sounds perfect... Now, come on. Time to work up an appetite.' She smiled, turned and disappeared under the water.

Patrick took a deep breath and followed. By the time he caught up with her, she was treading water. Looking back at the shore, they saw the bay was still quiet. The day-trippers were yet to arrive by boat from the harbour round the headland and the walkers were passing on the narrow, grassy path that ran high above. A handful of other groups had made it down the steep path to the beach but they'd all, predictably, turned left towards the widest part of the shore.

But the tide was on its way out, opening up the other end, and with it a series of caves and stretches of golden sand.

Over the summer, this end of the bay had been the back-drop to Patrick and Julia's blossoming love affair. They had known each other for years, having spent every summer holiday they could remember in the same Cornish village. But as soon as Patrick had set eyes on Julia, sitting on the wall of the stone bridge in the middle of the village, with her legs dangling over the side, he knew this summer would be different.

* * *

She'd greeted him with a wide, unguarded smile but he was suddenly nervous around her, not quite sure what to say. Next to her sat Maggie, a little wild and enormous fun. She lived in the big house on the hill. Then there was Richard, Patrick's oldest friend. Like Patrick, he was down for the summer, and was earning some holiday money working on his grandparents' farm before heading back to university in the autumn. Clouds puffed gently across the sky as seagulls bossed each other about above their heads. A cigarette dangled from Maggie's mouth, her eyes hidden by black cat's-eye sunglasses.

'You're here at last!' Maggie called out to Patrick as he walked to join them. 'What took you so long?' She offered him her cigarette.

'I got here as fast as I could.'

'How's Oxford?' Julia looked up at him, squinting her eyes from the sun as she did so.

'It's good, thank you, really good.' Given that he was studying English Literature, he was surprisingly stuck for words. A pause. 'How about you?'

'Oh, you know. Thrilled to be out at last.'

'God, yes, *at last*,' Maggie added, before taking a long drag on her cigarette and blowing a line of smoke out of her perfectly O-shaped mouth. 'School is such a bore.'

'So what's your plan now?' Richard looked from Maggie to Julia.

'Absolutely nothing, at least for the next few weeks.' Julia grinned at him. 'But I am thinking of going to college to study fashion next. Obviously my parents are horrified.'

'Why? That's a wonderful thing to do,' said Patrick.

'Oh, I think they had their sights set on me going to help them in the shop. But I don't want to stay in the same town where I grew up. I want to go to London, get my own flat, live a proper life. Not just the one they want me to live.' She sighed heavily. Julia's parents owned a large hardware store back home in Lincolnshire. 'I mean, I think what they've done, what they do, is all well and good. It's just not what I want to do. And I'm not sure they understand why I don't.'

'Well, we've got the next few weeks to not think about anything but having a blast. And I, for one, intend to have one. So, who's up for a party at mine later?' Maggie clearly had plans of her own.

'What about your parents? Aren't they at home?' asked Richard.

'Yes, I think so but they've got about a million people staying. I doubt they'll even notice we're there.' Maggie flicked the end of her cigarette into the river below.

'I promised my mother I'd be at home for dinner tonight but I'll come up after that. How about you, Julia?' Patrick tried not to sound too keen. He failed.

'Yes, I'll be there but not until later.' She didn't want to admit that she'd have to wait until her aunt was asleep before climbing out of the window and shimmying down the drainpipe to get there.

'Brilliant, I'll find something for us to drink.' That was

Maggie, she'd never knowingly under-cater even if it was without her parents' knowledge.

'I tell you what; I'm dying for a swim. Anyone up for a quick trip to the bay?' Richard was really hoping Maggie would say yes.

'Can't.'

His heart sank.

'Definitely, yes, please.' Julia swung her legs back over the wall to stand.

'Me, too.' Patrick couldn't bear the thought of Richard heading off with Julia alone.

'Right, I'll get the car. See you here in a mo. Maggie, see you later.' Richard turned with a wave and headed up the hill towards his grandparents' house.

'Yes, see you later!' Maggie called after him.

'Maggie, you do know he is mad about you, don't you?' Julia spoke quietly, even though Richard was by now out of earshot.

'Yes, of course I do. And I think he'll do very nicely for the summer, thank you.' She climbed off the wall.

Patrick looked at the ground, hands in his pockets, not sure what to say in the face of such an honest declaration of intentions.

'You mustn't break his heart, Maggie. He's such a softie,' Julia gently pleaded with her friend, knowing already it was bound to end in tears – and probably not Maggie's.

'Oh, come on, Julia. Don't be so serious. He's not a boy. He can look after himself. See you later.' Maggie kissed her friend fondly on the cheek, waved to Patrick and headed after Richard up the hill.

'Right, looks like it's you and me.' Patrick smiled nervously.

'Patrick, are you all right?'

'What do you mean?' He looked at Julia, wanting to both gaze at her for ever and hide away at the same time.

'Did something happen on the way? Is everything OK?' Julia looked into his eyes, wondering what it was he was hiding from her.

'Yes, fine. Really. I'm just, you know. Long trip. Bit tired. Nothing a swim in the sea can't fix. Come on, let's go and meet Richard.'

Later that night, as they danced in the hall of the big house on the hill, one of Maggie's many siblings played 'Great Balls of Fire' on the piano that stood in the huge reception hall of the house and they all sang along at the tops of their voices. As Patrick swung Julia around, her red dress flying behind her, he knew he didn't want to be just friends with her any more. He was in love with her.

Hours later, Maggie was still dancing despite her piano-playing sibling falling asleep at the keyboard, head on his arms across the keys. Party guests lay crashed out on various sofas; a few had curled up in front of the huge fireplace alongside dogs of various shapes and sizes.

Patrick and Julia walked back across the fields towards the village, the blue-grey light of the early morning surrounding them. Mist sat on the village like an eiderdown. Julia's aching feet were bare and wet from the dew-drenched grass.

'Patrick, there's something I need to tell you.' Julia stopped, turned towards him. 'I'm not sure we can be friends any more.'

Patrick felt his stomach lurch. 'Why not?'

'Because I think I might love you. I mean, I'm not sure because I've never actually been in love before. But, well, I've never felt like this.'

'Well... er...'

'Oh God, I'm sorry... I thought I should—'

'No, no, I'm glad you said that. Because... I think I love you, too.'

'You do?'

'Yes, I do. I definitely do. Seeing you on the bridge earlier, well, I was so happy you were here. Not that you'd know it, given that I practically lost the power of speech. And tonight I wanted that song to go on for ever.'

'I think I might wake up tomorrow without a voice after all that singing.' Julia laughed. 'So what do we do now?'

'This.' Patrick held her face gently in his hands and kissed her.

Standing in her red dress with his coat over her shoulders, shoes in one hand, she looked at him. 'This changes everything.'

'Yes, I think it does.'

* * *

Julia had set her alarm at the usual time. She liked to have the coffee percolator on the stove by the time Aunt Tessa came in from her studio at the end of the garden. Julia had stayed with her mother's sister for a month every summer since she was little and loved her time with Tessa more than anything else in the world. Her mother and aunt were so unalike, Julia thought it might be funny were it not for the fact that they clearly didn't get along. And compared with her mother's ridiculously organised approach to life, Aunt Tessa was a whirlwind.

After the perennial neatness of home, Julia adored the chaos of the Cornish cottage. The whitewashed walls outside were in stark contrast to the colourful mess within. Paintings, pottery, piles of books, stacks of newspapers and magazines, a sink filled with dirty dishes, and a kitchen table covered with jars crammed with wild flowers, empty cups and always an overflowing ashtray.

Every morning Julia cleared the table, emptied the ashtray and stacked up the books and newspapers. She stood at the sink, her back to the kitchen, looking out of the little window onto the road outside. If she leaned to the right and looked left, she could just glimpse the stone bridge where she'd sat the day before. She smiled, but her eyelids felt heavy, desperate to shut. She'd crept in with the dawn chorus but was sure she hadn't woken up her aunt.

'You came in early.'

Julia swung round to see Tessa standing at the open back door. She was dressed, as usual, in her paint-splattered faded blue overalls with her long grey hair pinned up in a bun, wisps escaping as they'd done for years. Tessa's blue eyes were bright. In one hand she held an empty cup, in the other an unlit cigarette.

'Oh God, you heard me. Aunt Tessa, I'm so sorry. I went up to Lyn House to dance. With Maggie...'

'I know you did. I might be old but I'm not stupid.'

'It was just a dance.'

'Look, Julia. You're sixteen...'

'Nearly seventeen.'

'Exactly. And I trust you to make sensible decisions but you must promise me one thing. You must be honest with me. If this is going to work – you staying here, helping me out – then I need you to tell me what you're up to. As long as there are no secrets, we'll be just fine.'

'Will you tell Mother?'

'Of course not, but keep something from me again and you might not be so lucky next time. Understood?'

'Oh, thank you!' Julia crossed the room to hug her aunt. 'Thank you! I'm so sorry. I promise, no more secrets.'

'Well, by the look on your face you've clearly got something else to tell me. What happened at the party?'

Momentarily, Julia was stuck for words. 'It's Patrick. How did you know?'

'I was young once too, remember.' Tessa crossed the kitchen to pour herself some coffee before sitting in her usual chair at one end of the table. 'So, go on then. What happened?'

'Well, we danced. Aunt Tessa, we danced all night. And I know I've known him for ever but seeing him yesterday was like seeing him for the first time. He's always been my friend, but this time I felt different. God, I'm not sure I can explain it...'

'Well, I think you just did. Perfectly, as it happens.'

'So, what do I do now? I mean, I know we've got some time now but then he'll go back to Oxford...'

'So you just enjoy every minute that you have. Make the most of it. And if you really do love each other you'll make it work, wherever you are.' Tessa lit her cigarette, took a sip of her coffee. 'Just don't go and get yourself pregnant, whatever you do. Your mother really will kill me.'

'Aunt Tessa!' Julia was used to her aunt's blunt proclamations but this one took her by surprise. 'Of course I won't! I mean I've never even, you know...'

Tessa held up her hand, looking away. 'What you've done is your business. All I ask is that you don't get pregnant on my watch.' Then she turned back, wrinkling her nose at her niece, smiling broadly. She didn't have children of her own but, to her, Julia was as dear as anyone could be. 'Anyway, what's your plan today? I thought we might walk along the river on the other side, up to the farm at the end. They've got eggs going spare, apparently. Thought they might do for tonight's supper, what do you think?'

'Sounds lovely.' Julia couldn't help but think about how she was going to fit in meeting Patrick. Even though she'd said goodbye only hours ago, the thought of not seeing him until tomorrow felt like a lifetime.

'Don't worry, I won't stand in the way if you have other plans.' Tessa drained her coffee. Sunlight streamed through the window, catching the thin curl of smoke from her cigarette as it did.

'No, not at all! I'd love that, really I would.' Julia meant it.

* * *

It was a long, hot summer. At the start the days seemed to stretch ahead of them like a swathe of bare, untouched sand. Before long they fell into a glorious pattern of late afternoon swims in the sea, early evening picnics at the beach and endless warm nights dancing up at the big house.

In the beginning, all four – Julia, Maggie, Richard and Patrick – would head down together to the bay, but as the summer went on, Patrick and Julia found themselves alone at the beach more often than not. It was as if Maggie and Richard realised they were surplus to requirements. Not that either of them minded; a few weeks into the holidays Maggie had indeed grown tired of Richard's company, just as Julia had predicted. And he, in turn, had moved seamlessly, if a little surprisingly, on to Maggie's older sister.

At one end of the bay was a rock with a series of hidden caves set in the cliff behind. Each day the tide would come and wash away their footprints from their last visit. It felt like this particular spot on the beach was in on Patrick and Julia's secret.

They were happiest together, hidden from view, with nothing but the sea, sand and seagulls overhead to witness them.

For hours they talked, lying side by side on the rock. About their favourite books, music, people, places they'd been, places they wanted to visit, about what might be ahead for them. And for hours they stayed hidden from view inside a cave, their bodies pressed against each other as they lay on the cool sand. They kissed, exploring each other's body with their hands and mouths until every curve and mark on their skin became familiar to the other.

The summer raced on and as it did, both became aware of time coming to an end. Neither wanted to think about it. Instead, Julia had insisted they lived in the very moment, just as Aunt Tessa had told her to.

But that day, when they'd found themselves lying on the rock drying in the sun before lighting a fire on the beach to cook the mackerel, eat the tomatoes and drink the cider, both knew that something between them had changed. Together they'd made a small fire from driftwood collected after their swim. And as they sat on the sand by the fire, Julia carefully turning the mackerel, their silence was charged. Patrick was the first to speak.

'I know we only have a few days left but I want you to know—'

'Patrick, don't. I can't bear to think about it.'

'I want you to know that I love you. And even though I have to go back to Oxford, I will write, all the time. And we can see each other in the holidays. You can visit. I'll come and see you, wherever you are.'

'I know, I *know* this isn't the end. But I can't bear that it's the end of this time together.'

'Yes, but this is just the beginning, Julia. Just think, you could go to college, do your course and then when you're qualified we can go anywhere, anywhere you want.'

'What I want is to be with you. Right now. I mean really be with you. Patrick...' She held his gaze.

Patrick set the bottle of cider down on the sand and reached for her hand. 'Julia... are you...?'

'Yes Patrick, I'm absolutely sure. In fact, I've never been so sure about anything in my life.' She took his hand and together they left the fire behind and headed into the cool of the cave. Lying on the sand, her hair spread out as if she was floating in water, Julia had never looked more beautiful, Patrick thought. Their bodies responded to each other's touch, their mouths on each other's as words became futile. Outside the cave the clouds rolled slowly across the deep blue sky, the waves washing lazily over the shoreline. Flames continued to flicker in the fire, the mackerel scenting the rising smoke with the smell of the sea.

Afterwards they lay wrapped in each other's arms in the cave, Patrick's fingers in Julia's hair. She traced her fingers gently across his back.

'How did that manage to feel so right, when everything I've been taught is that it's wrong?' Julia wondered aloud.

'I can't even begin to answer that.' Patrick laughed gently, turning his head to look into her eyes. 'All I know is that I love you. And I want us to be together.'

'Well, thank goodness for that...' Julia's eyes crinkled as she smiled right back at him.

But what now bound the young lovers together would become the reason they were soon to be forced apart.

9

Jess slowly opened her eyes but the brightness forced her to shut them again. The taste of something alcoholic clung to the inside of her mouth, coating her tongue. She opened her eyes again, taking in the unfamiliar surroundings. With a lurch in her stomach, she saw that this wasn't her hotel room.

The white sheets were soft and cool under her skin, the pillows soft as marshmallows. She glanced at her watch, barely able to focus on the tiny hands. It was early, really early. The small bedroom was quiet, the open window letting in a gentle breeze. The furniture was simple: an old armchair in the corner of the room, draped with clothes. Including her orange silk dress. She moved her hand down her body, relieved to find she still had her underwear on.

She moved her feet, slowly shifting her aching frame to sitting. Placing her bare feet on the cool tiles, she pulled back her hair, twisting it to one side of her face. She grabbed her dress from the back of the chair and put it gingerly over her pounding head, looking around for her shoes.

Assuming they must have been discarded before she'd made

it to the bedroom, Jess moved towards the door, gently opening it so as not to make a sound. Still silent, she thought she might just be able to get out of here without re-meeting whoever it was she'd obviously met last night. Spying her brown leather sandals by the long sofa in the sitting room, she crossed the room, scooping up her bag from the coffee table as she did so.

Jess slipped her feet into the sandals and with one hand on the handle of the front door, turned the latch with the other.

'You are leaving already, Jess-ee-ca?'

She turned to find a man standing there, towel wrapped around his waist.

'Hey! I thought you'd gone already. I...'

'Is no problem, really. I made you coffee but if you'd rather go...' He smiled, his dark eyes fixing hers. He took a sip from the small white cup in his hand, pushing back his wet jet-black hair with his free hand. 'It's Vito, by the way. Just in case you forgot. Honestly, I understand if you need to leave. You must get back to your sister.'

Jess wasn't entirely sure how much she'd told him. 'Thank you, I will. And thank you for the... drinks.' She hoped this was all she needed to thank him for.

'Thank you for the dancing!' He laughed. 'You were amazing. Seriously, I couldn't keep up.'

The club, the dancing, the heat, the beat of the music pulsing through her body... It was coming back to her now. And it was tequila she could taste. But then: nothing.

'Did we... did you sleep...?'

'I sleep here, Jess-ee-ca. On the sofa. You were asleep by the time I'd gone to get us a drink when we got back. So I lifted you into my bed. And I sleep here.' He looked at her face. 'Please, don't worry. I promise you. We drank, we went dancing, we ate, we talked. And then you fell asleep.'

Her voice was quiet. 'Thank you, Vito. I'm so sorry... I really must go.'

'Of course. *Ciao, bella.*' He kissed his hand and gestured towards her. 'But remember, your sister and your mother love you. And I know you love them. You told me. So don't be cross. Go and find them and tell them so.'

'Oh God, did I really give you my whole family history?' Jess was mortified.

'I think just the interesting bits.' He smiled at her. 'If you want to find good coffee on your way back, turn right at the bottom of the steps and go to the *caffè* on the corner before you turn left to head back to the bridge. Tell Elena I sent you.'

Jess wondered just how many customers Vito had sent to Elena over the years. But she couldn't help but be touched by his kindness.

'Thank you, I will. I'm just sorry...'

'Please, don't be sorry. I had a wonderful time, really.'

Jess returned his warm smile before turning and opening the door. She picked her way slowly down the steps. The sky was clear, the air gratifyingly fresh on her face. The streets were still quiet. The thought of food made her stomach turn but she longed for water and strong coffee. Pulling her thin scarf around her shoulders, Jess fixed her sunglasses in place and headed to the *caffè* at the end of the road.

A few moments later the smell of coffee and bread hit her before she'd even walked through the door. Elena – at least Jess assumed it was her – greeted Jess with a casual '*Ciao*'. All long dark hair and enormous brown eyes, Elena sat behind the cash register at one end of the long wooden bar. She motioned down to the other end where a young Italian man stood in front of the enormous coffee machine, talking over his shoulder to an older man propped at the bar.

'Elena?' Jess managed a smile and lifted her glasses. 'Vito sent me. Said your coffee is the best.'

'Ah, Vito. He's a very good customer.' Elena smiled back. 'Let them know what you'd like. And take a table, I'll bring you your coffee. We're still quiet.'

Jess ordered her coffee and took a seat at a small table by the door. With her back to the wall, she watched another young waiter carefully placing exquisite pastries in rows behind the glass counter, lined up like cake soldiers. The sound of the coffee machine, the chat at the other end of the bar and of Elena greeting locals as they came in for their morning caffeine fix was almost enough to take her mind off whatever was making Jess feel that familiar sense of shame prickling at her skin – but not quite.

Elena placed a white china cup and saucer on the table, along with a glass of ice-cold water. 'Are you sure you won't have anything to eat?'

'No, thank you. Though I'd kill for a cigarette.'

'I can't help you, I'm afraid. But if I were you, I'd have a *sfogliatella* – they fix ev-ery-theeng. Please, on the house.'

'Oh, no, I really couldn't...'

'No, you must. I promise you will feel better.'

Jess realised she wasn't going to get out of here without having to eat something. 'Thank you, I'd love that,' she lied.

A moment later a small fantail-shaped pastry arrived on a plate, dusted with icing sugar, delivered by the young waiter. Elena waved from her post behind the register. Jess raised her hand back, took a small slug of coffee and bit into the offering. Her mouth filled with wafer-thin layers of crunchy pastry and cinnamon-kissed, light custard. She closed her eyes momentarily, lost to the flavours and smells and feel of the food in her mouth. She took another small hit of hot coffee before going in for another mouthful of pastry. It was the most delicious thing she'd ever eaten for breakfast. In fact, it was about the only thing she'd eaten for breakfast for as long as she could remember. She looked up to find Elena grinning at her from behind the giant till.

* * *

On the other side of town, Annie woke up to the sound of her phone. She lifted her eye mask and tried to focus on the numbers on the hotel clock radio: 07:05 a.m. It was James. She hit the green button and the screen filled with the wide-awake faces of the boys.

'Mama! It's me!' Ned's face was smeared with jam. Rufus jostled behind him, trying to get a better look at the screen.

'Careful, Rufie. Let Ned talk to Mummy first.' Hearing James's voice in the background, Annie quickly rubbed her eyes and propped herself up against the pillows.

'Hi, darlings!' How are you? Are you being good for Daddy?'

'Yes! And, Mummy, when are you coming home?' Rufus asked out of shot.

'Tonight, darling. You'll be asleep, but by the time you wake up I'll be there.'

'Are you bringing us a present back?' Ned, as ever, got straight to the point.

'If you ask, you might not get,' James cautioned.

'If you don't ask, you don't get, more like.' Annie laughed. 'I'm sure there'll be something, boys.' She made a mental note to buy some T-shirts for them that day and not leave it until the airport. No doubt even a small fridge magnet would cost a small fortune there.

'How are you getting on?' asked James.

'Well, it was all going brilliantly but then...'

'Oh, no, what?'

'Well, we met Mum. And Patrick...'

'The old boyfriend? What's he like?'

'Yes, the old boyfriend. He's lovely, actually. He and Mum are sweet together. Like they've known each other for ever.'

'Well, they have, haven't they?'

'Yes, but they've not seen each other for *years*. Not that you'd know it. Anyway, we met up with them last night for dinner and, I don't know, maybe it was too much wine, or sun, or both. We'd had such a lovely day. But Jess and Mum had wound each other up within a matter of moments. About being late. About Ben. About being a serial bride...'

'Oh God...'

'I know. Then Jess had a go at me. Called me "lucky". I'm afraid I flipped.'

'When you say flipped...'

'You know, just pointed out that you make some of your own luck and she shouldn't assume that the only reason she is on her own is because she hasn't met the right one. She has. She did. And she didn't want him. Literally, the whole world loves her. But she doesn't love herself. And until she does, she'll keep deliberately pushing people away.'

'Wow, you really did flip.'

'I guess I did. I do slightly blame the wine but, to be honest, we've danced around this for so long. It needed to be said. The stuff about Ben, I mean. Possibly not in front of Patrick, but he was very good about it.'

'So what happened?' James dropped a piece of bread into the toaster.

'Well, she left the restaurant. It was all a bit awkward. I went after her but I couldn't find her. She wasn't answering her phone. I told Mum I'd found her, though; that we were in a wine bar. I didn't want her to worry.'

'Where is she now?'

'No idea. But she's a big girl. Probably lying in bed with a hangover, feeling sorry for herself.'

'Ouch.'

'Do you think I was unfair?'

'Probably not, but you can come across as a bit, you know...'

'No, I don't know. What do you mean?' Annie knew what he meant, but didn't want to hear it.

'Just don't let it carry on. It'll just get worse.'

'You were going to say smug, weren't you?'

'No... well, maybe. Sometimes, a bit. Only when it's you, your mother and your sister. It's like you two revert to being teenagers again when you're with her. Come on, you know that.'

Annie sighed. She knew he was right. 'I'll go and find her in a minute, wake her up for breakfast. Or coffee, at least. Anyway, where are the boys? It's gone quiet.'

'They've gone to watch telly.'

James! It's six in the morning there!'

'I know. But I'm in charge, so my rules.' He winked at her, taking a bite of his toast. He, too, was left with a smear of jam at the corner of his mouth.

'I dread to think...'

'See you later, then? What time does your flight get in?'

'Not until about eight-ish but I'll still have time to catch a train back. As long as there are no delays.'

'Well, enjoy your last day. What are your plans?'

'Find my sister, say sorry and then we'll see what happens.'

'Sounds good.'

'Love you. Tell the boys I can't wait to see them tomorrow. I've really missed them. Feels like I've been away for a week.'

'Missing you too. Safe journey home.'

* * *

As planned, Julia and Patrick had reached the Orange Garden on the Aventine Hill not long after the sun had risen. The park was practically deserted and perfectly tranquil. The city lay before them bathed in gold from the early morning sun. Clouds hung like candy floss in the sky. To the left stood the magnificent dome of St Peter's; to the right Victor Emmanuel's monument sat awkwardly, like an out-of-place wedding cake. Below them the Tiber cut through the city like a thick, grey snake.

Walking down a flight of grey stone steps, Patrick and Julia made their way to a hidden nook they'd found on their recce. Julia perched on the edge and peered over the low wall, looking at the city over her shoulder.

'There really is something about this city that feels eternal, don't you think?'

'Exactly that.' Patrick looked at the city through the lens of his camera.

'I think Richard would be very happy to be here.'

'I think he'd be very happy to know that we are here together. He always did have a soft spot for you.'

'Patrick, he had a soft spot for practically every available female in the village...' Julia laughed.

'Oh, come on, he was besotted with... what was her name? Your friend? The one who lived in the big house on the hill.'

'Maggie. Wonderful, mad Maggie. I wonder what happened to her.'

'Did you not keep in touch?'

'Sadly not. That was all part of the deal. No more trips to Cornwall after that.'

'Julia, are you sure about telling your daughters what happened? I mean, you must do whatever you think is right, of course. But it will mean they might want to know more.'

'After last night, I'm more sure than ever. I've kept it to myself for so many years. There was no need to tell them when they were small. But now that they're grown up, I feel like I'm keeping something from them that, really, they have a right to know. That they might want to know...' Patrick reached for her hand. She took it, turned her gaze back to the city. 'And to be honest, I just don't want to keep him a secret any more.'

He sat down next to her. 'What if they decide to look for him?'

'Well, that's up to them. I made a promise that I never would. That was my part of the deal.'

'But that promise was to your mother. She's not here any more.'

'Yes, but I promised. Besides, Aunt Tessa always told me that if, one day, he wanted to come and find me he would. And not a single day goes by when I don't think of him. What happened to him, where he might be... Actually, all I hope for is that he is healthy and happy, wherever he is. And that he's loved. That someone loves him.'

Patrick squeezed her hand gently. 'I know.'

'Now come on, we came here for Richard.'

'So we did. Right...' He stood up and looked around. 'Let's try not to get caught spreading our friend's ashes in a public park.' He took the metal flask from his canvas rucksack and started unscrewing the lid.

Julia slowly got to her feet, peered over the wall. 'Well, he's got a clear run if you do it now.'

Patrick tipped the container upside down over the side. A

thin, steady stream of grey dust poured out towards a small patch of grass below.

'Rest in peace, my friend.' Patrick spoke quietly. A nosy sparrow hopped onto the wall, clearly hoping there might be some crumbs to pick at. 'Sorry, dear fellow, it's not food.'

The last traces of dust fell from the flask, drifting down to the earth below. They stood for a moment, listening to the sounds of the city as it woke to a new day. A few scooters and cars now passed on the road down below as the *Romani* made their way to work.

'Are you OK?' Julia touched his arm lightly.

'I just miss him, that's all.'

'I know. You were a good friend.'

'He was a good friend to me too. He just took life as it came. That summer, after Cornwall, Richard was... there. For me, I mean. We never really spoke about it but I knew that he knew. And that was enough.'

'You're right. Sometimes that really is enough. Come on, let's go and find some coffee, something to eat.' Julia took the empty flask from Patrick, placing it in her straw basket.

Together, they climbed the steps and walked hand in hand slowly back through the still deserted park.

* * *

At first they didn't notice the woman sitting with her back to the wall. But she noticed them. As Julia and Patrick walked into the *caffè*, Jess's instinct was to head for the door. But she was yet to pay for her coffee. And if she bolted without paying she knew she'd feel even worse, especially since the staff had been so kind.

With her mother at the other end of the long bar, Jess reached slowly for her bag, hoping she had a note in there allowing her to place it on the saucer under her now empty coffee cup and leave. But as she reached for her bag, her glasses fell from her head onto the floor, clattering loudly onto the tiles. Patrick turned to pick them up, catching Jess's eye as he did so.

Jess motioned to him to keep quiet but it was too late.

'Jess, darling, what are you doing here?' Her mother was heading towards her, the two men at the end watching with sudden interest. Elena ducked her head and disappeared behind the till.

'Oh, hi, Mum. I just decided to, you know, come out for an early walk.' Jess took her glasses from Patrick, putting them back on her head. She felt about twelve years old, caught with her hand in the biscuit tin.

'In last night's dress?' Julia raised an eyebrow.

'OK, but it's not what it looks like. I lost Annie...'

'You left the restaurant...'

'You started having a go at me...'

'How about you order an extra coffee, Julia, and we'll join you for another, Jess?'

Jess looked at Patrick, surprised by the intervention but grateful nonetheless. She just didn't have the energy to argue any more.

'Good idea, you two go and sit back down, I'll be over in a minute.' Julia turned back to the man behind the bar and ordered one more coffee.

'Thank you, Patrick. And I'm so sorry, I don't think you were counting on this when you asked Mum to come here with you.'

'Honestly, it's fine. It's funny because I can see so much of her in you. When she was younger, I mean. You are very similar.'

'Is that a good thing?' It was Jess's turn to raise an eyebrow.

'It's a very good thing. You are both wonderful people.'

Patrick laughed softly. 'But it's why you two can't argue properly. It's like arguing against yourself.'

'Really?' Jess had never really thought about it like that before. 'But she's just so judgemental with me. You know, "typical Jess..."' She rolled her eyes for effect. 'I know I'll never be perfect enough.'

'You are absolutely enough. And none of us is perfect.'

Julia arrived back at the table, easing herself into the seat next to Patrick, carrying two coffees. Patrick got up to pick up the third steaming cup from the bar.

'What's your plan today, Mum?'

'Well, I think we're going to...' Julia turned to see Patrick drain his coffee cup in one quick gulp before placing it back on the saucer.

'I'll see you back at the guesthouse, the coffees are paid for,' he said, putting his hand on Julia's shoulder. He smiled at them both before slipping out of the door.

'Where's he off to?' Jess turned to watch him cross the road.

Julia knew that was the nudge she needed. 'Darling, there's something I want to talk to you about. To you both, actually.' She felt her stomach drop to the floor.

'What? What is it? Please don't tell me you're ill...'

'No, nothing like that, I'm absolutely fine. But there is something about my past that I've never told you. It involves Patrick. And it was a very long time ago...'

'You were married!' Jess cried out. 'I knew it. I knew there was more to it.'

'No, not married.' Julia took a sip of her coffee, picked up the small spoon and turned it over, staring at the reflection in the back. Her throat seemed to tighten, her fingers pressing heavily on the cool silver in her hand. She closed her eyes for a second, took a breath. Maybe she should wait until Annie was there, too? But Julia knew if she didn't tell Jess now, she might never pluck up the courage to say anything about it at all. 'Darling, Patrick and I had a son.' She brought her eyes up to meet Jess.

'What?' Jess's voice was barely a whisper. 'When?'

'It was a long time ago. We were very young. I was sixteen, almost seventeen, he was nineteen.'

'How? I mean, do you know him? Have you met him?'

'No, I haven't. And neither has Patrick. In those days, being pregnant out of wedlock was, well, it wasn't really...' Julia trailed off.

'So was he adopted?'

'Yes, he was. And I can't tell you where he is now because I honestly don't know. But I want to tell you what happened because I don't want to keep it a secret any more. Seeing Patrick, Richard's ashes, seeing you both here... it's made me realise that I have to tell you the truth. Before it's too late.'

'Mum, you promise me you're not dying or anything, because this all feels very... final.'

'I promise you, darling. I'm fine. It's just that I've kept this to myself for years. I put what happened away in a box. And I thought I'd never have to look inside that particular box again. But seeing you girls both here, how much I love you, I realise that keeping it from you isn't fair. All I can do is tell you the truth. What you choose to do with it is up to you. And Annie, of course.'

'Oh God, Annie.' Jess reached for her phone. 'I must call her; tell her where I am. She'll be awake now. And I really don't want her to know...' She ran out of words.

'That you didn't come back last night? Look, Jess. What you do is your choice, no one else's. I know your sister has a way of making you feel like you're doing the wrong thing but I'm sure she has your best interests at heart. As I do.'

'I know, Mum.' Jess sighed a long sigh, picked up her coffee cup and drained it. 'Thing is, I know she's right. She's bloody annoying like that.'

'I know.' Julia smiled across the table at her daughter, reaching for her hand. 'So, why don't we walk back now, you can go to your hotel and freshen up and we can meet a bit later, before you head back. I can tell you both at the same time. About your brother, I mean.'

'Really? Can't we talk about this more now? I mean, I want to know what happened. You can't just leave it at that.'

'And I will tell you everything, Jess. But I would rather do it when we're with Annie too, so you can hear it together.'

'Why don't you come back with me to the hotel now? We can get Annie and go and find somewhere to talk.'

Julia looked at Jess, her daughter's eyes pooled with tears. 'If we go back via our guesthouse I can leave a message for Patrick, let him know what time to meet me later.'

'Sounds good.' Jess wiped at her eyes quickly, then shoved the dark glasses back on and turned to wave her thanks to Elena at the till. She saw her watching a TV positioned just behind it, showing a football match. The camera cut to the pundits in a brightly lit studio. Jess squinted. The face on screen, talking animatedly to the other presenters, looked frighteningly familiar. She lifted her glasses back on to her head. 'Oh my God...'

'Yes, eez Vito!' cried Elena, pointing at the television. 'Your friend.' She drew out that last word longer than she really needed to. 'He is, how you say...'

'On television.' Jess could not take her eyes from the screen. The bright studio lights seemed to sharpen his features, giving him cheekbones as chiselled as any of the ones she'd seen on statues the day before. He looked devastatingly handsome, even if his suit was a little on the shiny side.

'Vito used to play, 'ee was a great footballer.' Elena winked at Jess. 'But now, 'ee does this. This was yesterday afternoon. I love heem.'

Looks like it, thought Jess, wondering if Elena had ever woken up in that same bed she had this morning.

'And 'ee 'as a nice wife.'

Jessica felt sick.

'Kids, too. They live in the country but they come and visit sometimes. I 'ave met them in 'ere.' Elena didn't take her eyes off the screen as she spoke.

Jess felt a lurch in her stomach. 'Yes, I'm sure he has.' She lowered her glasses onto her face once more.

Julia moved towards the door. If she had figured out what was going on, she wasn't letting on. Jess just wanted to get out of there as fast as possible but her feet felt like stone.

'Come on, darling. Let's get going.' Julia gently put her arm around her daughter and led her out into the cool air. They crossed the road and walked along the wide tree-lined pavement towards the bridge. The now cloudless sky gave them a heads up at the hot day ahead.

Jess stopped walking and turned to her mother. 'Mum, what's wrong with me?' Her voice was small.

'Nothing. Nothing at all, my darling. You are just not as happy as you could be at the moment, that's all. I promise you, things will get better. Just talk to me, tell me what's wrong.'

'I just feel like... I know people think I have everything I could wish for – the big job, life sorted – but the truth is, I'm lonely. And I want someone to love. Someone that loves me for who I am, not what they think I am. I had that. And I pushed it away.'

'Ben?'

'Yes, of course Ben.'

'But that was a long time ago. You've both moved on.'

'No, he's moved on. I feel I'm exactly where he left me. Except now I realise I was stupid to ever leave him in the first place. Oh, Mum, I'm such an idiot!'

'Jess, you're not. It's just that sometimes we don't appreciate what we've got until we haven't got it any more. That doesn't make you an idiot. It makes you human. What you need to do is figure out what you're going to do about it.'

'I know.' They stood in the middle of the bridge, looking down at the moving Tiber below. Jess lifted her face to the sky, filling her lungs with warm Roman air until she felt she couldn't fit any more in. She sighed a long, heavy sigh.

Julia squeezed Jess's hand between hers. 'Darling, it's never too late.'

10

Annie looked at the breakfast buffet laid out before her, wondering who on earth would choose to eat cold meats first thing in the morning. She plumped for a sad-looking croissant. Disappointing by Roman standards, she thought. Still, it made a change from a few cold crusts of toast and a lukewarm cup of tea.

She picked a small table in the corner of the room and sat down facing the window. Glancing at her phone, she couldn't decide whether she was more angry or worried that her sister had taken off into the night. She looked at her last unanswered text.

Please let me know you're ok.

Annie picked at the dry, papery croissant. The waiter brought a large cup of weak black coffee to the table accompanied by a small basket filled with little plastic tubs of milk. With that, she smiled apologetically at him. 'Actually, I think I'm going to go out for coffee. But thank you, I'm sorry to waste it.'

The young waiter smiled. 'Is a better idea, I think. The coffee here is terrible. Don't say I said that.'

'Of course not, thank you.' Annie moved out of her chair, gathered up her phone and key and headed back to the lifts by the front entrance. Standing there, pressing the button, was Jess.

Annie gently tapped her on the shoulder. 'Hey! Why didn't you answer me? I've been so worried!' Looking at Jess's face, Annie decided to change tack. 'And I am so sorry for saying the things I did.'

Jess looked at the floor. 'No, I'm sorry, Annie. I shouldn't have made out that you're the lucky one.' She looked up. 'But I had to get out of there. I couldn't face hearing it again from Mum, from you...' Fat tears began to fall from Jess's eyes.

Annie threw her arms around her sister. 'I'm so sorry. I just don't want you to be unhappy.'

Jess squeezed her sister hard, letting the tears come.

The lift door opened with a ping, depositing a couple of tourists into the lobby. The doors closed again, leaving the sisters where they were.

'Annie, Mum's got something to tell us...'

'Oh my God, is she OK? Is she—'

'No, she's not ill. She's fine. But she's here...' Jess looked over towards the hotel foyer. There, sitting in a red armchair by the side of the door was Julia. Annie waved.

'What? How come she's here? I'm really confused.'

'I bumped into her earlier this morning. She and Patrick had gone to the park with Richard's ashes.'

'Oh my goodness, I'd forgotten about poor Richard. Was she OK?'

'Yes, she was absolutely fine. But she's got something to tell us both. I think being here with Patrick... I don't know. I'll leave it to her. Anyway, give me fifteen minutes.' Jess motioned to her dress. 'Just want to have a really quick shower and change.'

'OK, be quick. I'll come up with you and get my bag.' Annie motioned across to Julia, pointing upstairs. Julia did a thumbs-up back at Annie. The sisters stepped into the lift together, Annie sensing Jess's fury from the night before had completely dissipated. The doors shut with the now familiar ping.

'So, what's the big secret?' Annie looked at her sister.

'Let Mum tell you. I think she wants to. I promise you it's nothing bad but it does explain a *lot*, I think. Patrick, this trip...' Jess ran her fingers through her long hair, pulling it into a knot on the top of her head.

'Promise I shouldn't be worried?'

'I promise. Give me ten minutes then come and knock on my door. We'll go down together.'

Julia sat in the chair, watching people come and go through the front door. Tourists ambled, staring at their phones. Others walked at pace and with purpose, on their way to meetings in this anonymous hotel, Julia supposed. She thought about the conversation that lay ahead of her. Her stomach tightened; her hands felt hot. But in her bones she knew this was the right thing to do.

She closed her eyes. There she was, standing in front of her, wearing a pair of thick-soled black shoes with tight laces. Moving her eyes slowly up, Julia took in the woman's blue uniform, like a matron's outfit. Everything else was blurred but those shoes were for ever imprinted in her memory. There was silence. Then a wail, but it wasn't a baby's cry. It was Julia, in the bedroom of Aunt Tessa's house. The baby was silent, sleeping, wrapped in a pale cream crocheted blanket.

'Mum? Are you OK?' Julia opened her eyes and smiled. Her two daughters stood over her, concern in their faces.

'Yes, darlings, I'm fine. But I do need some fresh air. Shall we go?'

Stepping through the revolving doors out into the already warm air, the sisters took an arm each and the three of them headed back towards the Eternal City.

* * *

They sat at a blue tablecloth-topped table outside a small café, the sisters on one side, Julia on the other, three steaming coffees between them. The narrow street was quiet compared to the morning rush hour buzz of people and vehicles they'd navigated on their walk in.

Julia picked up her spoon, stirred some sugar into her coffee. She took a deep breath and started to talk.

'I want you both to know that what I'm about to tell you is something that I've always wanted to share with you. But I felt, for years, that it was best not to. For all sorts of reasons, but mostly to protect you, to keep your lives as you knew them.'

'Mum, please just say what it is. I feel like I'm going to be sick.' Annie couldn't hide the slight irritation from her voice.

'When I was young, really young – seventeen – I had a baby. A son. Patrick was the father.' Julia forced her gaze upwards to look her daughters in the eye.

A beat, then Annie's words tumbled out. 'What? I don't believe this. You've got a son? So, what happened? Where is he? Do you know him?'

'No, I don't know where he is. I haven't seen him or had any contact since the day he was taken from me.'

'How old was he?' Jess reached across the table to take her mother's hand.

'He was six weeks old. I was allowed to have him for six weeks. Then I had to give him away.'

'What... what happened?' Annie asked again.

'Annie, let her—'

'Jess, you already knew about this. I want to know, too,' snapped Annie.

'Annie, that's all I told Jess, just this morning. What I'm about to tell you both, I've never told anyone before. Not even Patrick.' Julia turned her coffee cup in its saucer.

'I fell in love with Patrick when I was sixteen. He was nineteen. I was staying with my Aunt Tessa for the summer. She was Granny's sister and completely different from Granny. She was an artist and she lived alone in Cornwall. I used to go and stay with her every summer when I was little. Anyway, I'd known Patrick as a family friend for years but this was different. I know I was young but I also thought I'd met the man I wanted to spend the rest of my life with.' Julia closed her eyes, just for a moment.

'Anyway, we... I... well, I was obviously not quite as grown up as I thought I was. After the holidays finished Patrick went back to university. I went back to your grandparents' house. We were writing letters to each other every week, great long letters planning our future. Together we were going to travel the world. I was working at the shop when I noticed my uniform was getting tight. I know it sounds ridiculous but it took me a while to figure it out, but when I did, I was terrified.'

'God, Mum. What did you do?' Jess squeezed her mother's hand.

'I wrote to Aunt Tessa and told her. I was too scared to tell Granny. A few weeks later I was on a train back to Cornwall to go and stay with Tessa until the baby was born. I remember being told by my mother that I was to stay out of sight, not to tell anyone and that everything would be organised accordingly. I just did what I was told. Didn't ask questions. She was so angry.' Julia shook her head slowly at the memory, a palpable sense of her mother's disappointment still present after all these years.

'Did she not ask you if you wanted to keep the baby?' Annie's voice was barely a whisper.

'She told me I would ruin my life, hers too, my father's and the baby's. I felt I had no option but to do as she said. There was nowhere else to go. And to be honest, Tessa was the only other person in the world, apart from Patrick, that I wanted to be with.'

'What about Patrick, did he know?' Annie also reached for her mother's hand.

'My parents forbade me to ever make contact with him again. The deal was I would have the baby, they would find it a home and we would never speak of it again. If I did, I was on my own. In those days being an unmarried mother was just about the worst thing you could be, not least in my parents' eyes. I felt absolutely helpless. I had no money to leave and live elsewhere. So I went to Cornwall.'

'What happened?' whispered Jess.

'I had the baby, a beautiful boy. I called him William. He had enormous eyes, like Patrick's, with long, thick lashes and soft blond hair. He used to look up at me, fixing me with his stare. I'd spend hours looking at him. That first month of his life it was just Tessa and me in the cottage, with this adorable baby. My mother came to visit once; she spent an hour talking to Tessa downstairs in the kitchen. I remember hearing Tessa shouting at her, begging her to let us stay. But my mother refused.'

'God, Mum, I'm so sorry...' Jess wiped tears from her cheeks with a thick white napkin.

'So who took him?' Annie sat back in her chair.

'One morning, a woman arrived dressed in a matron's uniform. Black shoes. I couldn't look at her face but I'll never forget those shoes. I was told to bring William downstairs. Aunt Tessa came to help me. My legs felt like they were filled with air. I remember handing him to her...' Julia stopped; took a deep breath. 'And then I was told to go for a walk and not come back for half an hour. So I did. I walked to a spot where Patrick and I used to meet. A beautiful patch of grass surrounded by trees, on a bend in the river. I stood there, took off my shoes and walked into the water. I wanted to swim out towards the sea and not stop. I was just wading through mud, wanting the water to get deeper. Then someone was calling my name, pulling me from the water. It was Tessa. She took me back to the cottage. I don't really remember much after that apart from feeling utterly wretched. The cottage was so quiet...' Julia slowly stirred her coffee, watching it swirl around inside the small cup.

'I felt empty. Part of me was missing and I would never be able to get it back. But in time, Tessa helped me understand that I had to live my own life, that William would be well looked after wherever and whoever he ended up with. I had to promise to my parents, and to Tessa, that I would never try and find him. The thing is, I would have broken that promise if I'd made it only to my parents but I couldn't break it because of Aunt Tessa. She was so good to me, reassured me William would be OK. That he'd never know. And she said the best thing I could do was try to live a good life myself.'

Julia looked at her daughters across the table, squeezing

each of their hands. 'I am so lucky to have you both. And I wouldn't change anything if it meant that I didn't have you. I want you to know that.'

'We know, Mum.' Annie smiled.

'So why are you telling us now? I mean, you've kept it to yourself for so long...' Jess couldn't hide the hurt in her voice.

'Seeing Patrick, remembering Richard... I knew I couldn't keep it all to myself any more. I had to tell you. I feel you have a right to know. And like I said to you earlier, Jess, what you do with this information is up to you. I'm not going to look for him. I promised I wouldn't. I don't feel it's my right to simply walk back into his life.'

Annie let out a long sigh. 'What about Patrick, does he know?'

'Yes, he knows. Of course he knows. I wrote to him and told him everything once William was born. I remember sitting at Aunt Tessa's kitchen table, writing the letter. I told him that William was to be adopted and that I wouldn't be contacting him again. And I told him to not contact me, said that if he loved me he would do as I asked. Because, as I saw it, the only way I could ever live my life without the pain of losing William destroying it was to cut Patrick out, too. Seeing him would be a daily reminder of giving up my baby. Our baby. And I thought it was best for us to live separate lives, different lives, from then on.'

'But, Mum, you and Patrick were clearly so in love. Might you not have been happy together, in time?' Jess shook her head slowly.

'No, really. It just wasn't an option. I know it probably doesn't make sense to you now but I had no way out, nowhere to go. And I was so heartbroken. The day William was taken was the worst day of my life.'

'And did Patrick ever try to find you?' asked Annie.

'He wrote back, of course. Asked me to marry him. But it was too late for that. I felt that I had done enough damage. I just wanted to disappear. I was sent back home to work in the shop and that's what I did until a few years later when one day I simply walked out and headed to London. Soon after that, I met your father.'

'Did Dad know about William?' Jess wiped more tears from her wet cheeks.

'Yes, I told him. Of course I did. I was still grieving, really, when I met him. He was amazing, reassured me it was for the best. We didn't talk about it often but it was a great comfort that he knew. And he didn't think I was a terrible person for doing what I'd done. For that I will always be grateful.'

'And he told no one?' Annie's eyes widened.

'No, not a soul. And when you came along... eventually, it was quite a long time after...' Julia looked up from her coffee cup to Annie. 'I was so happy. I mean, over the moon. But of course it was a reminder of what was lost.'

'Oh, Mum, I'm so sorry. I can't imagine what it must be like keeping something like that to yourself for so long.' Annie reached for her napkin to soak up the tears in her eyes.

'*Scusi*, more coffee?' The waiter hovered behind Julia.

'No, *grazie*.' Jess smiled. 'I'd be able to fly home by myself if I have another one of those.'

'Of course! When's your flight?' Julia looked at her watch: still only just after nine o'clock in the morning.

'Later this afternoon. We'll have to head out to the airport fairly soon. When are you here until?' Annie remembered her unpacked suitcase back at the hotel.

'I'm on a flight later tonight. Patrick's here until tomorrow.

Time for one last late lunch and a few more paintings before I leave.'

'Mum, I know it's probably something you'll have to think about but... how would you feel if we tried to find him? William, I mean.' Annie spoke cautiously.

'Darling, as I said to Jess earlier, I'm not going to tell you what to do. My mother did that to me and I've had to live with it since the day I handed William over to a stranger. I'm not doing that. It's up to you.' She looked from Annie to Jess, a faint smile on her face. Both could see the hurt in her eyes, impossible for her to hide.

'Thanks, Mum.' Jess placed a note on the saucer, tucking it under the cup, moving from her seat round the table and wrapping her arms around her mother's pashmina-draped shoulders.

'Thank you, both. I can't begin to tell you what a relief it is to talk about him. He's felt like a ghost for so long, one that's always there, that only I can see. But he's real. And wherever he is, I love him. I just wish he knew that.'

* * *

The sisters sat on the plane in silence, the air between them filled with thoughts and questions. Jess turned her head to look out of the window as they climbed into the sky, leaving Rome behind. The now-familiar orange domes that loomed large above as they'd stood below them just a few hours ago now covered the city like a giant dot-to-dot.

Annie reached for the inflight magazine, hoping there might be something in there for the boys. The unexpected events of the morning had left her with no time to even buy a ridiculously overpriced fridge magnet in the airport. 'Jess, what do you think?'

'You don't need it.'

'What? No, I don't mean this,' she gestured at the magazine, 'I mean what do you think about looking for William? Do you want to?'

'Annie, I am so tired. My head hurts. My eyes hurt. Everything hurts. Can we talk about it when we land?'

'Of course.' Annie put the magazine back and reached for her book.

As they walked through security a few hours later, out through the doors into the arrivals area of the airport, Annie looked wistfully at all the dark-suited taxi drivers holding their signs with various surnames scribbled on them. There, at the end, was James, holding his own home-made sign.

SORRY FOR BEING A DICK

Annie ran to him, dropping her bag to the floor, throwing her arms around him.

'Annie, I am so sorry I forgot our anniversary.'

'It's OK, really it is. It's just a stupid anniversary.'

'No, it's not. Anyway, I'm really sorry. So much so, I made a complete tool of myself standing here with this.' He waved the sign.

'What on earth were you thinking?' Jess was laughing.

'Hi, Jess, how are you?' James gave his sister-in-law a hug.

'Good, thanks. I'm sorry I nicked your wife for a few days.'

'I think she deserved it.' James looked sheepish. 'How was it?'

'Amazing, actually, but exhausting. I need to fill you in on a few things...'

'Listen, I'm going to grab a cab back into town. I've got an early start tomorrow...' Jess kissed her sister on the cheek. 'Love you both. Call me tomorrow, OK?'

'Are you sure you'll be OK?' Annie squeezed her sister's arm.

'I'll be fine, honestly. I'll be fine.' Jess fixed her smile and gave them a wave, making a call sign at Annie as she went. 'Speak tomorrow!' And she disappeared into the crowd.

'So, tell me! What happened?'

She took a deep breath. 'James, I've got a brother. And I think I want to find him.'

PART II

PART II

11

'Are you ever going to open it?' Sophie tucked her hair behind her ears before starting to pile up the plates. 'God, you'd think they'd get at least *some* marmalade on their toast...'

'Here, I'll do that.' Ed got up from his chair, draining his coffee cup as he did.

'You didn't answer my question.' Sophie stopped, plates in either hand. 'You've had it for over a week.'

A thick white envelope sat in the middle of the kitchen table, propped up against the toast rack. Beside it, a small jug filled with a handful of slightly ragged dahlias added a dramatic splash of autumnal colour to the table.

'I know. I will, today.'

'Are you worried about what it might say? I mean, you wanted to know, didn't you?'

'Yes. I mean, no. No, I'm not worried. Yes, I do want to know. It's just that I wanted time to, you know, think about it. Prepare myself, or whatever...'

Sophie let the plates clatter back on to the table. She crossed the flagstone floor, stepping over a sleeping greyhound to stand in front of her husband. Slipping her arms through his and closing them tightly around his back, she looked up at his face. His hair fell forward as he brought his gaze to meet hers.

'You know, whatever happens, this doesn't change who we are as a family,' she said. 'Your parents – I mean, your proper parents, not your birth parents – loved you so much. We love you so much. So if it doesn't work out, well, we've not lost anything.'

'I know. Thank you.' Ed wrapped his arms around his wife. 'I mean it, thank you. I think, really, I've always hoped this might happen. I knew I wouldn't go searching myself.'

'Well, it's there when you're ready.' Sophie looked at the envelope, longing to know the secrets it held. But it wasn't her story to unfold. It was Ed's.

'I'll do it once we've sorted the fence. Cows got out again last night, apparently. All over the road by the pub; gave everyone a bit of a scare at chucking-out time, according to Tom.' Ed's farm manager had been ringing with updates all morning.

'OK, I've got to run. The kids are in the car. I'll be back later.' Sophie kissed him briefly, then scooped up her handbag and grabbed her coat from the back of a chair before heading for the door. 'See you at lunchtime!' she called. 'Bye, Billy!'

The greyhound lifted his head, looking to the now closing door before settling his head slowly back down to rest.

Ed looked around the room. It felt desperately quiet without his family in it. 'What do you reckon, Bill? Time to open it?' The dog looked up at him with his huge soulful eyes. 'Thought so.'

Ed picked up the coffee jug and refilled his cup. Sitting back down in his chair, he reached for the envelope, holding it in his hands, tracing the sharp corners with the tips of his fingers. The postmark was London. He knew it was from the agency, from the woman who'd been in touch about his birth family.

He took a slow sip from his mug, placing it gently back on the table before opening the letter, unfolding it slowly. Never had he wanted so much to know and not know, both at the same time. The words swam before his eyes, the name of the agency in blue across the top of the paper.

So this was it. How it felt to be wanted by your birth family. Ed let out a long sigh, closed his eyes. He dropped the letter on the table and put his head in his hands. His chest felt like it might burst, but whether with happiness or sadness he couldn't be sure. His phone lit up. It was a text from Tom, telling him the fence was fixed. Ed placed his head on his folded arms on the table and, for the first time since he could remember, started to cry.

* * *

Sophie battled with the car seat's buckle, as she did pretty much every morning, trying to release the wriggly two-year-old before walking her two eldest children down the path to the school gate.

'Mama! I do it!' Isla pulled at the buckle with her chubby toddler hands.

'No, baby, let me do it.' The fact that Isla had put on her enormous dusty-pink tutu over her trousers that morning made it an almost impossible task.

'Mum, come on! We'll be late!' Edie pleaded.

'We'll get a late mark *again*, Mum! Come on!' Johnnie tugged at his mother's arm, making it even more difficult to get the wriggly one out of her seat.

'Right, got you... Let's go.' With Isla on her hip, Sophie shut the door with a shove and followed the others, already halfway down the meadow path.

'Wanna WALK, Mama!' Isla squirmed, desperate to be on her own two feet.

'Of course you do,' Sophie sighed, dropping her gently to the ground.

'Hi, Sophie!' The shrill call of Amanda, the one mother guaranteed to make Sophie feel like she'd got dressed in the dark (which, to be fair, she practically had) was unmistakable. Sophie fixed a smile on her face, determined not to let her desire to disappear from view show.

'Hi, Amanda, how are you?'

'Running a bit late, actually. Not even had a chance to change after my run this morning!' Amanda laughed, gesturing to her get-up. Sophie wondered how anyone could look so glossy at this time in the morning, even in running gear. 'But I'm glad I've caught you. I wanted to ask if you'd be kind enough to run the second-hand clothes stall at the school Christmas Fair this year.'

Oh God, thought Sophie. She clearly thinks this is my calling.

'Er, well...I hadn't really thought...' She'd been warned about the second-hand clothes stall by her friend, Kate, and been advised specifically not to agree to take it on. 'Whatever you do, don't say yes to the second-hand clothes stall. You get inundated with bags and bags of stuff, most of it terrible. The only good thing about it is being able to nab all the second-hand school uniform before anyone else.'

'Oh please say yes, you'd be fantastic. And I thought you could do it with your friend, Kate, is it?'

As much as Sophie wanted to scream no, the thought of first dibs on cheap school uniform was impossible to resist, especially given how quickly the children were outgrowing theirs. 'I suppose...um, yes, OK. And I'm sure she'd be happy to help me.'

If Sophie was going to do this, she was taking Kate down with her. 'I'm seeing her later, I'll ask her then.'

'Perfect! Thanks so much, Sophie. I know you two will nail it.' With that, Amanda flashed her wide smile and turned to jog back up the path. Sophie watched her go, her glossy ponytail swinging behind her.

''Bye, Mama!' Turning back towards the gate, Sophie spied Johnnie and Edie waving. She waved back. 'See you at three! Have a good day!' Off they ran, down the path to school. 'Isla! Come back, darling. You can't go with them.' Sophie began to run down towards them, hoping to catch Isla before she disappeared into school along with her siblings.

* * *

'You did *what*?' Kate couldn't believe what she was hearing.

'I know, I'm sorry. But I just couldn't resist the promise of second-hand uniform.' Sophie shifted Isla from one knee to the other, handing her a cinnamon biscuit from the packet as she did so.

They sat in Kate's kitchen, which, with its toy-covered floor, felt like a home from home to Sophie. Kate's son, Gus, still in his pyjamas despite it being past midday, pushed a wooden train around the kitchen floor.

'I mean, I'd take the toy stall over the clothes stall.'

'I know, I'm sorry. But I think it'll be worth the pain.' Sophie said, brightly.

'S'pose. But still... Anyway, what's been going on?'

Sophie looked at her cup, unable to meet Kate's eye. They'd known each other since they were children. One look and Kate would know Sophie was hiding something.

'OK, what is it? You only ever don't look at me when you're

sitting on something you're not supposed to tell me. God, you'd make an awful poker player, Soph.'

'Kate, I can't.'

'Then don't.'

'It's Ed secret to tell. His family has got in touch.'

'Oh God, Sophie. When did this happen?'

Sophie let out a long sigh. She'd been holding this news in for weeks and now, finally, it was out. 'I feel bad even telling you but, honestly, carrying this around has been exhausting. He doesn't want to talk about it. But he obviously wants to meet them.'

'When did they contact him?'

'Last month, a letter from an agency arrived. They'd been contacted by Ed's sister... It feels so weird even saying that.'

'Not the mother?' Kate couldn't hide her surprise.

'No, it was from his sister. Or half-sister, I guess. I'm not sure. In fact, it was from his sisters. There are two of them.'

'Oh, wow. How does Ed feel about it?'

'Well, that's the weird thing. I honestly couldn't tell you. Not really, I mean. He says he wants to meet them. But he hasn't really talked about how he feels about it, about any of it. He always said he wouldn't look for her, for his mother. I assumed that was to do with self-preservation, you know. Having been given up once before, the idea of being rejected again was too much, perhaps. That and not wanting to upset his parents. But now that they are both gone, he must feel differently.'

'Why have the sisters got in touch and not the mother?'

'Apparently, according to the letter from the agency, the mother had never dared to assume Ed would want to be found. But the sisters felt strongly enough to take the chance and have said they would like to meet him, if he wants to, of course.'

Kate let out a long whistle. 'Soph, no wonder you've been a bit out of it. Poor Ed, it must be such a shock.'

'I think it really is. You know what he's like. He'd rather talk to animals than humans, anyway, let alone to humans about how he's feeling. Even me.' Sophie brushed a fat tear from her eye before it fell.

'Oh, come on, you two are heaven on earth together. He just needs time to let it sink in. And I know you would have said all the right things; you always do.' Kate squeezed her friend's arm across the table.

'God, I hope you're right, Kate. I'm just not sure how he'd cope with being let down. You know what he's like, solid as a rock. But underneath all that there is someone who's never known his roots, his real story, which I guess is why he's so determined to make ours so real.'

Isla slid off Sophie's lap to join Gus, picking up a stray wooden train as she did.

'That's mine!' shouted Gus.

'Hey, Gus, what did we say about sharing? Let Isla have that train and then you can play together.'

Gus stuck out his bottom lip, giving Isla a long, hard stare. In return, she held up her train in triumph.

'Now that's not the way to handle it, Isla.' Sophie gestured to the train track. 'Why not push yours round to meet Gus halfway?'

'Great idea! Put yours together and you can make an even better train.' Kate proffered the biscuits. 'And take a biscuit for your troubles.'

'Excellent tactics.'

'I know. I don't know how I do it.' Kate shrugged. 'Anyway, you were saying...'

'I can't remember. Just that it all feels like it should be good news, happy news. But it's also hugely unsettling. And I feel guilty that I'm feeling so unsettled by it when it's Ed who has to deal with it. I mean he has every right to meet his real family. I just can't bear the thought of him being at all disappointed by whatever he finds out.'

'Look, it's bound to be tricky in parts. But the fact that they've reached out to him shows that they want to know him, at least. And I guess it's up to him what happens next.'

'Exactly. The agency says it's completely up to him. They won't disclose anything about Ed, or us, to his sisters unless he wants them to. The ball's totally in his court.' Sophie gently shrugged. 'You won't say anything, will you?'

'Of course not, you know I won't. But I'm glad you told me. So what happens next?'

'He opens the letter, that's what.'

* * *

Ed stood on his favourite spot on the headland, the wind carrying the scent of the sea as it whipped around him. Billy raced ahead, along the narrow track towards the grass-topped promontory ahead. Far below, the waves crashed onto the rocks, sending up soft, low booms as they did.

Since leaving the house, Ed felt the letter was burning a hole in his pocket. Reaching his favourite rock, he sat with his back to the land and looked down at the letter, now in his hands. Slowly, he opened the envelope for the second time. This time, he told himself, he would read every word.

Dear Mr Duncan,

I'm writing to you on behalf of Jessica and Annabel, two sisters who would very much like to make contact with you.

You haven't met but they asked me to approach you in the hope that you might consider doing so. I would very much appreciate you getting in touch, either at the above address or by telephoning me at your convenience so I can give you more information.

Yours sincerely,

Alison Pearce

Ed read it again, stopping at their names. Jessica and Annabel. His sisters. No matter how hard he looked at the names, these people just didn't feel quite real. He glanced down at the dog, now sitting quietly at his feet, eyes closed, sniffing the air.

'What do you think, Billy? Time I met them?'

Billy looked at his master, then back out to sea.

Ed imagined Alison Pearce, sitting in an office opposite the two sisters, writing down what they knew in a notepad. Which made him think: what *did* they know?

He couldn't remember exactly when his parents had told him he was adopted but he also couldn't remember a time when he didn't know. And they'd made it feel like the most normal thing in the world, that he should be with them instead.

On his eighteenth birthday, his mother had asked him if there was anything he wanted to know about his birth parents. Deep down, he was desperate to know everything, but for the sake of his parents, for fear of hurting them, he decided that he wouldn't – couldn't – know. Even when they had died, both well into their eighties and barely a year apart, a couple of years before, still he hadn't felt he could go looking for his birth mother.

Once, when drunk after a wedding in Sophie's family, he'd opened his laptop and punched in his name and birth year into a family search website. But he'd drawn a blank before he'd even finished his whisky.

And now, sitting here on his favourite rock, in his favourite place in the world, looking out to the sea stretching far into the horizon, he felt on the brink. Excited at what he might find, scared at what he might not. His stomach lurched at the thought of meeting real people from his past.

He looked back down at Billy. 'Of course it's time. I mean, they've come looking for me, haven't they?'

Billy sighed.

'OK, Bill. No need to be sarcastic.' Ed folded the letter back into the envelope and placed it back in his pocket. 'Come on, let's go and check that fence.'

* * *

'Tea or coffee?' The smartly dressed woman with a neat helmet of blond hair stood behind her chair on the other side of the desk, smiling warmly.

'Water would be lovely, thank you.' Jess slid into her seat.

'I'm good, thanks,' Annie waved her reusable coffee cup. 'I'm already fully caffeinated.' She laughed, rather too loudly, she thought.

'Do you have any news?' Jess couldn't hide the impatience from her voice. Annie shot her a look.

Alison Pearce adjusted her glasses, reached for the jug of water on a tray on her desk and poured Jess a glass. Slowly, she took her seat.

'Yes, I do. Good news, in fact. As you know, this process can take months, years even. And it's not always successful. But in your case, luck has been on our side. The information that your mother's aunt left her led us almost straight to him.'

'Really? Have you found him?' Annie's stomach lurched.

'We have.'

'Does he want to meet us?' Annie hardly dared say the words.

'Yes, he wants to meet you.'

'He does?' Jess turned to Annie, squeezing her hand.

'Shit, he really does. God, sorry.' Annie smiled apologetically at Alison Pearce.

'Yes, he really does. I'm so pleased for you. And for your mother, of course; I know you're doing this with her blessing. But – and I know we've been through all this before – it's really important that you go into this with an open mind. He might not want to maintain contact once you've met. Or you might find that you don't feel quite as you might imagine when you do finally meet. Of course, every case is different but it's not always the happy ending you might dream of.'

'Oh, I know. I've been reading all about it.' Annie immediately regretted saying that out loud, worried that it sounded ridiculous.

'Great, read as much as you can; there are lots of brilliant books that can help you prepare for a meeting like this. As I said, it can be more complicated than you think. Your brother has his own life, and will have his own feelings about being given up for adoption. So you'll just need to bear all that and more in mind when you meet. Take your time, all of you. It's a big adjustment.'

'We quite understand, thank you, Alison.' Jess deployed her smile to make up for her earlier curtness.

'You are most welcome. Right, so I can tell you that your brother's name is Ed. He's married, with children, and lives in the West Country. I have a photo here. Would you like to see it?'

Alison took a photo from her file and pushed it flat across the table so the sisters could both see.

There, looking up at them, was a tall man with kind eyes and a mop of brown hair, standing on a wind-swept beach.

Annie gasped. 'Oh my goodness. Jess, he looks so like Patrick in the picture Mum showed me before we went to Rome.'

'Oh, wow, he looks so familiar!' Jess laughed, tears springing to her eyes.

'And he's got kids, you said?' Annie couldn't take her eyes from the picture.

'Yes, he's got three children with his wife, Sophie. Sadly his adoptive parents both died a couple of years ago. But he was very happy with them. They were obviously really lovely people.'

'And he'd never wanted to look for Mum?' Jess wiped at her eyes again.

'Well, no. He decided long ago not to look because he didn't want to upset his parents – his adoptive parents, I mean. I'm sure in time he might explain his reasons in more depth to you if he wants to.'

'Oh my God, Jess. That's him. I haven't stopped thinking about him since Rome, wondering where he is. How he is. What he looks like. And seeing him, he looks just as I'd imagined, even if I didn't know it. Do you know what I mean?'

'I know exactly what you mean. He looks so familiar, it's weird.' Jess pulled the photo closer to her face, as if studying it for clues. 'Where is this picture taken?'

'On a beach near his home. He can tell you more when you meet.' Alison Pearce opened the file on the table. 'Right, so the next step in the process is for me to set up a time for you all to do that. I suggest we say somewhere of his choosing. You've had a little more time to get used to the idea. For him, this really is a bolt from the blue.'

'Yes, of course, whatever suits him.' Jess placed the photo

back on the table. 'We'll meet wherever he likes. Just let us know when and where.'

'Will you be there?' Annie sounded hopeful that Alison Pearce would be.

'That's up to you all, but I don't think you'll need me there.'

'Oh, OK. We'll see what he says then, shall we? See what Ed thinks...' Saying his name felt so peculiar to Annie, yet she wanted to say it over and over again.

'So, can we tell Mum all of this?' Jess shifted in her seat.

'Yes, you can. And then when you meet him, you can ask him if he'd like to meet your mother. I've explained to him your mother's position.'

'I still don't understand why she feels she has to keep that promise, given that her own mother isn't around any more.'

'Jess, you know Mum. If she made a promise...'

'I know, but still.' Jess composed herself, fixing that smile back in place. 'So, Alison, when do you think we'll hear from you?'

Alison Pearce closed the file. 'Well, I'll talk to Ed, let him know you're happy to travel to a place that's convenient for him to meet you and we can take it from there.'

* * *

Back on the street outside, Annie glanced at her watch. 'I've got a bit of time before getting the train back. Fancy a bite to eat?'

'Can we have wine?' Jess took a surreptitious drag on her vape.

'I think I need it after that. How about that place over there?' Annie pointed at the restaurant on the corner of the small square in front of them.

'That'll do.' Jess grabbed Annie's arm and headed towards it.

Inside, the buzz of the brasserie washed over them like a warm wave. They were soon shown to a table by the window, Annie slipping into the seat with her back to the window so she could see the room. Jess immediately ordered their drinks and moments later a waiter placed two large glasses of chilled white wine and a small bowl of salted almonds in front of them.

'The Vermentino?'

'Yes, that's us. Thank you.' Jess picked up her glass. 'To meeting our brother.'

Annie raised her glass in return. 'To meeting Ed.' They clinked their glasses before each taking a sip.

'God, that's delicious.' Jess took another long sip. 'So, how do you think Mum is taking all this?'

'She seems fine. She did say that it was up to us and, to be honest, I think she was hoping we'd do this. She's probably always wanted to find him herself, but couldn't.'

'Has Patrick been down to see her again?'

'Yes, he seems to be around most weekends. I'm not sure I can really ask her exactly what's going on with him, though.'

'But do they look like they are together?'

'Well, they seem very happy in each other's company. But there's no obvious sign of romance, if you know what I mean.'

'Ooh, no. I don't even want to think about that. But we'll know when she announces she's going to get married. Again.'

'Oh, come on, Jess. Don't be like that. At her age she should be able to do what the bloody hell she likes.'

'I know, I know. I'm joking. Seriously, I *am* joking. Anyway, he's our brother's father, so that makes him our... What does it make him?'

Annie picked up her glass and drank a little more. 'I have absolutely no idea. Do you think Patrick will want to meet Ed? And vice versa?'

'I suppose we'll have to ask them. I guess Ed won't know his real parents are still in touch. Hopefully we can help fill in the gaps and then they can decide.'

'Bloody hell, this feels so strange.'

'Talking of which, I need to tell you something...' Jess held her vape in her hand, the knuckles betraying the pressure of her grip. Annie's eyes snapped up to meet her sister's. They held each other's gaze for a moment before Jess looked at her glass.

'Go on...'

'I've been in touch with Ben again.'

'Oh, Jess! Really? That's great news! I'm so pleased.'

'Wait, Annie. Hold on. Don't get too excited. He's only just moved back from New York.'

'But he's single – please tell me he's single, right?' Annie couldn't hide the joy from her face.

'Yes, he's single. Again. His marriage didn't work out, sadly.'

'Oh my God, you've had that conversation already? When did you see him?'

'I haven't seen him yet. We've just been in touch via email, catching up on each other's news.'

'This is so exciting, Jess! You two were—'

'Don't say it, please, Annie. I properly fucked it up last time and I can't even believe he's bothering to answer me but, well, he is. And I have to say, writing everything down has been so good. I mean, I've told him about Rob, about my job... everything.'

'Wow, Jess. Normally your emails are no longer than a couple of sentences.'

'I know. But since coming back from Rome, I've realised that I have nothing to lose. Well, apart from my dignity, but I lost that in Rome.'

'Why, what happened?'

Jess thought back to the television in the café that morning, the unmistakable heat of humiliation creeping up her neck. She shuddered at the thought. 'Oh, nothing really. I just decided it was time I ran towards something rather than away from it. It might come to nothing, but for now getting to know each other again this way feels right. And honestly, I think it's helped me make sense of everything that's happening.'

'Jess, that is brilliant news. I'm so happy for you.'

'Thank you.' They grinned at each other across the table.

'Here's to my sister.' Annie raised her glass to meet Jess's.

'To my sister.'

12

1963

The sound of the alarm clock battled its way through Patrick's dream, bringing him abruptly back to the surface. He sat up in bed, his breathing uneven, soaked in sweat. Another nightmare. This time he was running, but from what, he didn't know. The latest work assignment had left scars, far more than any before. Not that you could see them, bar the odd healing cut and bruise. This was more brutal. He'd taken to avoiding sleep in a bid to escape the images that flooded his head at night. Whisky helped.

He looked around the room, trying to focus on something, anything to remind him exactly where he was. The room was so dark. Pushing the covers away, he crossed the floor and opened the heavy curtains. He took in the grey stone on the quiet traffic-free street below. Paris.

Of course, he was in Paris. Since arriving back from Algeria he'd spent much of his time buried in the welcome silence of the darkroom at his studio. Some of the shots developing before his eyes were almost too painful to look at but he knew he had a job to do. That is, help tell the story of the people caught up in a bloody fight for independence, even if it was now technically over.

Throwing on some clothes, he headed for the door, hoping fresh air and strong coffee might help shift the fug in his head. He walked the now familiar route down the street, through the Jardin du Luxembourg, past his favourite jazz club he couldn't quite remember leaving last night and crossed the wide boulevard to the café. Chairs were still stacked up against the wall outside. He pushed open the door and slipped into the red leather-covered banquette seat at the table by the door, just as he had almost every morning since moving to Paris the year before.

'Bonjour, Patrick,' the waiter placed a small cup of coffee down on the table in front of him. 'Late one last night, *non*?'

'A little.' Patrick stared at the cup, dropped two lumps of sugar into it and stirred slowly. He reached into his pocket, putting a crumpled packet of cigarettes on the table. He felt around in the other for a lighter.

'Here...' The waiter held out a lighter.

'Thank you, Monsieur. Some eggs, too, please, when you're ready.'

'Of course.' The waiter turned and headed back to the long brass-topped bar behind him.

Patrick took a quick sip, the liquid burning his lips. He looked out across the street and realised for the first time for a long time that what he really needed was to go home. Not back to his parents but to Cornwall. To see the sea, smell and feel the prickle of sea salt on his skin. Running away, burying himself in work wasn't the answer. If he wanted to try to come to terms with what he'd had and lost, he needed to go back first.

Moments later a plate of fried eggs and bacon was placed on the table, the smell arriving before the food. 'I'm so sorry,

Monsieur, but I have to go.' Patrick stood up from his place, putting on his coat.

'Is everything OK?' The waiter looked concerned.

'It will be. Please, I don't want this to go to waste.' He put some coins on the table.

'*Merci, Monsieur*... if you are sure.' The waiter smiled and picked up the plate.

'Thank you. I'm so sorry.'

As Patrick walked back across the gardens, now filling with people walking to work, children running to school, he looked up at the pale blue sky and took in a deep breath of cool morning air. For the first time in months he felt a heaviness lift from his shoulders. He headed to the agency office, his pace quickening as he rehearsed what he might say to his boss, Henri. Since joining he'd not turned down a single job, knowing – as the rookie photographer – it wasn't his place to say no.

By the end of the day he stood on the tarmac at the airport, small suitcase in hand, camera round his neck. Just as he'd hoped, Henri had told him to clear off for a few weeks. 'And, Patrick,' he'd said, cigarette smoke curling from his mouth as he spoke, 'don't come back until you've had a proper night's sleep. You look like shit.'

* * *

Two days later Patrick stood on the steps of the big house on the hill. He knocked quietly. No answer. He knocked again, still nothing. He walked around the side of the house, peering into the windows. Inside, the place was in darkness. Dustsheets covered the furniture and, despite the gloom, he could see thick cobwebs hanging in the corners of the room.

'Can I help you?' A gruff voice came from behind him,

catching Patrick by surprise. He turned to see the old gardener standing, secateurs in hand.

'Ah, yes... Hello, I'm Patrick.' He held out his hand, dropping it slowly when his gesture was ignored. 'I'm looking for Maggie. She was a friend of mine, but I haven't seen her for a few years.'

'The family aren't here any more, I'm afraid. Moved out a few months ago now. Sad, really. They'd been here so long.'

'Oh, right... Do you know where they've gone?'

'I don't, I'm afraid. The new owners kept me on, though. Told me to carry on as usual. So that's what I'm doing.' He raised the secateurs by way of explanation.

'Ah, OK. Thank you anyway. I'll head off then.' Patrick looked into the room once more, then back across the field. For a moment, he could almost feel the touch of her hand in his as they'd stood on that slope gazing down at the village below. The grey sky sat heavily above, the smell of impending rain in the air.

'Right you are.' The gardener waved a hand and wandered off towards the rose garden.

As Patrick started the long walk back to the station he cursed himself for being so naïve. Why on earth had he thought it would be as easy as knocking on Maggie's front door to ask where Julia might be, how she was? Earlier he'd walked quickly through the village, past Julia's aunt's cottage. As much as he'd wanted to, he didn't dare stop. He'd carried on, taking the path to the left towards the river. As he went, he remembered the times he and Julia had walked along this very path, planning their future. One that was full of ideas, of promise, of hope. When he reached the corner he stepped out onto the small bank, looking first up the river then down. He wanted to cry out but the stillness stopped him. It all looked just as it always had, even though things could never be as they were. Julia had made it very clear in her letter that they were not to see each other again; that if he did indeed love her, he would let her get on with her life.

All he knew was that his baby, a healthy son, had been born and within weeks sent off for a new life with people he'd never know. But at least he – little William – had been in that small white cottage, with roses around the door, in the arms of the woman he loved. Not for long, but for a short while. The thought gave him some comfort, at least.

He carried on up the hill, the station a good twenty-minute walk away, so lost in his thoughts he didn't hear the loud revving as a car slowly crawled up alongside him.

'Patrick!'

He turned to see a familiar face behind the wheel of the Morris Traveller.

'Tessa?' Patrick saw she was smiling at him, familiar grey wisps of hair escaping the scarf keeping it back from her face.

'Darling, won't you at least let me give you a lift? I presume you're heading to the station. Come on, get in before this thing starts rolling backwards.' Tessa reached across to open the door for Patrick.

'I didn't expect to see you...' He folded his long body into the seat, his legs practically touching his chin.

Tessa floored the clutch and got the car moving again. 'I could say the same. But then I saw you walk past earlier, or at least I thought it was you. I came out after you but you'd gone. I've been looking for you ever since. Where did you go?' She had to shout for him to hear her over the roar of the engine.

'I'm not sure, really. The house, the river... I wanted to go to the beach but I couldn't get there. Tessa, I... I'm not sure what to say. I'm so sorry. I know you must know everything and I'm not here to interfere. Julia made me promise not to find her, not to try to get in touch but I just had to... see...'

'Oh, darling boy, I'm so sorry things didn't work out as you'd both hoped, as you both deserved. But her parents, my sister...' Tessa screwed up her face, shook her head slowly, '... is very old-fashioned, I'm afraid. This was one battle Julia was never going to win.'

'What's he like? William?' Patrick stared ahead, hoping he hadn't pushed her kindness too far.

'He looks like you, Patrick. Enormous eyes, a sleeper, thankfully. Julia was so happy to have him even for just those precious few weeks. They had such a bond, really they did.' Tessa closed her eyes, remembering the smell of his head, the clench of his little fists.

'And what about Julia – how is she?' Patrick looked at Tessa now, trying desperately not to let the tears behind his eyes fall.

'She's good, Patrick, a lot better than she was. It has taken time but she's getting there. She desperately wanted to go to college in the September after William was born but her parents needed her to stay with them and work in the shop. Her father wasn't well for a while and her mother couldn't manage on her own. She's been living there ever since but she's planning on going just as soon as she can. She's been saving up and when she's ready, she will fly, I know she will.'

'And does she...? Do you think she really doesn't want me to get in touch?'

'I think she would love that more than anything in the world. But because of what's happened she says she can't face you. I remember her saying that if you were together, she thought you'd both always be reminded of what you had lost, not what you had. Honestly, Patrick, this almost destroyed her. Giving up William was the hardest thing for her to do. It's a miracle it didn't destroy her, to be honest. I think she's determined to try to have a life. She hasn't been here since – I think her mother's still terrified of what people will say, which is ridiculous, I know – but Julia and I write to each other all the time.

'Please don't tell her I came, Tessa. I'm desperate to see her, to talk to her, but I know she doesn't want me to, and for that reason alone I don't want her to know I was here. I don't want her to worry.'

'Of course not, Patrick, but I think it's a good thing that you came.' Tessa put her hand on his, squeezing it as she did.

'I will try to move on, too, try to have a life, Tessa. Thank you. And I'm sorry... I never wanted to—'

'No more apologies, Patrick. Listen, how about I drive you to the beach, leave you there for a bit? I know it doesn't look like it now but I think the sun will break through soon. You can walk down to the cove.'

'How do you know about the cove?'

'Listen, you can't do much around here without being spotted.'

'Right. Well, I would love to go. But...' he looked at his watch, 'I'd miss my train.'

'Then unless you're in a hurry, you can stay with me tonight and I'll put you on the first train back to London tomorrow. I think that if you're really going to lay some ghosts to rest, you need to go down there and put your feet in the sand, watch the waves for a while, listen to the sound of the sea. What do you say?'

'Tessa, really, I couldn't put you out like that. You must have things to do.'

'Nothing would make me happier than knowing I've helped you in some way. And I'd love the company over supper tonight.

Not that it'll be anything more exciting than some bread and cheese and a bottle of red, I'm afraid.'

'That sounds absolutely perfect, Tessa. Thank you.'

'Right, I'll turn round at the top of the hill. If we make it up there, that is...'

Tessa drove back towards the coast and dropped Patrick by the edge of the road. 'I'll pick you up back here in an hour. I need to pop into town. Might see if I can find something a bit more exciting for us to eat tonight.' She waved as Patrick headed off towards the beach down the path across the field.

He walked towards the point, lifted by the sight of the sea far below. The sky was still grey – no sign of the sun – but the sound of waves on the shore soothed him. Picking his way down along the narrow path, he remembered how Julia would always run ahead, her bare brown legs moving quickly between rocks and gorse. There wasn't a soul on the beach. Now he was on the shore, the noise of the sea surrounded him and he watched the waves washing first up towards him before gently rolling back. Over and over, a soundtrack to his thoughts of her, of the way they were. And of William, a small boy made by them both. A gift they hadn't been allowed to keep. Patrick's sense of loss left him weak. He looked out towards the horizon, a huge black cloud spreading before him. The sea breeze had picked up, now whipping around him. He threw back his head and let out a long, desperate yell, the wind picking it up and carrying it up into the sky. He closed his eyes and felt the first drops of rain on his skin. Within moments, he was drenched, his hair sticking to his face. He held the heel of his hands to his eyes, hoping to stem the tears but they came anyway.

Patrick turned and looked back along the beach, first one way, then another. Still empty. The tide was out far enough for him to reach the cove round the corner. He walked slowly, his feet sinking in the stones but the wind at his back pushed him towards the small opening of a cave: their cave. Stones gave way to damp sand and he took his place on a rock just inside, where he'd once sat turning mackerel on the fire. How could it be so fresh in his memory and yet feel like a lifetime away?

He sat looking at the sea, watching until the rain stopped and the wind died down. The black cloud had all but disappeared and the grey clouds slowly gave way to glimpses of blue behind. He got up and walked to the shore, ready to walk back up the cliff path. The gulls wheeled overhead. Just as they always had and just as they always would. Taking a deep breath he started towards the steps.

Tessa waved from the top of the hill. He waved back.

* * *

The following morning, as he sat on the train heading east once again, flashes of Cornish coast soon giving way to sweeping moors, he thought of Julia. She had made her decision, asked him to go ahead and live his life for all their sakes. And no matter how much he wished he didn't have to accept it, he knew deep down he owed it to her to do as she'd asked.

For the first time he felt a sense of acceptance, a kind of perspective he hadn't known he'd needed. He'd spent so long running away from the facts, filling his days with anything other than the ordinary. Now he knew, things were as they were and the best he could do was to start living properly again, holding the memory of Julia and their son in his heart and cherishing it. He'd spent the last two years trying to forget, pretend nothing had happened. Now he knew he'd have to learn to live with it if he was going to have any life at all.

'I'm sorry... were you...? I didn't mean to disturb you.'

He looked blankly at the woman sitting opposite, now speaking to him.

'I just wondered if you knew how long it is until we get to Exeter?' She smiled, her brown eyes framed with glasses.

'Ah, not too long, but we're here for a little while at least, I'm afraid. You haven't done this journey before?' Patrick pulled himself back to the present, returning her smile.

'No, I haven't.' She extended her hand. 'I'm Katherine, by the way. Kathy, usually... Nice to meet you.'

'I'm Patrick. Pleased to meet you, too.' He took her hand and shook it.

'Well, if we're stuck here, how about tea?' She took a flask from the large tartan bag at her feet and placed it on the table alongside a tin. 'And by the looks of it, my mother has made enough biscuits to fuel an army.' She lifted the lid and peered inside. 'Or two.' She passed the tin across the table to Patrick. At that moment he realised he hadn't eaten a thing since supper with Tessa the previous day. He took a biscuit, a thick slab of yellow, crumbling shortbread, and bit into it.

'Thank you, delicious.' He wiped the crumbs from the corners of his mouth, watching her pour out two cups of steaming tea from the flask. 'So, what takes you to Exeter?'

'I'm going for a job, actually. And I'm quite nervous. I'm afraid that's why I came to talk to you. Sitting there on my own, I was overthinking it. I need a distraction.'

'Oh, right. Glad I can help.' Patrick laughed gently. 'So, what's the job? Or don't you want to talk about it?'

'Oh, no, I do. It's for a position on a research project. I'm probably far too young for them to even take me seriously but, honestly, I think this job was made for me. It's a project on Thomas Hardy, working through his correspondence, documenting new finds, figuring out as much as we can about his influences, his inspiration. It's a mammoth task, but to me it sounds like heaven.'

'Goodness, that does sound a huge undertaking. I love his books.'

'What's your favourite?'

'*The Mayor of Casterbridge*.' He hoped she didn't ask any more questions. It was the only one he'd read and that was at school. 'Yours?'

'*Tess*, obviously.' Kathy passed him a small Melamine cup of tea. 'What about you, what brought you to Cornwall?'

'I had a few days off work so thought I'd head down here to, you know, clear the cobwebs.' Patrick hoped she couldn't hear quite how hard he had to work to make this lie sound casual.

'Oh, good idea, quite the best place to clear the head. And what's work for you?'

'I'm a photographer.'

'How fascinating. What sort?' Kathy reached into the tin for another biscuit.

'I'm a photo journalist. A war photographer, specifically.' He was used to this being met with a few polite but slightly awkward questions but Kathy was anything but stuck for words. She asked lots of questions. Not just the usual ones – where had he been, did he get scared – rather she wanted to know why he'd gone into it, how he felt when taking photographs on the front line. On and on they went and, for once, Patrick was grateful for the opportunity to talk about it, not least because it kept his mind occupied.

As the train pulled into Exeter Kathy started packing away her things, carefully screwing the lid back on the flask and pushing the top of the tin down hard before putting them back in her bag.

Patrick watched her as she scribbled on a piece of paper,

wondering how this encounter might end. He'd enjoyed her company.

'So, it was lovely to meet you, Patrick.' Kathy extended her hand again. Patrick took it.

'And you. Good luck with the job interview. I think this one's got your name on it.' He smiled at her, meaning it.

'Thank you, I do hope so. It would be wonderful to be able to settle for a while. I do love it here. Here, this is me...' Kathy pointed at a small scrap of paper on which she'd written her name in neat black letters. 'And my number in Exeter. I'm staying with my godmother and I'll be here for a while, I hope. Just in case you want to get in touch when you're next passing through.' She handed it to Patrick.

'Gosh, thank you.' He was momentarily taken aback, unsure what to say. He looked at it before putting it in his pocket. 'I mean, thank you very much. I'm not sure when I might be back this way but...'

Her smile stayed in place but he saw her eyes lose their shine a little. 'Yes, of course. You're bound to be off somewhere far-flung by this time next week. Still, I really enjoyed talking to you.' Kathy picked up her bag. 'Good luck, Patrick, and thank you for your company.' She turned to head towards the carriage door.

'Kathy...' Patrick reached out, touching her gently on the arm. She stopped and turned back towards him. 'Thank you. I can't tell you how much I've appreciated your company, too. There's so much I would like to have told you but now definitely isn't the time.' He lowered his eyes.

Kathy looked at his face, sensing the untold hurt. She spoke softly. 'I thought there was a story but I figured you weren't ready to tell it. You looked so sad when I first saw you, and I couldn't bear it. That's the real reason I came over. Look, I'm not expecting you to—'

'No, Kathy, you have been so kind. I'm going to give you my number too and really, I would love for us to meet up again.' He took a pen from his coat pocket and hastily scribbled a number on the back of his cigarette packet. 'Here, this is my number in Paris.'

'Goodness, how very...chic.' Kathy took the packet from Patrick. 'I'd love to go to Paris one day.'

'Well, I hope that one day you do. Because I think you'd love it.'

'Well, goodbye again.' Kathy smiled at him before turning back to head to the door.

''Bye, Kathy, safe journey.' He waved as she walked past the window a moment later and she waved back, the shine back in her eyes.

13

1964

'Are you going to put those on or are you waiting for them to do it themselves?' Julia's mother called across the shop to her. Julia stood motionless at the foot of a ladder with a pricing gun in her hand.

Turning back to her customer, Jeanie Shield rolled her eyes. 'Honestly, that girl lives in a world of her own sometimes.'

'Oh, don't worry, Mrs Shield, mine don't listen to a word I say either. How's your husband doing, anyway?'

'He's much better, thank you. Almost back to normal now, thank goodness. Of course, he was very lucky. Not everyone his age survives a heart attack.' Jeanie handed a paper bag over the counter to the customer. 'There you go, Mrs Robinson. All yours.'

'Thank you, take care now.' The bell on the door tinkled as she left.

With the shop empty of customers again, Julia braced herself for a telling-off.

'Honestly, Julia, it seems to take you twice as long to do anything as anyone else. Once you *finally* finish doing that please can you make yourself useful and go and see what your father wants for lunch? He's upstairs. Go in quietly, though. He might be resting.'

'Yes, Mum.' Julia faced away from her mother, closing her eyes as she spoke. Making her way upstairs, she stopped at the door of the sitting room, pushing it slowly open.

'Dad?' she whispered.

'I'm awake, love. Come in.' Her father sat in his chair by the window, head resting against the side. He turned to look at her, his eyes lighting up a little.

'How are you feeling?' Julia spoke softly, kneeling down beside him. He'd aged quickly over the last few years and Julia couldn't help but feel it was partly her fault.

'Oh, don't look like that. I'm not dead yet.'

Julia checked herself, smiling. 'Sorry, Dad.'

'How's your mother doing?'

'She's OK. It's been quiet this morning, only a handful of customers.'

He looked at his daughter, her eyes to the floor. 'Listen, I don't know how many times I have to say this to you.' He lowered his voice. 'You don't have to stay here, you know? We'll be fine without you.'

'But Mum says—'

'I know what she says. But you can't stay here for the rest of your life, Julia. Listen to me...' He gestured at the door. Julia got up and crossed the room to push it shut. She sat back down beside him. He took her hand in his. 'I've watched you practically disappear over the last few years. I know what happened was... a terrible, terrible thing for you but, Julia... life goes on.' He nudged her shoulder. 'And it's about time you went and lived it, my girl.'

'Henry?' Julia's mother's voice rang up the stairs.

Julia quickly opened the door and called back, 'I'm just asking what he wants for lunch. I'll be down in a minute!' She turned back to her father. 'Thank you. I know you're right but I have no qualifications, nowhere to go.'

'That's because you've hidden yourself away here for too long! And I know we haven't helped as much as we could have done, but I think it's time you looked to the future. Your mother might take a bit of time to get used to it but she'll come round, I promise. Now, I suggest you go and make some enquiries into getting a proper job, something you want to do.'

'But it's too late, surely.' She looked at him, her eyes full of tears.

'Julia, it's never too late. Go on, I'll help your mother this afternoon. Why don't you start making some phone calls? You know where the phone book is.' He winked at her, smiling.

Just then, Julia's mother came into the room.

'What are you two up to?' She went to the window, peering down.

Her father quickly handed Julia a handkerchief. 'We were just talking about how quiet it is in the shop today, Jeanie.'

Julia wiped at her tears whilst her mother's back was turned.

'That's lucky, given she was too busy daydreaming to be much help.' She let out a short laugh. 'Right, you go on back downstairs. I'll make lunch for your father.'

'Go on, love, off you go. I'll see you later.'

Julia smiled back at him, though more tears were threatening to fall. Desperate for her mother not to notice, Julia made for the door.

'You can make a start on unpacking the delivery by the door. And try not to take for ever this time.' Her mother's voice followed her as she went down the stairs.

The shop was empty, shut for lunch. Julia looked at the big

cardboard box just inside the door and turned on the radio behind the counter. If she was going to spend the next hour stacking shelves, she decided she might as well do it to music.

The piano notes drifted from the radio, gentle and measured, almost dreamlike. Julia stared at the box but her feet wouldn't move. Instead, she let the melody surround her, carrying her thoughts to a place she rarely dared visit: the sight, smell and sound of her baby in his cot, his tiny feet in pale blue booties. Julia allowed herself to sit with these thoughts for a while, the music seemingly pulling at the memories. Tears now rolled down her face but instead of feeling shame, with her father's words ringing in her ear, she felt something a little more like hope.

As the music faded, Julia found herself taking off her tabard, folding it gently and putting it on top of the counter. She took a handful of coins from the till, unlocked the shop door from the inside and headed out along the street towards the phone box at the end of the high street. She made two calls, the second to her aunt.

'Aunt Tessa, it's Julia.' Julia whispered down the phone.

'Julia, is that you?' Tessa hollered back.

'Yes, it's me. I'm leaving, Tessa.'

'Leaving where?'

'Home.'

'Speak up, darling girl. I can't hear you very well.'

'I said I'm leaving home.' Julia couldn't help but laugh a little. She'd never felt as free as she did in that moment.

'Do your parents know? Where are you going to go?'

'No... well, I think Dad knows. He's kind of told me to go – nicely, I mean. And as for where I'm going, I have absolutely no idea exactly where but I'm thinking I want to head for London.'

'When?'

Julia looked at her watch. 'In about an hour's time.'

'Well, I'm not having you walking the streets of London. When you get there, go to a pub called The Admiral in Chelsea and ask for Charles. He's an old friend of mine. I'll tell him you're coming. He'll give you a room for a few nights, I'm sure.'

'I've actually got myself an interview at a secretarial college next week; I just rang. I thought that might be a good place to start. Then I can get some work, at least.'

'Oh, Julia, I am proud of you. I've been waiting for you to do this for a while. I knew you would at some point.'

'It's just taken me some time to figure it out but I can't stay at home any longer. It's killing me, Tessa.'

'Just promise me you will call me when you get to London so I know you're safe.'

'Of course I will. Thank you... I don't know what I would do without you.'

'Julia, I saw Patrick. He came here last year... to lay some ghosts to rest.'

'How is he?' Julia gripped the receiver in her hand, her knuckles turning white.

'He's fine. At least, he will be. I wasn't going to say anything but I think now it's better that you know.'

Julia remembered writing that letter to Patrick like it was yesterday, telling him that if he loved her, he'd move on. Her heart felt as if it might break – again – but she knew it was time for her to do the same. The line started beeping. Julia fished in her pocket for more change. 'I'm going to have to go.'

'OK, darling, but promise me you'll call me when you get there. I'll let your mother know you're all right.'

'Thank you, Tessa.'

Julia returned home and quietly put a few belongings in a bag. Reaching into the back of her wardrobe, she took out a shoebox from which she extracted a small notebook. Tucked in the back was a black-and-white photograph of Patrick, smiling with his eyes, his hair whipped by the wind. She held the photo in one hand, in the other a letter from him, sent on to her from Tessa not long after Julia had left Cornwall almost three years ago. She'd read it so many times she almost didn't need to look at the words. Her heart ached but there was at least some comfort in knowing that he was going to be OK. She allowed herself to think of William, smiling at how much like Patrick he'd looked. It hurt to think of him but, as Julia was learning, it hurt more to try to pretend William didn't exist at all. She tucked the letter and photograph back into the notebook, placed it in her bag and crept back down the stairs and out of the house.

That night Julia's parents sat in silence at the table eating dinner, an empty space where their daughter used to sit.

* * *

A few weeks later Julia lay on her bed in her room, her fingers tired from typing. She was still living above the pub, paying a small rent in return for hours put in behind the bar in the evenings. Charles, it turned out, was one of her aunt's old flames and clearly still carried quite the torch for Tessa, taking Julia in like an old acquaintance.

Glancing at her watch, she saw she had just twenty minutes until her shift started downstairs. She walked over to the sink in the corner of the room and splashed cold water on her face. She pulled her hair up into a ponytail and put on a clean white shirt, tied a purple scarf around her neck and applied a touch of lipstick.

In the bar downstairs, the regulars had taken up their usual positions, standing at the front or tucked away at favourite tables.

'How was your day?' Charles called from the other end of the bar.

'Good, thank you. Everything all right here?'

'I've just got to go and get something from out the back. Can you see to that gentleman who's just come in?' Charles nodded his head towards the door.

Julia turned to see a young man in a blue suit. She watched him pick a seat at the table by the window, putting the suitcase he carried on the chair and carefully placing his newspaper on the table. Walking up to the bar, he smiled at Julia.

'What'll it be?' she said.

'David...' He held his hand out, rather formally, Julia thought. It amused her.

Julia shook it, smiling back. 'What'll it be, David?'

* * *

After that first meeting, David came by the pub more frequently on his way home. What's more, Julia started looking forward to him walking through the door. It turned out that David had only come into the pub that first time by mistake; he'd meant to be in the one at the other end of the street to meet a friend. And it wasn't even really on his way home. Not that Julia knew that until he confessed over dinner one evening a few months later.

'Did your friend mind that you didn't turn up?'

'Not really, not once I explained that I wouldn't have met you if I had.' David smiled at her. For the first time for what seemed like an eternity, she felt her heart lift.

Two years later they were married, a small reception at a London registry office with just their parents and a small group of friends. After the ceremony they'd headed to The Admiral for lunch, sitting at a long table at the back. It had been a wonderful day but Julia's abiding memory was her mother's face, deploying a convincing smile for the wedding photograph but otherwise carrying a look of barely concealed disappointment throughout.

Just before the newlyweds left the pub to head back to David's flat for the night (their budget hadn't allowed for a night away) her mother had taken Julia's hands in hers. 'Congratulations, darling. Now, let's just hope we don't have to wait too long for a baby, eh?'

Julia's heart shattered into tiny pieces.

It was years before Julia did have another baby. In fact, she and David had almost given up hope that they would ever have children, despite doctors telling them there was no medical reason why they shouldn't. But then Annie was born, Jess following just eighteen months later. And eventually Julia learned to live with the guilt she felt every time she looked at her daughters, only to see her son.

14

'Which turn-off is it again?' Jess punched at the radio controls, trying to find a song she liked.

'Not the next one, but the one after.' Annie squinted at the map on her phone. 'Says we're only ten minutes away. It's not been too bad, really.'

The late afternoon light had faded fast, the sky now deep blue and cloudless. With each turn, the roads seemed to narrow further.

'Are you sure this is the right way?' Jess tried her best not to sound like she didn't trust Annie's directions.

'Promise this is the way. Look, that's got to be the coast up ahead.'

As they went over the brow of the hill, the landscape, hidden behind thick hedges until now, revealed itself. Fields swept away to either side and, up ahead, the grey-blue sea stretched out to the horizon, looking calm and cold. On the other side of the road, at the T-junction ahead, sat a pub the colour of turmeric. The windows glowed with warm yellow light and to the right, the pub's sign told them they were indeed in the right place.

'Told you!' Annie was triumphant, prodding her sister gently in the arm in celebration.

'Never doubted you.' Jess drove into an almost empty car park beside the pub. 'Right, what time are we meeting him?'

'In an hour.' Annie's stomach flipped at the thought of meeting this man, her brother, for the first time, despite having had six months to get used to the idea. 'Are you not nervous?'

'God, yes. What if he doesn't like us? Or we don't like him? I mean, you can tell with a person pretty quickly if you're going to like them or not, but when they're actually related to you, there's so much expectation.'

A moment of silence fell between them.

'Come on, let's go.' Annie slowly unfolded herself from the low, leather bucket seat of Jess's car.

They carried their bags through a low door into the pub. A fire crackled gently in the grate to the right of the old wooden bar, throwing an orange glow across the worn flagstone floor. Behind the bar, bottles of spirits fought for space and the whole room smelled faintly, and deliciously, of wood smoke and sausages.

An old man sat at one end of the bar, his face ruddy, eyes bright. He nodded at the sisters standing in the doorway. 'Evenin',' he offered, before going back to his beer.

'Hi, there.' A younger, rosy-cheeked man appeared behind the bar, his face friendly, hair a mess. 'You must be booked in tonight.' He looked at their bags, still in their hands. 'You're the only ones so you've got the two best rooms. It's pretty quiet in here during the week at this time of year.' He wiped his hands on his apron. 'Sorry, just been changing kegs downstairs. I'm Harry.'

'Hi, I'm Annie.'

'And I'm Jess.'

'Nice to meet you both. Right, follow me and I'll show you where you are.'

They followed him through the dimly lit dining room and up a wooden staircase. Their rooms were at the end of a short corridor, floorboards creaking at every step. Harry opened the door to the first room, which was tiny and practically all bed. The duvet and pillows, encased in fresh white cotton, looked as soft as clouds. At the end of the bed, a neatly folded checked woollen blanket lay ready to take off the chill. But the room was warm, with a small window looking out towards the sea.

'Oh, look! How beautiful is that, Jess?' The darkening sky hosted a bright moon that hung casually above the calm water of the bay below them. 'And there's a bath?' Annie hoped she didn't sound too desperate.

'There certainly is, round that corner.' Harry motioned over the other side of the room.

'Oh my goodness, it's gorgeous! Jess, look!'

'I believe you, Annie.' Jess smiled at Harry. 'Guess I'll take the other one, then.'

'Great, follow me.' Harry opened the door opposite to an equally small but beautifully furnished room. 'I'm afraid you don't get the sea view. But you do get fields.'

Jess went to the window, her gaze taking in the bare trees outside, branches stretching up to the sky.

'It's perfect, Harry. Thank you.'

'Great. You've got a bath too, just round the corner there. Now, I think you're booked in for dinner? You'll have the dining room to yourselves tonight.'

'Yes, we are, thank you. We're not sure if we'll be two or three, does that matter?' Ed was coming to the pub to meet them at seven o'clock, but they hadn't dared to mention dinner in the correspondence, just a meeting time.

'Not at all, whatever suits you. I'll leave the key here for you. Come down when you're ready. No hurry.'

'Thank you. See you in a bit.' Jess smiled back, completely won over by the warmth and comfort of the place.

Annie's voice rang out from across the corridor. 'Oh my God, Jess. Have you seen the toiletries? Really nice stuff. I'm shoving the whole lot in the bath!'

Jess smiled at Harry. 'She's quite excited, you might have gathered.'

'I'm glad she likes it!' Harry pushed his hair back from his face. 'Right, I'd better get back to it. Bert will be wanting a refill by now. See you later.'

He disappeared off down the corridor, floorboards squeaking beneath him as he went. Jess poked her head back through her sister's door. 'Annie, I'm going to have a bath. I'll see you in the bar. Let's get there just before seven, shall we, so we can find a quiet corner?'

'I don't think we'll have a problem doing that. Ed must have known it was quiet when he suggested meeting here in the first place. Do you think it's his local?'

'Must be. He lives really nearby, I think. See you in a bit.' Jess went back to her room, slipped off her shoes and lay on the bed. A wave of tiredness swept over her, the softness of the sheets drawing her in. But her mind raced with thoughts of the evening ahead and as much as she wanted to close her eyes, she knew sleep wouldn't come. Instead she hauled herself off the bed and headed for the bathroom, hoping a long hot bath might help calm her mind.

* * *

'Ed, are you sure you're OK about this? I could wait in the car...' Sophie stood at the old Rayburn, watching to make sure the toast didn't burn. At the table, Johnnie sat expectantly. Sophie turned to look at him. 'Darling, please can you go and give your sisters a shout? I think they must be in the sitting room.'

Johnnie stayed exactly where he was. 'Edie! Isla! Tea's ready!' he bellowed, as loud as he possibly could.

'Johnnie, no. I asked you to go and get them, please. I can't move from here or your toast will turn to burnt cinders the moment I take my eyes off it.'

'Yes, I'll be fine, I promise. I'm meeting them at seven at the Gunner's. It'll be quiet so hopefully we'll have the dining room to ourselves.' Ed gently pushed Johnnie from his chair. 'Go and get your sisters, please, Johnnie.'

Sophie knew Ed was nervous from the way his fingers played with his shirt cuffs. 'OK, if you're sure. But call me if you decide to stay, have a drink or whatever. I can come and get you.'

'What about the kids?'

'I'll ask Mum to pop over; you know she wouldn't mind.' Sophie's mother had moved down from Oxford to be nearer to her family earlier that year and had proved indispensable ever since. Not just as a support to Sophie and Ed; the children absolutely adored their grandmother.

'Thank you, but I'm sure I won't need to. I'll go and find out where the girls are...'

'Ed, stop stalling. You need to get going. You can't keep them waiting. They're your sisters, after all.' She laughed gently, hoping her attempt at humour wouldn't fall flat.

'I know, I know. I'm going. I'll see you later.' He pulled at his cuffs for the umpteenth time and made for the door.

'Good luck!' Sophie called after him, wondering if that was quite the right phrase. But this was unchartered territory. She had navigated his feelings as gently as possible, adjusting her course accordingly as he came to terms with the knowledge that his mother was alive and well and that he had two siblings who wanted to meet him. But she also knew Ed's ability to put his head in the sand when it came to dealing with anything remotely uncomfortable was unparalleled. It had taken him over a week to open the letter from the agency. In the back of her mind, Sophie couldn't help but worry that he might not be able to bring himself to walk into that pub, even though these two people, his sisters, had come all this way. Still, she'd done all she could. The rest was up to Ed. Sophie reached for the fridge door and poured herself a small glass of chilled Sauvignon Blanc.

'Think he'll be OK, Billy?' The dog looked up from his bed, gazed towards the door and sighed heavily. 'I'll take that as a yes.'

Ed drove to the pub in silence, his mind so preoccupied with thoughts of what lay ahead he didn't even turn the radio on. The lanes were now in complete darkness, leaving drivers to rely on lights from oncoming cars to warn them of anything round the tight corners. The sky was studded with stars and the moon shone brightly, not a cloud to contend with.

The drive was short, barely ten minutes. Soon he was pulling into the car park alongside the only other car in it, a long, sleek Mercedes. His heart jumped. His sister's car, he thought.

As he walked towards the familiar door, he took a deep breath. He'd given his friend Harry the heads up he was meeting old family friends tonight – he hadn't elaborated, of course – and hoped Harry had managed to seat them in the quiet dining room. He opened the bar door, the warm air inside a welcome contrast to the cold outside.

The bar was empty save for Bert, of course.

'Evenin.' He nodded his greeting to Ed.

'Evening, Bert. Harry around?'

Bert pointed behind the bar. 'Taps playin' up.'

'Ah, OK. I'll er...' Ed looked towards the open door to the dining room. He unclenched his hands, took a deep breath and walked in.

* * *

Annie and Jess had met in the bar; Annie still flushed red from her hot bath. Both now sat with large, chilled glasses of house white in front of them.

'I know it sounds ridiculous, Jess, but this feels like some sort of weird blind date,' Annie whispered. They were at a small table by the open fire.

'I know what you mean. But he wouldn't be coming unless he wanted to meet us. And the letters mean we're not finding out everything for the first time.' Jess took a small sip of her wine. She screwed up her nose and looked at her glass. 'That tastes... a bit strange.'

Annie picked up hers and swirled the glass gently, before putting her nose in and taking a long sniff. She winked at her sister before taking a short sip. 'What are you talking about? It's delicious!'

'It tastes funny to me. What is it?'

'Chenin Blanc, I think.' Annie looked around the room. 'Do you think we should move next door to the table? Then we're not quite so public when he comes in.'

'But there's no one here.'

Annie motioned to the old man at the bar.

'Annie, he's not going to mind.'

'No, I think we should go to the dinner table. Have a room to ourselves, just in case.'

'OK, whatever you prefer.' Jess picked up her glass.

Harry appeared behind the bar again, his hair more wild than before, in one hand a tea towel and in the other a screwdriver. 'Sorry, had to get that fixed. Take a couple of menus with you and there are some specials on the board next door. Let me know if you need anything.'

'Thanks.' Annie picked up the menus. 'We won't be eating quite yet; we're having a drink with a... friend... first. But we'll eat after, thank you. He might stay, we're just not sure.'

Harry looked at the woman with the menu in her hands. She looked familiar but he couldn't quite place her. 'Absolutely. Whatever suits you. I'll bring you some bread and olives to keep you going.'

'Thank you, that would be lovely.' Jess followed her sister.

They sat at a table in the bay of a window, neither of them quite sure what to say. The room was small and dark, painted the same yellow colour as the outside. Paintings covered the walls, some dramatic, others almost poetic. There was an enormous seascape, complete with crashing waves against craggy rocks. In another, an old man sat at his desk in a crowded study surrounded by piles of books and paper. He looked lost in his task; Annie wondered what he might be writing.

'You OK?' Jess sounded like she was reassuring herself.

'Yes, I think so. A bit light-headed, actually. Do you think he'll come?'

'I hope so. I'm not sure I could bear it if he didn't show now.' Jess looked about the room, twisting her hair around her fingers as she did.

Just then, a man appeared at the door. He stopped, looking across at the sisters, seemingly rooted to the spot. Slowly he raised his hand at them, his expression unsure.

Jess got up slowly out of her chair. 'Hello, you must be Ed.'

She awkwardly extended an arm, dropping it quickly back by her side. 'I'm Jess and this is my sister, Annie.'

Annie stood up, a nervous smile on her face. She didn't know whether to laugh or cry.

'Hello... I'm Ed...' His voice wavered a little.

'Hello, Ed,' Annie sprang forward. 'It's so lovely to meet you...' She went to hug him but he took a step back. 'Oh God, I'm so sorry. I promised myself I wouldn't do that.' Annie's cheeks reddened.

'Hello, Annie. It's OK, really. I'm just... I'm not very good at...' Ed ran his fingers through his hair with both hands, laughing nervously. He exhaled deeply. 'I'm sorry.' He held out his hand to Jess. 'Hello, Jess.'

Jess took his hand in hers and looked at him. 'It's really, really good to meet you at last.'

'I know, it's been... there's a lot to take in.' He looked from one to the other again.

'Oh my goodness, you look so like them,' Annie whispered.

'Annie,' Jess touched her sister's shoulder, 'don't spook him again.'

Ed smiled. 'No, it's fine. I've always wondered about that, actually.' He laughed again, whether through nerves or relief he couldn't tell.

'So, where on earth do we start?' said Jess.

'I can't even... I'm so glad you're here.' Annie shook her head slowly, grinning at Ed.

'Pint, Ed?' Harry popped his face round the corner into the room.

'Yes, please, Harry.'

Harry looked at the two women standing either side of Ed and he could see there was something about their features that united them.

'Harry, these are my...' Ed paused briefly, 'half-sisters, Annie and Jess.'

'Of course you are, just look at you,' Harry laughed. 'Can I get you anything?'

'No, thank you, we're fine for now.' Annie smiled warmly at Harry.

'Right, I'll be back with your pint in a mo, Ed.' Harry headed back to the bar.

Ed tugged at the sleeves of his jumper. 'So...' He felt completely lost for words. Which, given that he had so many questions, seemed quite ridiculous. 'How was your journey?' He cringed inwardly. Was that really the best he could do?

'All very easy. Thank you for suggesting here. It's so lovely.' Jess gestured at their surroundings.

'It really is,' Annie agreed enthusiastically. Sensing his discomfort, she suggested they sat.

Ed pulled out chairs for them in turn. 'I'm sorry to make you come all this way but the woman from the agency suggested it. I hope that's OK?'

'Yes, of course.' Annie put her hand on his arm, feeling it tense up immediately. Too soon, she reminded herself.

'I'm sorry, I really do have so many things I want to ask you but I don't seem to be able to...' He trailed off, looking at them apologetically.

Jess spoke softly. 'I know, this is strange for all of us, most of all you. We could start by giving you a letter from Mum. She wanted us to deliver this to you. If we ever found you, that is. Obviously you don't have to read it now. Annie, have you got it?'

'How is she? I mean, was she pleased you decided to come and look for me?'

'Yes, I think she really was.' Annie reached for the letter in her bag, pushing it gently across the table to Ed.

He picked it up, holding it carefully in his fingers, looking at the name on the front of the envelope. William. It felt so strange to see something other than his name and yet feel such a connection to it.

'When Mum told us about you – we were in Rome, long story; we'll fill you in – she said that when she had to give you up for adoption, she also had to promise not to come and find you. Apparently she was forbidden to put her name on the adoption register...' Annie's voice broke a little.

Ed put the envelope back on the table. 'I did wonder if that was the case. I don't think my parents knew much about her at all.'

'And when she told us about you, she said it was up to us if we wanted to find you.' Annie smiled at him. 'I hope you don't mind that we did.'

'How could we not? Knowing you were out there some-where, we had to come and find you.' Jess looked at him, forcing Ed to meet her gaze.

'What made her tell you?'

'You explain, Annie.'

'I think, to be honest, she'd kept it to herself for so long. She and Patrick, your father, who's wonderful, met up again after all that time apart and I think she just couldn't keep it in any longer. I think she wanted us to find you because she couldn't. Anyway, she asked us to bring you this.' Annie tapped the envelope on the table. 'She wrote it to you when you were a baby and her aunt, Tessa, promised to keep it safe for her.'

'And hidden from her witch of a mother, our grandmother.' Jess couldn't help herself. 'Sorry...'

'Well, yes. That, too, but anyway, when her aunt died the letter made its way back to Mum. But read the letter. We don't know what it says, obviously. She just wanted you to have it and read it when you were ready.'

'Thank you.' He picked up the envelope and put it in his coat pocket. As much as he wanted to open it there and then, he knew he needed to be on his own when he did. 'So, are they... together again now?'

'Well, we're not exactly sure. They're spending time together, but whether they are *together* together or just friends, we don't know. It's not something one can really ask one's mother.'

'Oh, Annie, if you don't ask her I will the next time I see her. I mean, come on! It's not like old people don't do romance.' Jess laughed. 'Basically, they hadn't seen each other for years and then, quite out of the blue, Patrick got in touch, inviting Mum to Rome.'

'They had to bury an old friend... spread his ashes, I mean. So she went...' Annie picked up her glass.

'... And we followed because, well, we were a bit worried about her going on her own with someone we – or she, for that matter – barely knew.' Jess spoke quickly now. 'But as it turns out, she did know him. Just hadn't seen him for a long time and now we know why. I think she knew that if she did then all that pain, all those feelings, she must have had giving you up for adoption against her will, would come back.'

'But something changed in Rome. It was like...' Annie reached across towards Ed's arm once again, unable to stop herself. 'I don't know, maybe she just knew it was time to tell us. And I think she wanted you to know she's there...' Annie blinked, trying to keep the tears threatening to fall in check.

'And obviously that's completely up to you.' Jess continued softly. 'We'd understand if you need more time to think about it, let it all sink in. But please know, Ed, that our mum is a good person. I know she's lived with this for years and we think she just didn't want to have to do that any more. More than that, she thought we all had a right to know.'

'And with Patrick, she's happier than she's been for years. It's like whatever happened... they know they can't change it. But perhaps she's hoping that it's not too late for her to make up somehow for all that time lost. Only if you want to, that is.' Annie gently squeezed his arm.

'Yes, it's a lot to...' He looked up at them both, their faces full of hope. He took a deep breath. 'Of course I do.' His smile made his eyes crinkle at the edges.

* * *

Hours later, Jess lay on Annie's bed. Annie stood at the basin in the little ensuite, brushing her teeth.

'Oh my God, Annie. I never thought it would be so...'

Annie stuck her head round the door, mid-brush. 'Normal?'

'Exactly! I mean, I know it was awkward at the beginning – poor thing looked like he was actually going to be sick – but then once we got talking he definitely seemed to let his guard down a bit.'

'I think that was more damage limitation, but once he realised we just wanted to let him know we're here,' Annie came to sit on the other side of the bed, 'the whole thing was amazing. I can't wait to meet his family. Sophie sounds absolutely gorgeous. And his kids looked so sweet in the pictures.'

'I know, didn't they? And can you believe he was in a band? What were they called again?' She stabbed at her phone. 'What's the wifi code? I'm going to Google them.'

'It's there, on the table in the file.' Annie pointed over at the desk under the window. 'He did say he wasn't in it for long. And they only had him because he was the only guy at school who could play the drums. Made me sad, the thought of him spending hours on his own in his room playing the drums.'

'Oh, Annie, don't jump to conclusions. You heard him. He said he had a very happy childhood. His parents – his adopted parents, I mean – they sounded heavenly.'

'They were obviously quite a bit older. Sad now they're gone that he didn't have any other siblings.'

'He said he didn't know it any other way, remember? And now he's got us.'

'But that's the thing. I can't help feeling like this is quite selfish of us. We were the ones wanting to find him. He might not have wanted to be found.'

'Annie, listen. If he didn't want to, he didn't have to. That's the point. Just like Alison Pearce said, he could have always said no. And we just mustn't rush it. Rush *him*, rather.'

'Jess, he suggested a reunion with Mum before Christmas. Doesn't that feel too soon?'

'If you'd been waiting for more than forty years to meet your birth mother, do you think you might not want to get on with it as soon as possible?'

'I guess you're right. I know!' Annie pointed at her sister. 'It was Ten Green Bottles! The name of the band, Ten Green Bottles. Look them up. I want to see what he looked like when he was in the band.'

Jess tapped away intently at her phone. A few taps later and she passed the phone across to her sister. 'Look, there he is on the left.'

Annie peered at the phone. 'Oh, look at him! He was *gorgeous*! You could cut meat with those cheekbones. How old do you think he was then? Nineteen?'

'Early twenties, he said. By the time they were famous,

anyway. I do remember them, funnily enough. Not my kind of music: too tortured art student for me.'

'Ha! I know what you mean. Still, how cool to have a brother that was in a band!'

'Half-brother, Annie.'

'Whatever. Right, what time are we off tomorrow?'

'Early-ish, I'm afraid. I've got to get back to London by late afternoon but can drop you off on the way. I'll pop in to see Mum quickly, too.'

'Have you called her yet? She'll be dying to hear.'

'I've just texted her to let her know everything was fine. I didn't want to say too much but I told her all's good and that we'd fill her in tomorrow.'

'Great, if you don't mind. I've got to get back for the school run so I'll pop in after that but we can call her from the road tomorrow. Clare's taking the boys in the morning for me. God, I really owe her.'

'Right then, bed. See you in the morning. I'm bloody knackered.'

'Go on, off you get.' Annie shoved her sister playfully with her foot. 'Otherwise you'll fall asleep here and I won't get the bed to myself after all.'

'All right, I'm going.' Jess laughed, blowing her sister a kiss. 'See you in the morning.'

'See you in the morning.' Annie blew one back. The door shut softly behind her sister. Within minutes, face hastily splashed with water and teeth brushed, she climbed into bed, delighting in the feel of the heavy duvet. Looking up at the ceiling, Annie imagined Ed back at home telling his wife how it had all gone, hoping he felt as happy as she and her sister did.

* * *

'So, how was it?' Sophie sat at the table, her back to the range cooker. Billy lay at her feet, stretched out in peaceful slumber on the warm floor. The house was quiet bar the soft sound of a lone cello coming from the radio on the shelf on the corner.

'Well, it was quite amazing, really.' Ed looked a little bewildered but he did have a wide smile on his face.

'Were you nervous?'

'Really nervous. Thought I might actually be sick at one point but once I'd managed to walk into the room, it felt... strange but OK. I was just really happy to meet them, not that they probably realised it at first. It's funny because they're total strangers to me and yet once we got over the initial weirdness of it all, it was relatively easy to talk. And we talked about so many things... about my birth parents...'

'So do you think you'll meet them, too?'

'Yes, I hope so. I have a letter here from my mother.' He patted his coat pocket. 'She gave it to them to give to me.'

'And you haven't read it yet?' Sophie's eyes widened.

'I wanted to read it here, with you.'

'Well, go on then.' She stood up. 'Do you want a whisky?'

'Yes, please.' He took a seat and went to open the letter. Sophie returned to the table with a bottle and two tumblers.

'So? What does it say?'

Ed unfolded the letter slowly but read quickly. He sighed. Sophie could hardly breathe. He handed the letter to her. 'Can you read it to me again?'

She took the letter. Ed poured two generous measures, adding a dash of water from a jug on the table to each. He took a sip, the heat and smoke hitting the back of his throat instantly. Sophie spoke the words softly, quietly.

16 June 1962

My darling William,

First of all I want you to know that I love you so much and that I'm so desperately sorry that it has to be this way.

Looking at you lying in your cot beside me now, blanket tucked up under your chin with your head of soft hair, I wish we could stay here for ever. Your eyes are mostly shut tight (you sleep a lot!) but when you open them, and I look into them, I'm lost and found all at once.

This past month has been so precious, watching you grow every day, taking in the world around you. You love the sound of the gulls outside the window, turning your head to listen. And your grip – so strong! But I know that by giving you to another loving family, one that can take care of you properly, I will be giving you the best start in life that I possibly can.

I also want you to know that your father is a wonderful, kind man. In another life, we would all be together, for ever. But in this one, it cannot be.

I just hope this letter reaches you one day, as promised, and that you know that you were loved, always. I will think about you every single day that goes past.

Eternally yours,

Mummy x

Sophie looked up from the letter to meet Ed's face, huge tears pooling in her eyes.

Smiling, he took her hands in his. 'It's fine, really. I'm happy. And to be honest,' he looked at the letter, now on the table, 'she's told me all I've ever wanted to know.'

15

Julia felt hot and unsettled. Sleep had evaded her for much of the night. The radio came on; people discussing farming with far too much enthusiasm for this time in the morning.

Moving slowly, she sat up, sliding her feet into her slippers at the side of the bed. She reached for her dressing gown, held her palms to her eyes and pressed them to her head for a moment. Stars swam before her.

She looked towards the window. Through a narrow gap in the curtains, she could see a flash of pink sky behind dark grey clouds. Slowly, her thoughts gathered. She remembered the text from Jess the night before, reassuring her everything had gone really well and that they'd call first thing. Julia wondered if he would have read the letter by now. She took a deep breath, closed her eyes, let the air out slowly.

She went downstairs, stepping over the cat on the step halfway down as she did so. Lancelot – a present for her birthday a few years ago from her grandchildren, masterminded by Annie – always slept at the end of her bed. But by the time

Julia awoke he'd be in position on the stairs, where he'd wait for Julia to come down and open the door to the garden.

'Morning, Lance.' He looked at her, reaching out a paw to catch the bottom of her dressing gown as she passed. 'Come on, then. Silly thing.' Filling the kettle at the sink, Julia looked out at the view. A few fat camellia buds sat among the leaves of the bush just outside the window. The stillness of the early morning outside pleased her enormously.

As she put the empty wine glasses on the side in the dishwasher, she acknowledged she had been grateful for Pam and Dicky's company last night. Supper and a game of cards had been just what she needed to take her mind off other things. She looked at the clock. It wasn't yet seven.

Taking her steaming cup of tea into the sitting room, she put it on the table and went to the hidden cupboard behind an old oil painting. There, behind stacks of old board games and half-drunk, long-forgotten liqueur bottles, was a brown wooden box. She reached for it, took it out; went to the small red pot on the chimneypiece and reached inside for the key. Taking it, she sat in the chair next to the still warm embers of the fire and unlocked the box.

Julia's stomach flipped as she opened it, a wave of nausea hitting her hard. Again, she closed her eyes and took a breath, long and slow. She reached inside and lifted the photograph on the top from the pile, bringing it closer to her face and looking at it properly for the first time in years. His features so familiar, a tiny, clutched fist, eyes clamped shut.

She picked up the next photograph. It was of Aunt Tessa looking at him, smiling, her little finger clenched tightly by the boy in the blanket in her arms. And another: William in a pram with his arms and legs splayed in peaceful, deep sleep.

Julia picked up the envelope underneath. She saw her mother's unmistakable spidery writing on the front.

TESSA.

She took the letter out. She'd read it only once before, having been given the box by her father, along with the key, after her mother had died. The box had been returned to Julia's mother after Aunt Tessa had passed away just a few years before that. In the letter, her mother had asked Tessa to keep the photos safe. But – and she knew the words before she got to them –

DO NOT give them to Julia. The situation is bad enough. Her having these will only make it worse.

Julia stared at her mother's name at the bottom. As much as she'd told herself over the years they'd acted in what they believed were her best interests, as much as she knew Tessa had only been keeping a promise, she couldn't help but feel wretched at the thought of what could have been, what might have been.

But what Julia would never know was just how often Tessa had gone to the box, unlocked it and spread the photos across her kitchen table, her tears falling uncontrollably.

The sound of the phone ringing pulled her back to the now. Julia put the box to one side and went to the kitchen to answer it.

'Hello?'

'Mum?'

'Annie! How was it?'

'I'm so sorry we didn't call you last night but it was really late by the time we finished. I know Jess sent you a message...'

'How is he? What did he say?'

'Mum, he wants to meet you.' Annie sounded as if she were smiling.

'Really? He does?' Julia steadied herself with a hand on the kitchen counter. She felt suddenly weak, almost winded.

'Yes, Mum, of course he does.'

'So... how is he?' Julia's voice was barely audible.

'He's fantastic, Mum.' Annie laughed with delight.

'Happy?'

'Yes, really happy and with a beautiful family. Three kids and a wife he obviously adores.'

'Oh my goodness... that's...'

'Amazing, I know. I don't know what we were expecting but it was definitely much easier than I had imagined. I mean, I think we were all so nervous but the minute he walked in...'

'And he wants to meet me?'

'Yes, Mum, I told you. He can't wait.'

'So, what happens now?'

'We've got each other's email addresses so we can organise something with him, for you to meet him. Or you and Patrick. I'm not sure how it'll work but I guess it's up to Ed. I mean, William. You know what I mean.' Annie laughed apologetically.

'OK, that's...' Julia hardly dared to believe it.

'Mum, it's OK, really. He's very happy we found him. There's no anger on his side – not that we could tell, anyway. I think he's just relieved to know he'll get to meet you at last.'

'Darling, thank you.' Julia closed her eyes. She felt tension flood from her body.

'Anyway, we're leaving soon. Jess has got to get back to London but she's dropping me on the way, kindly. She said she'd call in if the traffic's not too bad, to fill you in.'

'OK, I'll be here.'

''Bye, Mum. Love you.'

'Love you, too.'

Julia walked back into the sitting room, sat back in the chair next to the fire. The smell of warm ashes scented the air. Lance padded across the room, jumping onto Julia's lap and turning a few times before curling up and settling in.

'Can you believe it?' The cat looked at her briefly before returning to his resting position. 'I can't. I really can't.' Her tears began to fall. But unlike Tessa's all those years ago, Julia's were not tears of pain. They were tears of relief. And she was happy to let them fall.

* * *

Jess pushed the plate away from her, the sight of the uneaten eggs making her feel suddenly queasy.

'You OK, Jess? You look pale.' Annie sat back down at their breakfast table by the open fire in the bar.

'Yes, just not feeling brilliant, I must admit. Do you think you could drive back as far as yours? Hopefully I'll be feeling better by then. I've just pushed back my meeting till later this afternoon so I'm not in a hurry.'

'Of course, no problem. What's the meeting?'

A pause. 'Hopefully, I'm selling.'

'What, your company? Really? Jess, that's so exciting. Why didn't you say before? What will you do?'

'Not have to work like a dog and have absolutely no life of my own, hopefully. They've been after me for a while. I'll have to work with them to hand over the business for a period of time, but other than that I'm not entirely sure.'

'So, what's brought on the sudden change of heart? You always said you weren't interested in selling?'

'Nothing to do with the heart, Annie.' Jess fixed her sister with a smile.

'Bullshit. It's Ben, isn't it? Why do I get the feeling you're not telling me everything? I thought you said you were taking it slowly.'

'We are! But I'm not the bloody Virgin Mary...' Jess suddenly looked at her sister, eyes wide. 'Oh, shit.' Jess put her head in her hands.

'What? What is it?' Annie whispered, grabbing Jess's arm.

'Fuck! FUCK!'

'Oh my God, do you think you're pregnant?' The words came out a little louder than Annie intended.

The young waitress behind the bar dropped the cutlery she had in her hand. 'Sorry,' she mouthed, before turning and scuttling off to the kitchen.

'Yes. Fuck. I think I must be. I've been feeling a bit sick for weeks.'

'Do your boobs hurt?'

Jess squeezed her arms across her chest. 'Yes, they do.'

'And have you got like a weird metallic taste in your mouth?'

Jess screwed up her nose and swallowed. 'How the hell did you know that?'

'How do you think, you idiot? Boobs, sickness, everything tastes weird. I'd say you're about two months gone, maybe three. Didn't you miss a period?'

'Annie, I've been on a diet since 1992. My periods are hardly regular.'

'Oh. Right, well, I think you'd better get a test and then see a doctor as soon as possible. Oh, wow, Jess. That's so exciting!'

'Is it? I'm not sure Ben will see it that way. How am I going to tell him?'

'Come on, you're both grown-ups, for goodness' sake. Just tell him. What's the worst that can happen?'

'He legs it?' Jess shrugged.

'Well then, that's one way to find out if he's a keeper or not.' Annie stifled a smile.

'Annie, this isn't funny. I'm being serious. I'm no spring chicken.'

'Well you're hardly bloody ancient. Look, say you are pregnant. Forget Ben for a moment. Do you want a baby or not?'

Jess sat back in her chair, looked at her stomach and sighed.

Annie waved her hand. 'Whatever. Take a test. Go to the doctor, find out, tell Ben, see what happens.'

'Annie, it's not that simple.'

'Yes, yes, it is, actually. It couldn't be simpler. Come on, Jess! This is exciting! I'm excited!'

'Well, I feel sick so can we hold that thought and I'll let you know as soon as I've done a test.'

'Done. We can get one on our way home.'

'No, I'll do one later when I'm back in London. After the meeting.'

'Seriously? How can you bear to wait that long?'

'Well...' The thought of having to tell Ben that despite being back in his life for only a matter of months they might be having a baby together was just too awful to even think about.

'OK, whenever you like... but I think it's amazing. Thank God I didn't know before speaking to Mum.'

'How was she?'

'She sounded fine, actually. I wasn't really sure what to expect. Quiet but relieved, I think. Probably a bit freaked out by the speed of it all. Call in if you can, she'd love it.'

'OK, I'll see how we go.'

'Everything all right for you?' It was Harry, the friendly face from the night before.

'Lovely, thank you,' said Jess, despite the largely untouched breakfast that sat on the plate in front of her.

'It's so heavenly here, I slept like a baby,' said Annie. Jess shot her a look.

'Glad you liked it.' Harry started removing the plates from the table. 'Did we not do your eggs to your liking?'

'No, honestly... I think I'm just still full from last night. Could we have the bill, please?' Jess was relieved the egg was out of sight.

'It's all done, actually. Ed, your... brother? He paid.'

'Really?' Annie couldn't help but laugh.

'Well, he didn't need to do that,' said Jess, sounding faintly annoyed.

'Oh, come on, Jess. That's really kind of him.' Annie looked at Harry apologetically. 'Thank you. We'll just grab our stuff, then.'

'Great. It was really nice to meet you both. Ed is a... well, I don't need to tell you, but he's a good man.'

'Thank you, Harry,' said Annie. 'I'm glad we got to meet him here. This place is like a giant hug.'

'Excuse me a moment.' Jess pushed her chair away. 'Where's the...?'

'Loo? Over there.' Harry nodded at the door to the side of the fireplace and Jess made a dash for it. 'She OK?' Harry looked concerned.

'She will be.' Annie looked at Harry, a great beaming smile on her face.

* * *

Four hours and seemingly endless dual carriageways later, Annie was back at home throwing still-damp swimming things into a bag and a few hastily scooped-up ingredients into the fridge. She looked at the clock. She had precisely two minutes to get to school. The trip took ten. The events of the previous evening suddenly felt like a distant, extraordinary dream. One she couldn't wait to share with James. She reached for her phone to call the school, reassure them she was, in fact, coming to collect her children. An unread message: it was from Clare.

See you at swimming. I'll grab kids. You bring snacks.

'You bloody angel!' Annie shouted at the phone as she punched in her reply.

Half an hour later, with blue plastic covers on their shoes, Clare and Annie sat poolside in deep conversation, faces flushed pink from the heat of the stuffy, chlorine-infused air.

'Then what happened?' Clare could hardly contain her delight at such a dramatic storyline.

'Well, then... he walked in.'

'And?'

'And it was like meeting an old friend. I mean, it was a bit strange to start with, obviously. I was so nervous. We both were. But then, he looked so familiar, so like Mum. And Patrick. He's just... so... I don't even know. That's the thing. In theory, I don't know him. But I feel like I've known him for years. Does that make sense?'

'It really does, Annie. They say there's always a connection of sorts.'

'Exactly, a bond. And it feels like it doesn't matter that it took so long to find each other because we've got the rest of our lives to enjoy it.'

'Mum! MUM!' Annie looked up across to the other side of the pool to see Rufus signalling madly for her to watch.

'Watching,' she mouthed back. The noise of the swimming pool when lessons were in full swing was akin to the seventh circle of hell, as far as Annie was concerned. Rufus plopped into the pool with a pencil dive, resurfacing seconds later with an enormous grin on his face. Annie clapped her approval.

'Anyway,' she continued, an eye on the pool, 'he's asked us to go down to meet his family. Once he's met Mum and Patrick, of course.'

'Really? Does he have a family?'

'Yes, wife and three kids. His parents – adoptive parents, that is – both died a few years ago. They were quite a bit older than Mum and Patrick, apparently. They sounded lovely, though. He obviously had a happy childhood. But,' Annie dropped her voice to a whisper, 'you'll never guess what?'

'What?' Clare whispered in return.

'OK, I know this makes me sound shallow but I have to tell you because I know how much you'll appreciate it.'

'Oh, come ON, what?'

'He used to be a pop star.'

'FUCK. OFF.' Clare wasn't whispering now. Heads turned disapprovingly. Annie smiled at the other mothers apologetically.

She turned back to Clare. 'No, I'm serious. He was the drummer in Ten Green Bottles. Remember them?'

'Oh my God, yes! The gorgeous one at the back! With the cheekbones! I always thought he should have been the front man.'

'No, he was very happy to be at the back. Honestly, the way he tells it, he was an accidental pop star. He's a farmer now.' Annie felt ridiculously proud telling Clare this, even though she realised that just a few days before she'd known next to nothing about Ed.

'Mama, I'm cold...' Clare's daughter, Eve, stood in front of her.

'Come here, sweetie.' Clare wrapped a towel around her. 'Right, let's go. Where's your brother?' Eve pointed at the boys, still messing about in the water.

'Rufus, Ned, come on, it's time to go. Max can come back for tea with us.' She turned to Clare. 'I'm doing their tea tonight.'

'You've only just got back. Please don't—'

'Look, it's only fish fingers, with an Angel Delight chaser if they're lucky. It's the least I can do. I definitely owe you.'

'Will there be wine?' Clare looked hopefully at her friend.

'Abso-bloody-lutely.'

* * *

Julia sat on her garden bench. The air was cool, perfectly still. An aeroplane left a long, thin trail of smoke high in the clear sky above and she watched it until it disappeared out of view. She'd hoped a few hours in the garden would help her feel better but her limbs felt heavy.

Long-tailed tits crowded round the birdfeeders hanging from the branches of the magnolia tree. They worked quickly, helping themselves to food before taking flight together, only to return a few moments later.

Julia heard the garden gate open. She stood slowly, pulling her thick wool cardigan tightly around her. 'Jess, is that you?'

'It's me.'

The voice wasn't one she knew. Julia turned towards the gate to see a tall man standing before her, smiling a little.

'I'm sorry to come unannounced but I just couldn't wait any longer.'

'William?' Julia turned towards him, her hands covering her mouth in shock. 'It's you...'

For a moment, they stood rooted to the spot, neither daring to believe the other was there.

'You're here!' Julia put her hands on Ed's shoulders. Then she hugged him with all her might. 'How did you know where to find me?'

'They told me the name of your village last night, about your cottage on the green. Luckily, there's only one Wisteria Cottage here.'

'But how...? When...?' Julia stood back, her hands around his. She looked into his eyes, so new to her and yet so utterly familiar.

'Well, after I met Annie and Jess last night, they said you'd hoped to meet me sooner rather than later but that it was up to me. And this morning, Sophie, my wife, took one look at me and told me to get in my car and come straight here. So I did. I'm sorry if—'

'Oh, William... Ed. Should I call you Ed?' Julia looked at him, studied his face. 'I think I should call you Ed.'

'Well, that would definitely make things simpler.' They both laughed gently, nervously.

'Honestly, please don't say sorry. I'm the one who's sorry, for goodness' sake. I'm just so, so sorry.'

'Listen, I've been thinking about this for a long time. Not just since I got the letter from the agency, I mean long before that. And I know you will tell me in due course what happened, fill in the gaps. But I promise you, I don't want or need you to apologise for anything. In fact, it's the last thing I want.'

'OK, no more apologies.' Julia wiped at her eyes briefly with the back of her hand. She looked at him, his eyes framed with the same long lashes as his father's were. 'Come on, let's sit.'

They sat side by side on the bench, a small silence between them. 'So, the girls tell me you have a wonderful family.'

'I do, I really do. Sophie – who made me promise to tell you that she can't wait to meet you, too – and the children.'

'What are they called?'

'Edie's our eldest, she's eight; Johnnie's five, nearly six, and Isla is two.'

'And your parents?'

Ed looked at the ground. 'They were lovely, really they were.'

'Oh, that's so good to hear.' Julia put her hand on his arm. 'I just wanted you to be happy. To be loved and looked after, because I could give you the love but I had nothing else to give. Not a roof over your head, food to eat.' She shook her head. 'And not a day, a moment has gone by when I haven't wondered how you are, hoping you are happy wherever you might be.'

Ed met her gaze. 'I promise you I have been very lucky. Of course I often wondered about you and about my real father... more as I got older. After we had Edie, to be honest. In fact, I almost started looking for you then but there was something that stopped me, and it would have felt disloyal to my parents. I just couldn't ever quite pluck up the courage to do it. Sophie says it was my way of avoiding disappointment, in case you couldn't be found. Or didn't want to see me. Annoyingly, I know she's right.'

Julia laughed. 'I think she's right, too. And on my side, I had to promise *not* to look for you. My mother...' Julia looked out across the garden.

'Look, I honestly don't feel anything but relief to have found you. When I first learned your daughters were looking for me I admit I did wonder whether it was all better left as it was. I think, perhaps, I had... feelings about being adopted in the first place I didn't know were there. Or perhaps hadn't allowed myself to think about. But since the moment I met Annie and Jess, it has felt...' he searched for the right words, 'strangely inevitable.'

'And my letter. I want you to know I wished you'd had that years ago but I was never allowed to...'

'I know. Jess and Annie told me the story. Well, what they knew. I want to hear it from you too one day, but please don't feel you owe me an explanation. That's not what this is about.'

'I understand, thank you.'

'I can't imagine how hard it must have been for you.' Ed's voice caught in his throat. 'I mean, I look at my own children and the thought of...' He stopped himself. 'Sorry, that's probably a really insensitive thing to say.'

'Not at all.' Julia thought of those black shoes and laces, blinking the memory away. 'I will always feel sadness for those missed years, but the most important thing is that we've found each other. And we'll have plenty of time to talk about the past.'

'But there's also the future to think about, too.' He took her hands in his. 'Can I introduce you to my family one day soon?'

'My darling boy, there's nothing I'd love more.'

* * *

Jess looked out of the rain-covered window, watching the blur of lights outside. The traffic moved slowly but she was grateful to be cocooned in the warmth of the cab. Ahead, the lights changed from green to amber to red and back again. Cars edged slowly forwards, horns sounding in frustration.

'I'm going to go up and round, if that's all right with you. Otherwise we'll be here for hours.' The cab driver glanced at her over his shoulder.

'Good idea, thank you.' She went back to looking into shop

windows, watching people walk along the street hunched over their phones. She looked up, seeing the Christmas lights lining the street up ahead. 'When did they go up?'

'A couple of weeks ago, love. Can't believe it's that time of year already. Mind you, I swear it gets earlier every year.'

She wondered how on earth she could have missed them, given she walked along this stretch of road almost every day on her way to work. Her phone buzzed in her hand.

'Hi...' Seeing his name on her phone was still taking some getting used to.

'Hi, what time can you be here? I've got a table, last minute, but we've got to be out by half eight. Is that OK?'

'Perfect. I'm a few minutes away.'

She pulled the band from her hair, letting it fall loose onto her shoulders. Adding a slick of red lipstick before the taxi stopped, she waved her card at the machine and thanked the driver, hopping out onto Piccadilly.

As she walked through the doors into the packed restaurant, the noise, a joyous layering of conversations, seemed to fill the room.

'I'm meeting someone here, he's just been given a table...'

The waitress smiled. 'Yes, I'll take you over. Can I take your coat?'

Jess shook her head. 'I'm OK, thanks.'

'Follow me.'

They weaved through the tables until they reached one at the back, to the left. A small booth clearly meant for more than two.

'How did you manage that?' Jess asked as she slid into the seat opposite him.

'Front of house is an old friend.' Ben grinned, standing up to greet her. 'How did the meeting go?'

'Well, I think. I mean, there's still a bit of work to be done but I think we'll get there.' Jess sat down, reaching straight for the bread.

'Can I get you a drink?' asked the waitress.

'Gin and tonic?' Ben looked at Jess.

'Water's fine, thanks.'

'Just another beer for me, thanks.' Ben knew Jess didn't order water unless something was wrong. 'So, how was last night? Did it all go OK? Did he turn up?'

'Yes, he turned up.' Jess laughed. 'I mean, we had dinner...' She trailed off, tears coming to her eyes.

'Oh, Jess, I know it's a lot to take in but he's only just found out who you all are. It's going to take time...'

Jess shook her head. 'It's not that. Ben, I've got something to tell you and I'm going to say it all at once. I'm going to close my eyes whilst I say it and then keep them closed for a moment when I've finished. And when I open them, if you're not sitting there any more I will completely understand. Seriously. Go. I won't come after you. I mean, again... ever.'

'Jess, please. What is it?' Was that fear in his voice?

'OK.' She looked at him, let out a long breath, closed her eyes gently and clenched her fists under the table. 'I'm pregnant. I did a test earlier today, halfway up the M3. Not on the side of the motorway, obviously. I mean at the services. Anyway, I'd been feeling a bit weird for a week or so, just put it down to a bug or something. Then when we were at the pub this morning Annie realised what it might mean. I thought I'd wait until I got back to London but then I couldn't stop thinking about it and I had the meeting this afternoon and we'd just spent an evening with my brother – who really is lovely, by the way – and I was supposed to stop in and see Mum, but I just couldn't think straight, about this, about you, about anything. So I dropped

Annie, stopped at the motorway services on the way back to London, did the test in the loo and... here I am. Pregnant. And feeling slightly sick. Still with my eyes closed. And hoping with all my heart that when I open my eyes in about thirty seconds that you're still there...'

Silence.

Suddenly the noise of the rest of the room resurfaced. She could hear every conversation around her. But she couldn't hear him.

Slowly, she opened her eyes.

16

Patrick stood in his room, staring at his small suitcase. For someone who'd spent years throwing things in a bag at the last minute he was surprisingly indecisive about packing to head to Cornwall for a couple of nights.

'Dad! Are you nearly ready?' his daughter called up the stairs. 'Come on, we're all waiting!' She sounded so like Kathy, he thought. Ever since her mother's death Emma had been the one to keep an eye on Patrick, visiting him every other week. She was infuriatingly bossy, always telling him off for not having the right food in the fridge or letting the washing pile up. But she was also a complete tonic: funny and bright and hugely entertaining. Introducing her to the idea of Julia, let alone a half-sibling, had caused Patrick endless worrying. But Emma and her husband, Monty, had loved the idea of coming with him to Cornwall to meet up with everyone – and to meet Ed for the first time.

'Did you speak to Ollie?' Patrick came down the stairs, small case in hand.

'Yes, he's asked us to FaceTime when we're there. He doesn't want to miss out, obviously.' Emma stood at the bottom of the stairs. She was, as ever, a colourful sight, draped in a long, deep red linen coat, a cream cotton scarf around her neck and a bright blue silk scarf somehow holding the majority of her blond curls off her face and out of her piercing blue eyes.

'It's such a shame he couldn't come back for this.'

'Dad, he's on the other side of the world in the middle of a job. He'll be back in a few months.' Ollie was filming a wildlife documentary somewhere in South America; Emma wasn't entirely sure where. 'Anyway, we don't want to throw too many of us at the poor guy all at once. We might scare him off.'

Patrick smiled at his daughter. 'You're right, I'm sure.' Indeed, she usually was.

It was Emma who'd been so supportive from the beginning, sitting quietly opposite her father as he read that first email from Ed confirming his wish to meet. It was Emma who'd persuaded Patrick to suggest a meeting, at a time and place of Ed's choosing. And it was Emma who'd driven him down to the country pub where they'd arranged to meet just a few weeks later.

Patrick and Emma had arrived early and she'd left him alone in the quiet pub garden, waiting for Ed. He'd never known time pass so slowly as it did that day, waiting for his son to walk through the door. And when he finally did, Patrick felt he was looking at someone he'd known all his life.

Ed walked towards him, a cautious smile on his face. Having done this once already with Julia, Ed wasn't nearly as nervous as before, knowing he was meeting a man whom his mother clearly adored. 'You must be Patrick. I'm Ed.' He held a hand out.

Patrick took it, tears in his eyes. 'I am. And I can see that you are Ed.'

Both stood looking at one another for a moment before Ed put his arms around his father and the two men embraced. Relief flooded through Patrick's body.

'Thank you.' It was all Patrick could manage.

'You really don't have to thank me.'

Patrick stood back from him, looking at Ed's face. 'I'm just so happy you're here.'

'Me, too. I wasn't sure I'd ever get to meet you, either of you. But to then find that you're both still very much here... I just feel very lucky.'

'You do?' Patrick was stunned. For years he'd carried his guilt with him. Even when he'd tried to escape it by going to some of the worst places on earth, it followed him like an unwanted rucksack on his back. The fact that he'd had no choice in the matter was of little comfort. And yet here was his son, standing in front of him, saying he felt lucky.

'Yes, I really do. My parents were devoted to me and I didn't know any different. Of course they told me what had happened when I was a bit older but I think I felt guilty wanting to know who my real parents were when they'd been so good to me. So I left it and the longer I did, the better I got at burying it... wanting to know about you, I mean.' Ed sighed. 'But then I had my own children and I guess that brought things up I hadn't dared think about for years.'

'I'm just so sorry—' Patrick shook his head.

Ed quickly cut him off. 'Please don't say sorry. I promise you the last thing I want is for anyone to be sorry about anything.'

'Well, that is an extraordinary thing for you to say. I'm very grateful.' Patrick smiled. He reached across the table and put his hand on Ed's arm. 'Now, can I get you something to drink?'

When, an hour later, Emma had arrived as arranged, she'd

walked into the garden to find the two men deep in conversation.

'Am I interrupting anything?' She smiled at them both.

'Emma!' Patrick beamed at her. 'This is Ed.'

Ed stood, taking her hand in both of his. 'Emma, it's so lovely to meet you.' He looked earnest, she thought.

'Likewise, Ed.' She smiled warmly. 'Goodness.' She looked from one to the other, shaking her head and laughing a little at how similar they looked.

Since that first meeting Patrick and Ed had been in regular contact via email (both preferring email to phone calls) but this would be the first time Patrick would be meeting Ed's family. His heart lurched at the thought.

They headed out of the front door towards the car. 'You go in the front, Patrick.' Monty, Emma's husband, called over his shoulder to Patrick as he opened the passenger door.

'Are you sure?' He looked across at Monty, perfectly dishevelled in his old, faded blue linen suit and thick glasses, smiling his usual conspiratorial smile.

'Yes, please do. I suggest you pick the music before Emma makes us listen to some dreary play.'

'Right, for that, Monty, I'm going to make you listen to a dreary play...' Emma reached forward through the seats to turn the dial on the radio.

Soon, they were on the long A roads heading west. The sun shone intermittently behind cotton-wool clouds strewn across the warm May sky.

'You all right there, Dad?' Emma proffered a tin of travel sweets from the back seat with one hand.

'All good, thank you.' Patrick ignored the ache starting to settle in to his knees and hips, a cruel reminder that he was getting really quite old.

'So, come on, what else can you tell us?' asked Monty. 'I mean, you find your first love, then find your first child. Can we expect any other surprises this weekend?'

'Monty! Stop being deliberately mischievous. Poor Dad is worried enough about this without you making it worse.'

'No, no, it's fine. I know, Monty, that in your own weird and wonderful way you're actually trying to make it better.'

'Exactly, Paddy!' Monty laughed. 'Em, have you got the directions?'

'Darling, concentrate on the road.' Emma shot him a disapproving look. 'Yes, Dad forwarded the email to me from Ed. The accommodation looks amazing. Seriously, Dad, are you sure you're OK with all this?'

'Look, I'm the one who should be worried about you. I mean, it's a lot for you to take in.'

'Dad, we're fine. Excited, even. Sure, it was a bit of a shock but really, how wonderful that you all found each other again! Before it's too late, if you know what I mean.'

'I do, thank you, Emma.' Patrick laughed gently.

'It might have been more tricky if Mum were here but you know what? I think she would have understood. She would have been happy, for you. Really, I do think that.'

'Thank you, Em. You always know what to say.' Just like your mother always did, he thought. The thought of Kathy reassuring him she'd be fine as he left for another stint away, God knew where, not knowing if he'd ever come home, still physically pulled at his heart. She had been an amazing woman, not least to put up with him and his barely there presence. And the one thing that she had always said to him, whenever he returned, was, 'Well, you're here now.' As if that was all that mattered.

* * *

'Rufus! Ned! Will you PLEASE stop arguing! We've got three more hours in the car and I'm not listening to this all the way there.' Annie shot James a glance, looking for backup. His eyes were fixed on the road.

'Stop that now, boys, otherwise we'll leave you behind.'

'Why don't we play I Spy?' Julia sat in the back with the boys – her choice – and promptly picked something beginning with P. The boys immediately yelled out 'POO!' with glee.

'Did you leave food for the dogs for Mum?' James asked Annie over the noise in the back.

'Yes, and food and wine in the fridge.'

'So where are we going, exactly?'

'I told you, darling, it's a big self-catering place. Ed knows the guy who used to live there, Harry. Remember, the man who ran the pub Jess and I stayed in when we went to meet him for the first time? Apparently Harry's mother's family used to live there but they sold it many years ago. Anyway, it looks gorgeous. Big garden, beautiful views...'

'And this is on Ed?' James had already voiced his mild discomfort at this arrangement.

'Yes, he insisted. Said that if we were all going down there, he at least wanted to find us somewhere to stay. Sophie's sorted out the food, apparently. I did offer. I've made lasagne and we've got a ton of cheese. And everyone's bringing wine, obviously.'

'Who else is going to be there apart from your sister? What about the rest of Ed's family?'

'Well, he hasn't really got any on his parents' side. I think there's an aunt but I'm not sure if she's coming. Sophie and the children, obviously, but then it's really just us. And Patrick and his daughter, Emma, and her husband, Monty. Is that right, Mum?'

'Yes, they left earlier this morning so they'll probably be

there just ahead of us. Emma is delightful – she's an artist – and Monty's a journalist, I think. Not sure what he writes about. They're both adorable, anyway. Where exactly is it we're going again? I couldn't hear you properly.'

'Boys! Quiet a minute!' Annie snapped. It worked. She continued over her shoulder. 'I was just telling James. It's like a big holiday rental but Ed knows the old owner. Says the house is perfect for us all for a couple of nights. We'll probably leave before lunch on Sunday, though, if that's OK with you.'

'Of course, we'll still have plenty of time.'

'How's Patrick feeling about meeting Ed's family?' asked Annie.

'Good, I think. A bit nervous but excited.'

'Mum, I need a wee,' Ned piped up from the back.

'Seriously? But we've only been going for about twenty minutes!' Annie closed her eyes and took a breath. 'Didn't you go before we left?' Annie turned and looked at him, trying not to sound too irritated.

'Yes, but I need to go again.'

'OK, we'll have to find somewhere to stop. Darling, how long until the next services?' Annie looked at James.

'There's one in about ten minutes, I think.' James glanced in the rear-view mirror, recognising Ned's wriggle as quite severe on his scale of needing to go. 'We'll stop as soon as we can, fella. Just hang on in there.'

'How about another game of I Spy to take your mind off it? You start, Ned.' Julia thought distraction was their best chance. 'Come on, I Spy...'

'With my little eye...' continued Ned, still wriggling. It was going to be a long journey.

* * *

The sky was dark by the time James was navigating the small, winding Cornish country lanes. The boys were both fast asleep in the back, either side of Annie. Julia now sat in the passenger seat, piecing together the landscape outside. The lights from houses were few and far between.

'Annie, text Ed and let him know we're nearly there.'

She reached for her phone, the glare lighting up her face in the dark space of the car. 'No signal.'

'Let's hope the sat nav's right, then. The turning should be just up here on the left.' James swung the car slowly into the next left-hand turn, picking up a beautiful tree in full blossom in the headlights as he did so.

Julia looked at it, the sight prodding at something in her mind. As they drove down the long tree-lined drive to the house, Annie started to wake the boys. 'Rufus, darling, we're here at the house. Time to wake up... Ned,' she shook him gently, brushing the hair from his hot forehead, 'wake up, my sweet.'

They turned a corner, the house temporarily hidden by thick rhododendron before it came back into view, a sturdy Georgian house with large windows throwing warm light onto the gravel drive.

'Wow, look at that,' Annie whispered. 'What's it called again?'

'Lyn House,' replied Julia. She looked up at it through the windscreen. 'I've been here before.'

'When?' Annie gazed at it, mentally moving in.

'With Patrick. Years ago. This is near where Aunt Tessa lived.'

Annie looked at her mother, her eyes wide. 'Really? Does Ed know?'

'No, I don't think so. I know I've told him about Tessa, how I spent summers down here but I just said it was on the south coast. I don't think I ever mentioned Porthlyn, or the house. Too many ghosts.'

'Ghosts?' Rufus said sleepily.

'No, not ghosts. Granny said "hosts", didn't you, Julia?' James looked round at his mother-in-law. 'Do you want a moment whilst we take the kids in?' he asked.

'No, no, it's fine. Just... I wasn't expecting it, that's all.' Julia slowly undid her seatbelt, not taking her eyes off the house.

As they got out of the car the enormous red front door opened and there, in the light at the top of the steps, was Ed. Next to him – same long legs, wide shoulders – was Patrick. Julia looked at them standing together, the sight of father and son making her heart soar.

'How was your journey?' Ed called out as he came down the steps. 'Hi, Julia.' He kissed Julia on the cheek.

'Hi, darling.' She held her palm to his face for a second. 'How are you?'

'All good, everyone's very excited. Come on, you go inside, I'll help James with the bags.'

'Hi, Uncle Ed.' Ned and Rufus stood grinning up at them.

'Hey, boys!' The novelty of their newly acquired uncle was still evident as demonstrated by their excited faces. 'Go on inside. I think Emma has got plans for hot chocolate and marsh-mallows by the fire for you boys.'

The boys ran up the steps into the house, shouting a cheery hello to Patrick on their way past. Julia embraced Patrick before she followed them inside.

'Hi, Ed!' Annie gave him a big hug.

Ed knew Annie dealt in hugs, not kisses. 'Hi, Annie. Hello, James.' Ed extended his hand. 'How was the trip?'

'All good, thanks. Wow, what a place!' James took in the scale of the house. 'You know Julia knows it?'

'How funny, Patrick said he knew it too.' Ed looked at Annie. 'How come?'

'We're not really sure. She just said as we drove in. Knew the name of the house. James, did she seem OK to you?'

'I think so. She mentioned Aunt Tessa. I think she must have lived near here. I'm sure she'll fill us in.' James picked up the boys' bags from the back seat and closed the car door. 'Remind me of Patrick's daughter's name again?'

Ed took a bag from James. 'Emma, and her husband's called Monty. They're brilliant. So, Julia's been here before too, then?'

'She must have been, I suppose.' Annie shrugged her shoulders. 'I'm sure they'll tell us. When did you arrive?'

'Earlier this evening, enough time to put food and wine in the fridge and light the fire in the sitting room. It's a bit draughty. Sophie made a cottage pie for tonight. there's plenty keeping warm in the Aga, if you're hungry.'

'Is Sophie here?' Annie couldn't wait to see her again.

'Yes, she's inside. Our kids are in bed but definitely not asleep. They're too excited. I think she's probably showing your boys to their room unless they've been sidetracked by hot chocolate.'

Annie and James followed Ed up the steps into a reception hall. The ceilings were impossibly high and a staircase swept up one side of the room. On the other, to the side of an enormous fireplace stood a piano. And in the middle of the room, Julia and Patrick stood as if frozen to the spot.

'Is everything OK?' asked Ed.

Julia turned to look at them in the doorway. 'We know this house. We used to come here.' Her voice was quiet.

'We knew the person who owned it,' said Patrick.

'Hang on, I'm confused,' said Annie.

'You knew Harry's mother?' Ed tried to process the connection. 'Why didn't you say?'

Patrick looked at Julia. 'I thought I'd better wait until Julia was here.'

'Maggie,' said Julia. 'She was a friend of ours.'

'You knew someone who lived here?' Annie's eyes lit up.

'Yes. Maggie was, briefly, the girlfriend of our friend Richard. The one's whose ashes we took to Rome,' said Patrick.

'Hang on, who's died?' Emma came into the room, Monty behind her. 'Oh, hi! You must be Annie! I'm Emma.' She crossed the room and greeted Annie warmly. 'And this is Monty.'

Monty ambled over, glass of red in hand. He proffered the other hand to first Annie, then James. 'Pleased to meet you both.'

'Hi, Julia. You look so well, as always.' Emma kissed Julia on the cheek. 'What's Dad on about?'

'Hello, darlings.' Julia looked at Patrick. 'We were just saying we've been here before. In this house, I mean. Years ago. We spent a summer here. Well, we spent lots of summers here in Porthlyn, but our last summer here... We loved this house.' Julia looked around the hall, taking in the familiar walls despite the lack of paintings.

'Careful!' Sophie shouted from the top of the stairs, children in pyjamas racing down ahead of her. 'Sorry, ours heard the words "hot chocolate" and there was no stopping them.' Sophie came down the stairs, realising halfway down that everyone was standing still, like a game of grown-up musical statues. 'Hey, what's going on? Is everything OK?'

'Well, yes. But I think we're about to be told something we didn't know.' Ed looked at his parents.

'Not until I've said hello to Annie and James.' Sophie crossed the room to hug them both. 'Right, sorry, go on.'

Patrick looked at Julia before speaking. 'Well, it was in this room that I first danced with Julia.'

'So you did.' Julia smiled, holding Patrick's gaze.

'It was our last summer together. Back then, I mean.'

'What an extraordinary thing!' exclaimed Monty. 'Well planned, Ed!'

'But it wasn't... I mean, I didn't know.' Ed shook his head in disbelief. 'So, you knew Harry's mum?'

'Yes, she was my best friend down here. Well, that summer, anyway.' Julia laughed at the memory of her friend with her cat's-eye glasses and ever-present cigarette hanging from her red painted lips.

'We used to sneak up here for great parties.' Patrick looked at Julia and squeezed her hand.

'Well, I think this calls for a toast. I'm going to get some glasses. Come on, Monty, give me a hand. Sitting room in five!' called Emma as she turned and left the room.

'Oh my God, Mum, that's such a mad coincidence.' Annie shook her head.

Sophie hugged first Julia, then Patrick. 'Full circle, though, don't you think?'

Julia wiped an eye briefly with her hand. 'Come on, let's go and sit by the fire.'

* * *

An enormous – now decimated – cheeseboard lay on the low ottoman in the middle of the room; on one side an old vintage port-coloured sofa hosted Monty, Emma and James. On the other, Ed sat between Patrick and Julia. Sophie and Annie sat on the floor in front of the fire, their faces flushed warm on one side. Conversation flowed, as did the wine and the sound of jazz floated across the room from the record player in the corner. The children had finally fallen asleep, on a promise of more fireside stories from Emma and Monty before bed the following night if they were good.

They heard the front door open with a loud, echoing bang.

'That must be Jess.' Julia got up. Annie followed her into the hall. Jess was standing just inside the door, her bag at her feet.

'God, I need a wee. Where's the loo? Wow, this place is incredible... loo?' Jess screwed up her face, trying desperately to cross her legs despite the enormous bump she was carrying.

Julia pointed at a door just to the right. 'Nearest one's there.'

'Back in a mo.' Jess disappeared behind the door.

'Hello, Julia. Hi, Annie.' Ben appeared at the door carrying two large bags. 'I'm not sure how long she's planning on us staying but judging by these, I'd say a while.'

'Darling Ben! How are you?' Julia crossed the hall and hugged him.

Annie joined them. 'Hi, Ben, how's she been?'

'All good, thanks, Annie. I think, anyway. She's not sleeping that well but other than that she says she's feeling pretty good.'

'Not long to go now,' said Julia.

'Six weeks. Early July.'

'You both look so well. So exciting... Come and meet everyone. You must be tired from your journey. How was it?' Julia led Ben into the other room.

'I'll wait here for Jess,' Annie called after them.

A moment later, Jess came out from the loo adjusting her dress. 'God, I feel like a whale.'

'You look absolutely beautiful, my lovely sister.' Annie threw her arms around Jess's neck. 'How are you feeling?'

'Fucking knackered, to be honest. I mean, if I feel like this now, how on earth am I going to cope when the baby's out?'

'I promise you will be fine. We'll all be here to help whenever we can. The boys are so excited about this, I can't tell you. So, how's it all going?' Annie grinned, winking. 'Sorry, I don't know why I winked.'

Jess laughed. 'Good, I think. I mean, apart from feeling enormous.' Jess pointed at her stomach. 'But, to be honest,' she lowered her voice conspiratorially, 'I can't quite believe it. I mean I still can't believe he stayed. Poor thing takes me back and within a few months I go and get pregnant.'

'Of course he was going to stay, you moron. He loves you!'

'I know, but... I'm not a very dependable moron. At least I haven't been.'

'That's the point. It doesn't matter what's in the past with you two. What matters is now. You love each other and that's enough. Figure out the rest as you go. So stop worrying and come and sit down. Leave your bag there for now. I'll get James to show Ben where you're sleeping.'

Jess walked into the sitting room to find everyone already on their feet making their introductions to Ben. Before long more wine was poured and the noise of talking and laughter filled the room. For a brief moment, Patrick and Julia found themselves together on the sofa.

'Can you believe this is happening?' Julia spoke quietly so no one else could hear.

'I could never, in my wildest imagination, have imagined this is how our story would end.'

'End? Patrick! We're not that old!'

'I know, it's just that I really thought I had lost you. For ever. And I came to terms with it, eventually. You don't know this but I came back here after Will... Ed was born. Not to find you. Well, that's what I told myself.'

'I know you did.' Julia smiled.

'You do? How? Tessa?'

'Yes. She told me that you'd come back, hoping to make sense of everything. I think she might have helped you do just that.'

'Yes, she really did, but I asked her not to tell you. I didn't want you thinking I'd gone against your wishes.'

'Darling, I understand why you came. Tessa told me about your walking past the cottage, going to the beach.'

'Julia, Tessa was quite amazing. It was what she did that was so intuitive. Not just words but driving me to the beach, as if she knew I had to go back once more if ever I was going to let go of you.'

'She really was an amazing woman. More of a mother to me than my own, in truth – and I know she loved you, too.'

'When did she tell you? That I came back here, I mean.'

'The following year. She wanted me to know how you were doing, as I'd asked. Moving on so that we all could. And it helped me in the end, even if it nearly killed me at first. It was the day that I moved out and away from my parents.'

'I just wish she'd seen this. Us all together, I mean. Back where it all started.'

'Oh, I think this would have made her very happy indeed.' Julia raised her glass to his and together they drank a silent toast to Tessa.

17

Annie heaved back the heavy curtains in their room. It was still early and a sliver of moon hung in the clear, pale blue sky like a forgotten decoration. It was blissfully quiet, the children still asleep, thanks to their late night. The view from the bedroom window looked down across the fields in front of the house to the village below. A lone oak tree stood in the middle of the field directly in front of the house.

Annie stood for a moment at the window, drinking in the view. She thought about Patrick, about Ed. How could it be that just over a year ago she didn't know either of them? And yet here they were, suddenly both a big part of all their lives. She thought of her own father, David; how he'd sent over the wine to bring down here for the weekend from his home in France ('so I can be there in spirit, or at least in wine').

Annie looked at James, still sleeping. She wanted to show him the moon but decided to go and make him a cup of tea instead. Padding down the stairs, she looked at the empty hall, imagining her mother and Patrick dancing there, years ago. She found her way to the kitchen, the flagstones cold beneath her feet. Jess was already at the table.

'You're up early.' Jess motioned to the Aga. 'There's a pot of tea on there.'

'Sod's law: the one time the kids do actually sleep in I wake up and can't get back to sleep. Sorry, I swore I wouldn't tell you the bad bits before the baby arrived.'

'Don't worry. I've had plenty of that from Ben's sister. Really didn't need to know her birth story, as she insists on calling it.'

'Just you wait, you too will become obsessed and I'll have to sit there listening to yours for hours on end.' Annie laughed.

'Rude.' Jess threw her a look. 'Anyway, what's the plan today?'

'There was talk of a walk on the beach, then lunch back here. That's as far as we got.'

'Can I do anything for lunch?' Jess realised this was somewhat overselling her cooking capabilities.

'Sophie and Ed have done most of it, I think.'

'That's very generous of them.'

'I've seen the quiche in the fridge. And she put the meringue for pudding in the oven before we went to bed last night.'

'Seriously? There are people who do that?' Jess couldn't help but sound annoyed.

'Come on, it gets us off the hook. You should be grateful.'

Jess reached for a piece of cold toast from the rack in the middle of the table, smearing it with a thick slice of butter and dropping a spoonful of marmalade on top. 'I'm only joking. Sort of.' She looked at her sister and pulled a face. 'Right, I'm going to take this and go and have a bath. See you in a bit.'

'Jess, can I ask you a question?' Annie had her serious face on.

'Oh God, you're going to do the marriage talk, aren't you?'

'Well, I just don't get it. Why don't you want to get married? I mean, he has asked you, hasn't he?'

'Yes, of course he has. Right after I told him I was pregnant. Well, not right after, obviously. He was in shock for at least a couple of days. But then he asked me – and he said it wasn't just because I was pregnant – but I said, can't we just *not* get married? I don't expect you to understand but, honestly, I don't want to be anywhere else, with anyone else, But I don't need him to marry me to prove it.'

'So you really don't want to ever get married?' Annie poured some tea from the pot.

'Not now, no... That might change, of course, but at the moment, I just don't want to. God, you're such a hopeless romantic, Annie.'

'Oh, come on, I just want you to have the happy ending.'

'But it's not about an ending. It's about now. And I'm happy now. You know?'

'Yes, I suppose so. But if you change your mind, lots of people have old bridesmaids nowadays.' Annie pointed at herself. 'Just saying.'

'Noted.' Jess laughed and left the room, piece of toast in hand.

Annie sat with her tea for a few moments, taking in the view from the kitchen window, then made her way back upstairs. She woke James gently. 'Cup of tea?'

'Ooh, thank you.' He sat up, plumping the pillows behind his head before settling back with his still steaming cup. 'God, I slept like a baby.'

'I know. And notice anything?'

'No, what?' He looked at her, then around the room, wondering what he was missing.

'Listen...'

James couldn't hear a thing. 'The boys! Are they still asleep?'

'Yes. Yes, they are.' She climbed back into bed with him, slipping her hand underneath the sheets.

'Well, what to do...?'

'Mama...' Ned stood at the door. 'I can't find Monkey.'

James sighed, putting his tea down. He looked at Annie. 'Thought it was too good to be true... Right, let's go and find him.' He turned back to her as he left the room. 'I love you.'

'I love you, too.'

* * *

The party sat under the shade of the terrace at the back of the house, roses cascading down the walls on either side, their scent heavy in the warm air. The table was set with a beautiful white linen tablecloth and strewn with freshly picked flowers from the garden, and Sophie put the pudding in the centre, the pavlova now topped with a thick layer of cream and a small mountain of raspberries dusted with icing sugar. The children ran around the garden, shrieking with delight as they chased Monty, who was happily playing the fool.

'He's so sweet with the children, Emma.' Annie watched them, noticing how Monty ran just fast enough to make them think he was making an effort but slow enough for them to catch him every now and again.

'I know. He would have loved children of his own but... it just didn't happen for us.'

'Oh, I'm so sorry. I didn't mean—'

'Please don't apologise, Annie. I'm not sad about it, really. I was for a long time, but it just wasn't meant to be. And I'm not sure Ollie, my brother, will have any either. He's certainly not showing any signs of settling down or having a family. Which is why it's even more wonderful that Dad's now got Ed and his kids. We feel like we've won the life lottery, inheriting you lot.'

'That's such a lovely thing to say! Thank you... I know, it's quite extraordinary. How we were all connected but never knew. And when you think that it was Richard who brought Mum and your father back together without even being here...'

'Yes, I suppose he did. How funny. Life is so much bigger than us, isn't it? My mum always used to say it was what you did right there and then that mattered. Not what went before, or what happens after. It was just about being present when you were together.'

Annie looked around the table. Patrick and Julia sat at one end, laughing together. 'Do you mind that they're together after all this time?'

'Why on earth would I mind? Annie, it's quite wonderful! I've not seen Dad so happy since, well, since Mum died. I know it's only a matter of time before he tells me he's moving down to live with her. I think the only reason he hasn't before now is because he's worried about what we'd think. But I've told him not to worry about us.' Emma topped up her glass. 'More wine, Vicar?'

'Lovely, just a splash.' Annie took a sip of the chilled white, the smell of cut grass in the glass matching that of the garden. 'And what about Ed – is he what you expected?'

'I'm not sure what I was expecting but it's almost as if he's totally it. Do you know what I mean?'

'I know exactly! I thought the same. And he's so like your father, I think.'

'Yes... his eyes. But look at the shape of his face. It's like your mother's. And yours.'

Annie looked at him, talking animatedly to Patrick. 'So it is.'

'So, you're a painter, too? Dad told me you used to work in a gallery.'

'Yes, I did... years ago, though.' Annie was suddenly embarrassed to be talking about her work, feeling like a bit of a fraud. 'I haven't actually painted for such a long time. Basically, I just do up bits of furniture and sell them.'

'Get much for them?' Emma was as direct as Jess, thought Annie.

'Not much, sadly... not for the time it takes to do them.'

'But you enjoy doing it, right?'

'Well, I guess. Not as much as painting, obviously. But I can't sell my paintings.'

'Why not?'

'Um... they're not good enough?'

'Says who?'

'Me!' Annie took another sip, a little larger this time.

'OK, not good enough for you. But how do you know no one else will buy them unless you try? Sounds to me like you're doing the furniture because you can't bring yourself to put your paintings out there.' Emma took a quick sip from her glass. 'Have you got any on your phone you can show me?'

'No I haven't, but the funny thing is, a friend of mine said the same thing.' Annie thought of Clare, her lovely loyal friend. 'And now you... and rather annoyingly, I know you're right. I just can't quite bring myself to—'

Emma held up her hand. 'Right, that's it. I've got a sketchpad and some paints upstairs. I always take them with me when I go away in case I see something I wish to paint. But you're going to go and paint something this afternoon. You don't have to show it to anyone. You just have to paint something. Anything. Deal?'

Annie realised she wasn't going to get away with making any other excuses. 'OK, fine, you win. Thank you, Emma.'

'My pleasure. I know someone who needs to paint when I see them.' She got up from the table and headed into the house through the open French doors.

James and Ed had left the table to take over playing with the children from Monty, now falling asleep in a deck chair in the garden. Annie took herself off on Emma's orders to sketch and paint under the oak tree in the field beyond the garden. Emma, Patrick and Sophie went to explore the gardens, leaving Jess and Julia together at one end of the table, Jess with her feet up on Julia's lap.

'How are you feeling, darling?'

'I'm good, Mum. You?'

'I can't quite believe I'm back here after all these years. But at the same time, it doesn't feel strange at all.'

'Would you change anything? I mean, if you could go back.'

'Of course, but I can't. If I hadn't had to give up... Ed, I wouldn't have had you. So no, of course I wouldn't change that. And I have you all here now and nothing could make me happier.'

Later that night, as they celebrated their reunion with a magnum of champagne shipped in at the last minute by Harry, Monty belted out songs on the slightly out-of-tune piano in the hall, mostly, and in parts thankfully, covered up by the reposi- tioned record player.

Ed twirled Edie around the makeshift dance floor; Isla perched precariously on his shoulders. Sophie danced with a delighted Johnnie, Harry flung a delirious Emma around and Monty whooped wildly at the piano. James and Annie tried their best to dance, hampered by Rufus and Ned, giggling madly as they clung to James's legs. Ben and Jess stood, arms around each other, laughing as they watched. Beside them, Julia and Patrick took in the scene together.

'Darling, I know we had to live another life until we got here. But I'm so happy to have found you again.' Julia looked at Patrick.

'And I'm happy that you said yes. To Rome, I mean. So what do we do now?'

'This.' Julia kissed him gently.

'How could I have ever let you go?' He held her face in his hands.

'Because you had to. I asked you to. But I'm here now.' Her eyes filled with tears. And then she smiled.

18

It was the kind of bright, January morning London does so well. The sky was cloudless, the air crisp. On the steps of the Old Town Hall a small group embraced each other warmly, all feathers and fake fur in stark contrast to the pale grey walls behind them.

'You do look gorgeous in that get-up, darling.' Annie grinned at her husband.

'Why, thank you.' James kissed the top of her head, narrowly missing the huge velvet flower she was wearing on the side of it.

'Annie!' Emma swept up the steps, resplendent in a scarlet cape, Monty behind.

'Hi, Em! Look at you... you look amazing!' More hugs were exchanged. 'Now, where's your father and my mother? I thought they'd be here by now?'

'Haven't you seen them yet? Honestly, they are bloody hopeless. I told them to leave enough time. The traffic was always going to be awful.'

'Hey, you lot! Are you coming to our wedding or not?' Ben

called to the crowd from around the side of the door at the top of the steps.

'Yes!' The crowd cheered and slowly made their way inside. Once upstairs, they were ushered into a small, formal room with rows of chairs and a dark wooden desk at the front.

'She's still got a few more minutes.' Annie put her hand on Ben's arm reassuringly.

'I know, it's just... it took us a while to get here, you know? Hey, Annie, you remember my parents?'

'Of course, lovely to see you!' Annie waved, Ben's parents waving back.

'Hi, darling.' Julia appeared on Annie's other side.

'Mum! You're here! Where were you two? I was worried about you!'

'Patrick's fault. He couldn't find the right tie this morning.' Julia gestured to Patrick, making his way towards them. 'I can't wait to see the bride. Is she here yet? Have you seen her?'

'Yes, earlier. She's with Dad on the other side of that door. Hi, Patrick!' Annie pointed to the heavy double doors at the back of the room before giving Patrick a warm hug. 'She looks so happy, Mum.'

'Would you all like to take your seats?' the registrar called over the noise. Slowly, the gathered guests hushed and did as they were told. 'Right, a few housekeeping notes...'

Moments later, the doors opened and in walked Jess on the arm of her father. He looked so proud of his daughter; Annie was in tears before Jess had made the short walk to the front. Julia's hand reached for Patrick's, and next to them Ed and Sophie beamed.

Simple vows were exchanged, Ben and Jess's daughter, Tessa, in Ben's arms throughout, charming everyone in her eyeline, even the ones who didn't like babies that much. The whole thing took less than fifteen minutes. It was wonderfully, refreshingly informal.

The newlyweds stood on the steps of the Old Town Hall and kissed, their guests whooping cheers of encouragement. Ben turned to Jess. 'Hello, you.'

'Hello, you.' She smiled back at him.

'Thank you for marrying me.'

'Thank you for saying yes.' Jess grinned. 'Come on, let's go and eat. I'm starving... haven't eaten since Tuesday to get into this.' She gestured at her outfit, a beautiful, belted emerald-green silk trouser suit. In her hand she held a simple bunch of winter roses and grey-blue eucalyptus leaves.

Slowly the crowd moved off down the street towards the restaurant, carried on a wave of love and the promise of a cold glass of champagne. Standing in front of the restaurant's familiar wooden revolving door, Jess and Ben urged their guests to go on ahead.

Ben squeezed her hand. 'You know, if I hadn't seen you that day, passing you on your way in, I think I might have carried on convincing myself that I was *definitely* over you.'

'Well, it certainly took me a while but... here we are. And I'm still not sure what I did to deserve you but somehow you seem to see the good before the bad, and my bad bits don't seem to bother you *too* much.' She pulled a face. 'But you make me feel like I can do anything. And all I want to do now is make our lives as good and as much fun as they can possibly be. This is where I want to be.'

'You could of course have said all that in your speech later.'

'I'm not making a speech, as you well know. And promise me you'll keep yours short.'

'Promise. Now in you go; our guests will be waiting.' They went in one after the other to be greeted with a great cheer.

A long table strewn with candles ran down the length of the room, with bunches of camellias, paper-white hyacinths and magnolia arranged along the middle.

In the corner a man played the piano as friends and family mingled, trays of champagne cocktails passing between them.

'Well done, fellow witness,' said Ed as Annie joined him by the bar.

'I know, who'd have thought it? I mean, the only thing more surprising than finding out I have a brother – a divine one, by the way – is Jess getting married.' Annie laughed.

'What made her change her mind, do you think?'

'Well I'm not really sure but maybe it's to do with meeting the right one? It's like all the walls she'd built up around herself over the years just fell away when Ben came back into her life. Or maybe she had changed even before he came back. I wonder if something happened when we were in Rome. Mum, Jess and I had a massive row – God, it was awful; poor Patrick must have wondered what the hell was going on – and it all came out. That's when we found out about you, too. In fact, Rome has got a lot to answer for. Good things, I mean. Anyway, I think she realised back then she was still in love with Ben. The rest, as they say...'

'Well, they look insanely happy now.'

'I know, don't they just.'

'And as for our parents...' Ed looked across at Julia and Patrick, chatting with cocktails in hand.

'I know, at their age. Ridiculous, but very sweet.' Annie laughed.

Champagne coupes were soon joined by enormous wine glasses and bottles of Burgundy, both red and white, on the table. Great pie dishes were placed on the table along with platters piled with roasted vegetables – artichokes, carrots, parsnips

– liberally sprinkled with Parmesan. As the light outside faded and the wine flowed, the room took on a warm glow. In one corner a small band set up their instruments. People started to move around, the smokers heading for the revolving door, others to the bar.

Jess leaned across the table, a mischievous look on her face. 'So, Mum, do you think you and Patrick might follow suit?'

'Darling, no, I don't think so.' Julia laughed and put down her glass.

Annie couldn't help herself. 'Really? But all these years we've basically banned you from getting married again and now you've found Patrick and you *don't* want to marry him?'

'Well, when you get to my age, darlings, you see things a little differently. I mean, when we first met, we were so young.' She looked across at Patrick, now seated between Sophie and Emma, on the other side of the table. They were talking animatedly, Sophie's head thrown back mid-laugh. 'Back then we thought we had all the time in the world. Turns out we didn't. But the difference between falling in love when you're young and falling in love when your old is knowing we might not have much time left.'

'Even more reason then, surely?' Annie raised her eyebrows at her mother.

Julia lowered her voice. 'The only man I married that I truly loved was your father.' Julia looked down the table to see David chatting with Ed and Monty on either side. 'The others, not so much, but your father is a lovely man. And he has been a good friend to me ever since. With Patrick, it's different. We lost so much time... but you can't change the past. And given the time we might have left, even more reason not to waste it worrying about it. I feel like I've been given a second chance with Patrick and I intend to enjoy every moment of it. Of course if he really wanted us to get married, I would. But it's not like that. Being together is enough.'

'Well, I think that's a gorgeous sentiment. Here's to enjoying the moment.' Annie raised her glass to her mother and sister.

'To the moment,' they chorused.

The sound of a teaspoon clinking against glass slowly brought the table to a hushed silence.

'Family and friends,' began Ben, standing, 'I just wanted to say a few words, if I may.'

Whoops and applause filled the room.

'Thank you.' He took a sip of water and cleared his throat. 'As most of you know, Jess is the love of my life.' Cue more loud applause. 'But as you also know, our path here was not exactly smooth. And that's OK because I believe that we met – again – when the time was right for us both.'

'Definitely *not* going to cry,' Jess laughed, looking at Ben.

'The point is, life has a habit of not always working to plan. And the best thing we can do is not to try and control it but instead be ready to just... take it on. And now that I'm with you...' Ben turned to Jess, 'I can't wait for us to do it together.'

There was a second of silence. Sophie squeezed Ed's hand. Another joyous round of applause followed.

Slowly, Jess stood up. 'I told Ben I wasn't going to do this.' She looked at him, smiling. More cheers, then: 'But the thing is, I thought luck was for other people.' Jess caught Annie's eye and her sister winked back at her. 'But then you came back. And if there's anything I've learned over the last few years it's that sometimes you just have to make your own luck and not let an opportunity go by.' She looked at Ben with Tessa, curled into his lap, gazing up at her. 'And this time, I'm going to make the most of it.'

Ed shouted, 'To Jess and Ben!' and together the company

raised their glasses and cheered.

Hours later, as the couple swayed gently on the small dance floor, the sound of 'Sea of Love' floating across the room, Annie and James watched, perched on a small sofa near the door.

'Don't they look so happy?' Annie sighed.

'They really do. Actually, Annie, I've got something to ask you, too.'

'What?' Annie turned, wide-eyed.

'Well, as you know, I'm not great at remembering certain things.'

'Like wedding anniversaries, you mean?' She raised an eyebrow at him.

'Well, yes, exactly. Anyway, I've gone early for our next one. Really early, actually... and it's kind of a very belated one from before as well but anyway... here. This is for you.' He reached for his jacket and pulled out an envelope from the pocket, handing it to her. 'Go on, open it.'

Annie took the envelope. Inside was a folded piece of paper. Slowly, she unfurled it and scanned it for information. One word jumped out.

'Rome?' she whispered, looking at James, tears springing to her eyes. 'Really, Jimmy? But how...? When did you plan this?'

'A while ago, but I thought it would be a good day to tell you. We go next month, for three nights.'

'But what about the kids?'

'All sorted, between Mum and Julia.' He grinned. 'Just us.'

Annie kissed him. 'Thank you. I honestly don't know what to say. I can't believe it. It's my favourite city in the world.'

'Well, that's why I want to see it too. Properly, I mean, with you showing me. I've been doing a bit of online research and we've got a lot to fit in...'

'I thought you just said I was showing you?' Annie laughed,

looking at him.

'You are, Annie. I'll just follow you around Rome.'

Jess appeared. 'Come on, you two! Definitely your turn to have a dance.'

'On our way! Just give us a second.' Annie indicated her glass.

'Promise?'

'Promise!'

Jess returned to the floor swaying to the music, one arm in the air holding her champagne coupe aloft.

Annie turned back to her husband. 'James, I know it's hard work sometimes with work, the kids, having so little time for ourselves... but I want you to know, I'm so happy I get to do it with you.

'Even with my terrible dance moves?'

'Especially with your terrible dance moves.'

He took her hand and led her to the dance floor, passing Patrick and Julia by the bar as they did.

'Are you two joining us?' Annie called out to them.

'We're happy here!' Julia shouted back, both raising their glasses as Annie went past.

Julia turned back to Patrick. 'Very happy, actually.'

Hours later, as Patrick and Julia sat in the back of their black cab, the lights of the bridge throwing a low orange glow onto their faces, Julia tipped her head onto Patrick's shoulder, listening to the music floating gently from the radio. It was a familiar tune taking her back to a moment years before, standing in her parents' shop, choosing a different path. She closed her eyes with a deep contented sigh. 'That was such a wonderful day, wasn't it?'

'It was. And now...' Patrick squeezed her hand gently, '... we have tomorrow too.'

BOOK CLUB QUESTIONS

1. Do you think Annie and Jess made the right decision when they followed Julia to Rome?
2. How has Jess's childhood affected her relationship choices?
3. Which of the three women in *This Changes Everything* do you relate to the most, and why?
4. In what ways has a lifetime apart made Patrick and Julia's relationship stronger? Do you think their love would have survived if they hadn't been separated?
5. How do Jess and Annie's expectations and hopes for their own romantic lives change throughout the book and by watching their mother reunite with Patrick?
6. What did you make of Ed's first meetings with his sisters, Julia and with Patrick? Which touched you the most?
7. Which location came alive most for you – Rome or Cornwall?
8. Did Julia's parents make the right decision when they

decided she was too young to have a child? How would her life have been different if she had kept Ed?

9. Everyone gets their happy ending as we reach the last page of *This Changes Everything*. Did you find the ending satisfying or had you hoped for any different outcomes?

QUESTIONS WITH ANSWERS FROM HELEN

1. Do you think Annie and Jess made the right decision when they followed Julia to Rome?

It was obviously a crazy, rash decision but I'm so pleased Jess called it. Obviously she had ulterior motives – needing to escape an awkward situation – and Annie was annoyed with James for forgetting their anniversary but both craved a change of scene. The idea of stealing time together, topped with a whiff of adventure, was impossible to resist (especially after a few big glasses of red in Annie's case)

2. How has Jess's childhood affected her relationship choices?

I think her parents' divorce left her unsettled by the idea of marriage. But I think her choices were as much a result of her own self-worth (or lack of) rather than just her childhood experiences. My own experience of having divorced parents was an increased determination from an early age to not let history repeat itself.

3. Which of the three women in *This Changes Everything* do you relate to the most, and why?

I'd love to be more like Julia or Jess in some ways but I know I'm definitely most like Annie. I relate to her as a mother, as someone who married someone she'd known forever and I identify with the friendships she has. I also live close to my own parents and in-laws and know how fortunate I am to have my close and extended family nearby.

4. In what ways has a lifetime apart made Patrick and Julia's relationship stronger? Do you think their love would have survived if they hadn't been separated?

I think the fact that they wouldn't change what happened whilst they were apart is key to them being so comfortable together again after all that time. And experience taught them both to appreciate the now rather than regret what might have been. I think Julia had no choice but to tell Patrick to leave back then. Living together, knowing what had happened, would have been incredibly tough for them to bear.

5. How do Jess and Annie's expectations and hopes for their own romantic lives change throughout the book and by watching their mother reunite with Patrick?

They develop as the story unfolds but Rome brings so many realisations to the surface for them all. For Jess, it's the fact that she still loves Ben and can't spend the rest of her life running away from happiness she doesn't feel she deserves. For Annie, it's that she wants her mother and sister to know that her seemingly together marriage and family life didn't just fall into her lap; she has to work at it. But seeing their mother and Patrick back together makes the sisters think about Julia as a person with a past, not just their mother.

6. What did you make of Ed's first meetings with his sisters, Julia and with Patrick? Which touched you the most?

Those scenes were really challenging to write. I so wanted to do it justice but obviously I haven't experienced it myself so spent a lot of time researching adoption stories and watching hours of *Long Lost Family* (one of my all-time favourite programmes). I think what touched me was the fact that so often in real life, no matter how many years have passed, in the very moment people are reunited it's not about the sadness of what's lost but about the joy of being together at last.

7. Which location came alive most for you – Rome or Cornwall?

I've spent many happy summers in Cornwall and one of my favourite pubs on the planet, The Gurnard's Head near Zennor, is the inspiration for the pub where the sisters meet Ed for the first time. For years we stayed in the same cottage on the south coast too, at the top of a river, so that really helped when writing about it. We went to Rome for our honeymoon, which I adored of course. But I loved it even more when we returned with our own children a decade later. For them it was mostly about the ice cream but it was one of our favourite holidays ever.

8. Did Julia's parents make the right decision when they decided she was too young to have a child? How would her life have been different if she had kept Ed?

It was Julia's mother's decision based as much on her own selfish concern about what people might think as the practicalities. If Tessa had been her mother, Julia would have kept the baby and Julia and Patrick's life would have been quite different. But that's the heart-breaking thing: their story was determined by another person's actions. Luckily, it's not the whole story.

9. Everyone gets their happy ending as we reach the last page of *This Changes Everything*. Did you find the ending satisfying or had you hoped for any different outcomes?

At one point it nearly didn't have a happy ending! But then I thought, hang on, life isn't always a f*cking fairy tale but if I want this particular story to have a happy outcome then it will. That's the real beauty of fiction. You can just make it up.

ACKNOWLEDGMENTS

So many people have helped me get this story on to the page and out into the world, not least my brilliant – and very special – agent, Heather Holden Brown. Thank you Heather and Elly James at HHB for all your support and encouragement always, I'm so grateful.

To Amanda Ridout, Sarah Ritherdon, Nia Benyon, Elly Foot and all at Team Boldwood, thank you so much for taking me into your family of authors and turning my fiction into reality. Sarah, you took the story and prodded it into shape so beautifully, thank you. It's been a dream and I'm beyond thrilled to now be part of your Boldwood story. Thank you too to Alice Moore for your beautiful cover design and to Yvonne Holland, Camilla Lloyd and Sue Lamprell for your expertise, encouragement and eagle eyes.

I really hope to have written about adoption with care and understanding. I read so many incredible accounts (and watched hours of *Long Lost Family*!) but special thanks to Julia Feast OBE for not deleting my random email asking for advice. Your help was invaluable and much appreciated.

To all my wonderful friends who've supported me with this book, thank you from the bottom of my heart. Special thanks to Alie, Gemma, Claudia, Charlotte and Sara for reading early drafts and telling me what you *really* thought. And to the One Day Mores, the Six o' Clockers, the Treble F and my brilliant Book Clubbers – thank you! I'm just sorry I've been talking about this for *so* long.

To my mother Christine and my sister Alex, the two funniest people I know: even though this story is completely made up, you were constantly in my thoughts. To my father Ken and step-mother Jo (sorry!) and to my wonderful in-laws Frank and Dru, I'm so lucky to have you all as my eternal cheerleaders. And to Tim, who might not *technically* be here any more – but is always with us – here's to you, little brother. I miss you every day.

Then there's my husband, Ross. (I think there's something in my eye). Thank you for *literally* everything, from the cup of tea you bring me every morning to the constant encouragement to do what I love. I'm so happy I didn't stop following you and, to paraphrase Elton, I love you more than life itself.

All love and quite possibly annoying hugs to my brilliant children – George, Xander and Alice – not least for making me understand what really matters in life. No, I don't mean always having biscuits in the biscuit tin (although come to think of it that actually really does matter).

Thank you to all the readers of my wine blog, The Knackered Mother's Wine Club, for your support over the last ten years. Promise to let me know what you think of this one (and what you're drinking whilst reading it, obviously).

Finally I really hope that you've loved reading this book as much as I loved writing it. Thank you SO much, it means the world to me. x

Instagram: @knackeredmother

Twitter: @knackeredmutha

Facebook: Knackered Mother's Wine Club

For more information (and regular wine recommendations!)
visit Helen's website www.knackeredmotherswineclub.com

MORE FROM HELEN MCGINN

We hope you enjoyed reading *This Changes Everything*. If you did, please leave a review.

If you'd like to gift a copy, this book is also available as an ebook, digital audio download and audiobook CD.

Sign up to Helen McGinn's mailing list for news, competitions and updates on future books.

https://bit.ly/HelenMcGinnNewsletter

ABOUT THE AUTHOR

Helen McGinn is a much-loved wine expert on TV and in print and an international wine judge. She spent ten years as a supermarket buyer sourcing wines around the world before setting up her award-winning blog (and best-selling wine book) *The Knackered Mother's Wine Club*. She is the drinks writer for the Daily Mail and regularly appears on TV's Saturday Kitchen and This Morning. Helen lives in the New Forest.

Visit Helen's website: www.knackeredmotherswineclub.com

Follow Helen on social media:

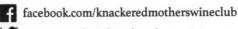 facebook.com/knackeredmotherswineclub

twitter.com/knackeredmutha

instagram.com/knackeredmother

ABOUT BOLDWOOD BOOKS

Boldwood Books is a fiction publishing company seeking out the best stories from around the world.

Find out more at www.boldwoodbooks.com

Sign up to the Book and Tonic newsletter for news, offers and competitions from Boldwood Books!

http://www.bit.ly/bookandtonic

We'd love to hear from you, follow us on social media:

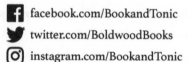

facebook.com/BookandTonic

twitter.com/BoldwoodBooks

instagram.com/BookandTonic